Headwaters

Headwaters

Jerry Leppart

1998
Galde Press, Inc.
Lakeville, Minnesota, U.S.A.

Headwaters
© Copyright 1998 by Jerry Leppart
All rights reserved.
Printed in the United States of America.
No part of this book may be used or reproduced in any manner whatsoever without written permission from the publishers except in the case of brief quotations embodied in critical articles and reviews.

First Edition
Second Printing, 1998

Library of Congress Cataloging-in-Publication Data
  Leppart, Jerry, 1945–
    Headwaters / Jerry Leppart. — 1st ed.
       p.   cm.
    ISBN 1–880090–66–X
    1. Indians of North America—Mississippi River Valley—Fiction.
  I. Title.
  PS3562.E6135H42   1998
  813'.54—dc21   98–6593
                                                                          CIP

Galde Press, Inc.
PO Box 460
Lakeville, Minnesota 55044–0460

To the Spirit of Wakantanka.
And to those who keep the Spirit.

Contents

Prologue	The Past	1
Chapter 1	Pickle One, Pickle Two	3
Chapter 2	Footsteps in the Rain	7
Chapter 3	Camp L3	15
Chapter 4	Beta	37
Chapter 5	An Offering to the Heavens	51
Chapter 6	Chad	59
Chapter 7	"I'll Tell the Director"	77
Chapter 8	Seemann	85
Chapter 9	Showtime	95
Chapter 10	"Tell Him Amjad Mustafa Is Here"	103
Chapter 11	On to Rome	111
Chapter 12	"Thank You, Florence"	121
Chapter 13	"Sometimes You Just Get Lucky"	127
Chapter 14	No Respect	141
Chapter 15	"No Problem at All"	147
Chapter 16	Entry	151
Chapter 17	"Better Buckle Your Seat Belt"	163
Chapter 18	"To Going Home"	175
Chapter 19	"Give It to Tonto"	187
Chapter 20	"Welcome to the Community of Cities"	197
Chapter 21	Ships Passing in the Night	205
Chapter 22	Ordnance	209
Chapter 23	Soldiers of Time	219
Chapter 24	Sweat Lodge	223
Chapter 25	The Cask	229
Epilogue	The Future	239
Note to the Reader		241

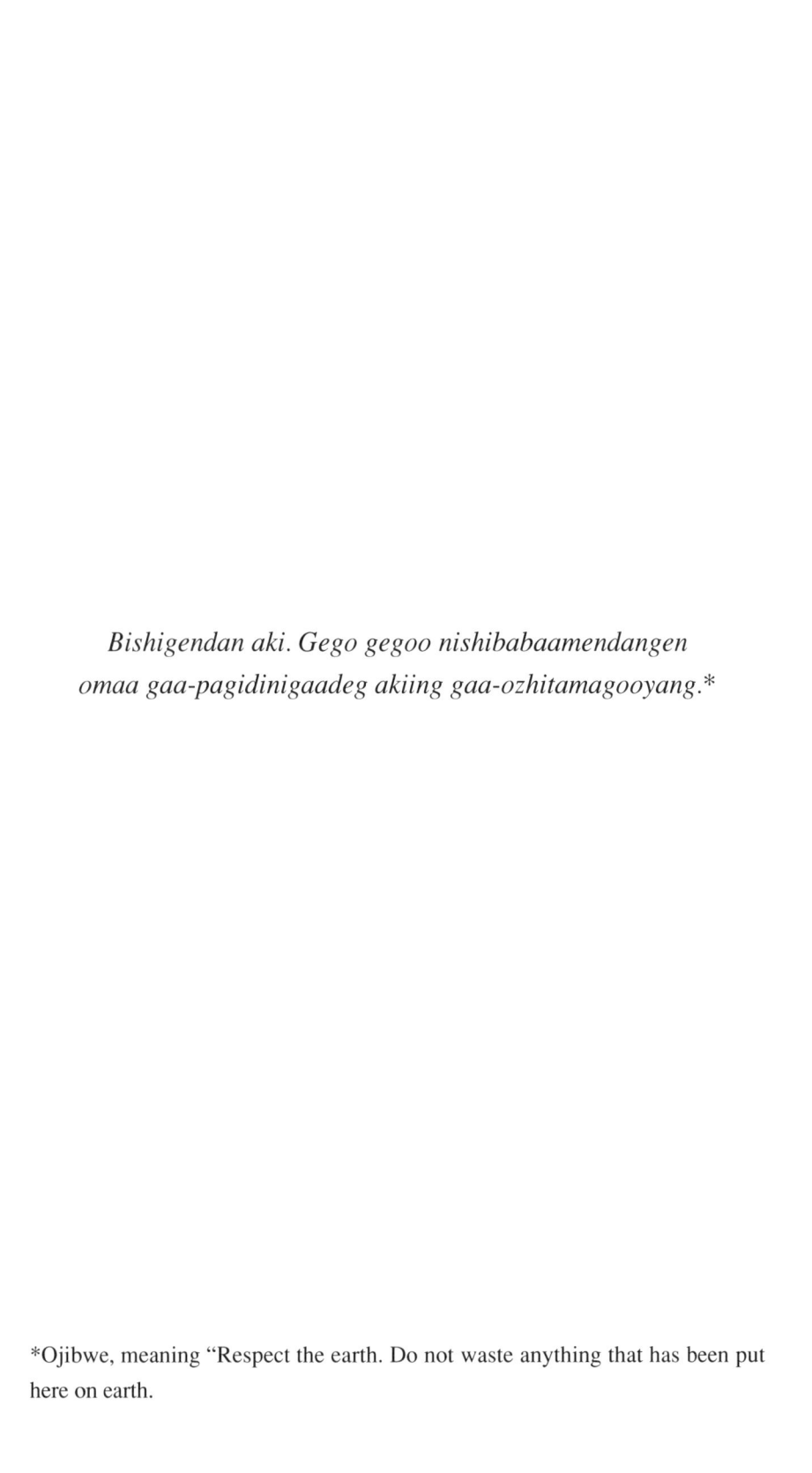

Bishigendan aki. Gego gegoo nishibabaamendangen omaa gaa-pagidinigaadeg akiing gaa-ozhitamagooyang.

*Ojibwe, meaning "Respect the earth. Do not waste anything that has been put here on earth.

Prologue

The Past

Morning does not waken quickly. It lies beyond the horizon, moving from its slumber. But before rising, it stretches out its painted fingers and touches far away clouds, coloring them with pinks, oranges, and fiery reds that burn in brilliance before giving way to the purples and grays of the morn. The sky behind the wispy clouds turns the color of robins' eggs announcing the arrival, the fresh start, the gift of a brand new day. The sun peeks its head over the horizon, meekly at first, then gaining confidence with each moment, arises boldly and, with its brilliant rays, trumpets its ascendancy, its sovereignty, its dominion.

It is dawn in the Upper Mississippi Valley. Women with dew laden moccasins gather wood for the upcoming fire. Men emerge from the tepees in their best ceremonial robes. Soon the campfire will send its flames dancing toward the heavens. Wide eyed children with mouths agape will sit in wonder as elders spin tales of yesterday's glories. And the drums will beat with rhythmical pattern that seems to match the heartbeat of the land itself.

They call themselves Dakota. They come to honor the Great Spirit, the Creator, Wakantanka. He is the creator of all things. He has created the balance. In this harmony they have all that they need. If they keep the spirit of Wakantanka, their medicine will be strong and their numbers will multiply. So they take only what they need and they put back what they do not use. And they honor Wakantanka whose spirit flows on through the land and the sky and the trees and the grass and the river. The river that will flow on to nourish a continent.

Chapter One
Pickle One, Pickle Two

"Bank right! Bank right!" Captain Kelly yelled into the intercom. Colonel James jammed the joy stick hard to the right, setting the jet on its right side.

"Jesus Christ!" yelled Captain Kelly as his helmet slammed against the canopy.

The surface to air missile passed beneath the left wing and exploded in the backwash of the jet, buffeting it slightly. Colonel James eased the stick to the left and brought the two-seat F111 fighter-bomber back on course.

"Damn, that was close!" said Captain Kelly, his heart pounding beneath his pressure suit.

"Welcome to Baghdad, son," Colonel James said into his intercom. "You got the target?"

Captain Kelly raised his visor and looked out into the cold, darkened sky. His breath was coming in short spurts and sweat was beading up on his forehead. As he closed his eyes, he brought up his right hand and quivering fingers pinched the bridge of his nose. He took in a deep breath and held it.

"You got the target?" Colonel James repeated over the intercom.

Captain Kelly released his breath slowly and opened his eyes.

"Captain?"

Captain Kelly looked down at an array of green and orange fluorescent gauges. In the middle of a round, gray scope, a point of light was transfixed in the silver cross hairs. "Got it, sir," answered Kelly.

"Is it lazed?"

"All lit up."

"Let's do it and get the hell out of here."

The F111 carried only two bombs. Both were laser guided. A laser was pointed at the target and the sensors in the nose of the bombs would guide them to the source of reflected radiation. Pinpoint accuracy was assured. The first bomb would blast a hole in the superstructure of the building. The second bomb would pass through the hole the first one had made. The second bomb also had a delayed five-second fuse which would allow it to penetrate deep into the building without being prematurely detonated. The effects of this bomb would not be wasted on super-structure. This bomb was anti-personnel.

Colonel James kept the F111 on a steady course. He had been awaiting the anticipated lurch of the F111 when the bombs were released.

"Problem?" asked Colonel James into the intercom.

Captain Kelly hesitated slightly.

"What if they're wrong?" he said.

"Whadaya mean?"

"Look, scuttlebutt has it that it's a baby milk factory." Captain Kelly took a deep breath from his oxygen mask. The air was sweet but dry. He swallowed to moisten his throat. "And it could be used as a bomb shelter. What if it's not what they say it is?"

"Intelligence says this is where all the big wigs hang out. We know they are using the top floor for military communications. They wouldn't be crazy enough to put a civilian shelter beneath a communications center. But even if they did, our bombs would only destroy the top floor. It may be disguised as a baby milk factory because it's a legitimate target. Who knows, maybe we'll get old Sadam himself tonight."

"Yeah, but what if they're wrong?"

"Look, this is not our call. Now pickle those babies and let's get out of here!"

Captain Kelly was sweating fully now and the perspiration touching his oxygen mask accentuated the rubber smell.

"Well, like you said, it's not our call."

Captain Kelly reached over and flipped a switch.

"Pickle One," he said.

The first bomb was armed. He flicked another switch and felt the F111 lurch.

"Pickle One released," he said.

Captain Kelly counted five Mississippis. He flicked a third switch.

"Pickle Two," he said.

He flicked a fourth switch and felt the plane lurch again.

"Pickle Two released," he said. *I hope you're right,* he whispered to himself.

The two guided bombs passed through the thin clouds, their nose sensors seeking the pinpoint of radiation emanating from a building below.

The first bomb found the source of the radiation and exploded. An enormous hole was created in the superstructure. Five seconds later the second bomb passed through the hole in the roof. But its momentum carried it through the upper floor and it came to rest wedged halfway through the bottom floor. The closest woman to the bomb turned her head, closed her eyes, and held her infant closer to her breast.

"Pickle Two" patiently completed its life sentence of five seconds.

And detonated.

Chapter Two
Footsteps in the Rain

It would not have mattered if he had been the first one there. The smoke and fire had kept all rescue efforts futile for some time. By the time he arrived, they had just started to pick through the rubble. There had actually been two bombs. The first was designed to make a hole in the superstructure and the second was guided through the hole the first one made. The second bomb was anti-personnel.

Amjad tried to stay low to keep under the smoke that remained as he crawled across the clumps of cement and smashed beams. The smell of explosives and burnt flesh was everywhere. There was light now from searchlights and lanterns. He scrambled over one pile and fell down the other side, choking from the smoke. He wiped his eyes and shook his head to clear the dust.

"Fata!" he yelled. "Fatima."

The creaking of the twisted beams grew louder as the weight they supported fought against the newly imposed positioning. There was a loud crash as another beam gave way and a pile of cement and steel smashed to the ground across the room. Dust from the pulverized concrete billowed through the room like a cloud of pestilence. Coughing, he put a handkerchief to his nose and mouth. His eyes, burning from the smoke and dust, started to water. From behind, a lantern was drawing closer. Its illumination cast his shadow onto a pile of rubble across the room. As he squinted in the half light he saw a glimpse of something red, partially buried in the pile right next to his shadow. He rubbed his eyes with the handkerchief and coughed again. The lantern was right behind him now, casting its light fully on the pile and the red object across the room. He gasped in horror.

"Fatima!" he called out.

He stumbled across the room to the pile of rubble and the red object. From ten feet away he could see it was a shoe. A red shoe.

"God, no!" he yelled. "Oh my God. No! No!"

He threw himself on the pile. Feverishly he dug out the shoe. Then the leg appeared and then the knee. He reached down, grabbed the shoe, and pulled.

* * *

"Happy birthday, Fatima," Amjad called as he walked through the door. It had been a hard day for all. In fact, it had been several hard days since the bombing had started. But it was her birthday and Amjad was determined to make her smile.

Fatima jumped up, her eyes open wide and, with a smile, ran to Amjad.

"Daddy!" Fatima yelled as she threw open her arms to give her father a hug. She had the same dimple in her cheeks that all six year olds seem to have, and the lisp created by her two missing front teeth made everything she said a treat.

"Daddy!" she squealed as she hugged his leg.

She had been too quick for him to put down his package so he could lift her in his arms. He switched the package to one arm, bent down, and lifted her with the other.

"Happy birthday, honey," he said, and squeezed her.

"Daddy, Daddy, what did you buy me?" she asked excitedly.

"Oh, nothing much," Amjad said. He always liked to play coy with his daughter. The fun was in the tease.

"Daddy, let me see."

"What's the magic word?"

"Oh, please, Daddy, please."

"Well, okay. Since you said please." He knelt over and let her down.

"Happy Birthday, hon. I hope it fits."

She grabbed the box from his hand and tore at the ribbon but it was tied tightly. It took *way* too long to finally force the ribbon over the corner of the box and down the side. The wrapping paper was a much easier task as she quickly found the seam and split the paper with one big tear. She tried to pull the cover off the box but it was taped shut.

"Daddy, can you help me with this, please?" she asked.

Amjad took the box and slid his thumbnail down between the cover and the box and split the tape with his thumbnail. Fatima grabbed the box and pulled the cover off. Inside was a white blouse, neatly folded.

"Oh, thank you Daddy!" she said, and pulled the blouse out of the box. Beneath the blouse was a red skirt. Amjad had guessed size six, but with the help of the saleswoman he was corrected to seven-eight. There should be a law, he had thought to himself, to make all countries have the same sizes fit the same way. Europe has one fitting, America another, and here in the Middle East still another. But, he guessed, that's what salespeople are for. Fatima pulled the skirt out and held it to her waist.

"Oh, Daddy, thank you."

"Look back in the box," said Amjad.

Fatima looked back in the box. There was a new pair of shoes. Red shoes. Fatima always loved it when her father bought her new things. He always brought back things when he went on trips. And they were always special. Times had been tough in Baghdad for some time now. The seemingly continuous war with Iran, the embargoes, and now the invasion of Kuwait. Food and medicine were scarce, but new clothes were impossible.

"Try them on, honey," he said.

She took off her worn brown leather shoes while still standing and grabbed the shoes out of the box. She sat down and slid the new shoes on her feet.

"A little small, are they?" asked Amjad.

"No, no, they're perfect," replied Fatima.

The glow on her face and the twinkling in her bright eyes gave proof that the choice was right.

"Daddy, can I go out and play and show Tarinda?"

"No, honey. I wish you could but it's not safe right now and I'd like you to stay here until we go to the shelter."

"That's right," said Fatima's mother, Fata. She had slipped out of the kitchen when she heard Amjad come in. "And besides, we haven't had birthday cake yet."

She held a rectangular pan in her hands. As she put it down, Fatima ran to the table.

"One, two, three, four, five, thix," Fatima said as she counted the candles. "That's because I'm thix years old," she lisped through the hole in her teeth.

"That's right," said Fata. "And we're so proud of our Fatima. Now, let's light the candles and you can blow them out."

She lit the candles.

"But remember to make a wish before you blow them out," said Fata.

"Oh yes, I forgot," Fatima said. She closed her eyes and went into deep thought.

"But don't tell us or it won't come true," said Amjad.

Fatima opened her eyes, took a deep breath and blew as hard as she could. All the candles went out on her first try.

"Okay, let's eat," said Amjad.

Amjad cut the cake and put a rather large portion on Fatima's plate. She giggled.

"But I don't understand," said Fata. "Where did you get these clothes?"

"I picked them up when I was in America for the seminar," said Amjad. "They've been sitting in my desk at the hospital for months."

"This is the best cake I ever had, Mom," said Fatima, chocolate cake crumbs falling from her lips, a piece of brown frosting clinging to her chin. She looked down at her new red shoes and touched her new skirt and blouse. "And thank you, Daddy," she said smiling.

As Amjad smiled back at her, a single siren started in the distance but was quickly joined by the wails of others as nighttime Baghdad came to life.

"Mom, do we have to go the shelter tonight?" Fatima asked, the smile fading from her face.

Fata turned to Amjad. "Do we have to go there tonight?" she repeated the question.

Amjad brought a piece of cake to his mouth and swallowed it in one gulp, but leaned forward to catch the telltale crumbs with his plate. He brought his napkin up and quickly wiped the frosting from his lips. "Yes, you do," he answered. He took a swallow from a glass of water and cleared his throat. "I have to go back to the hospital and you have to go to the shelter. The Americans have very sophisticated technology. And they seem to see everything. I'm sure they know it's a baby formula factory and they must know it's being used as a civilian shelter. They are very careful about what they bomb. They do not want civilian casualties." He reached over, took Fatima under the arms and lifted her over to him, sitting her on his lap. Pulling her plate over in front of him, he brought a fork full of cake to Fatima's mouth. She pecked at it like a hungry bird, then turned and with chocolate smeared lips and teeth, grinned at her father. He bent down and kissed her forehead.

"You go there tonight," he said. "You will be safe there."

* * *

Amjad pulled on the red shoe. It released and he fell backward against the rubble. He stared through the smoke at the shoe in his hands. He blinked as his eyes followed up the leg past the calf, the knee, and thigh until it ended in a bloody stump. His hands were shaking. As the horror swept over him, his jaw dropped and he gagged. The smoke and dust were burning his eyes, but he could not close them anymore. He could not blink. He could only stare; stare through the smoke and the dust, smell the burnt flesh, hear the wailing of the searchers and the cries of the dying. He stared at the stump until his hands stopped trembling. A peaceful calm came over him as the floor came up to meet his head and all was black and silent.

They did not find all of Fatima and Fata, but they found enough. The funeral procession filled the street to the point that it barely inched along. The procession was for all and all had come. Rows of coffins flowed on shoulders like a river of death. Each coffin was bedecked with flowers and each coffin bore a picture of its owner. The most pitiful were the half caskets, the three-foot containers housing the remains of the children. They were borne on the heads and shoulders of men but could easily have been held under the arms like half-filled sacks of groceries.

The air was filled with grief. Shouts and screams and sobs filled the air. Open-mouthed prayers and curses were accented with the staccato of small arms fire.

An American flag was burned for the benefit of the ubiquitous news cameras. Fists were clenched and shaking as they spit and stomped on the burning rag.

Most emotions were spent by the time the grave sites were reached. But once there, each grief fed upon another and rekindled the pain and sorrow until it reached a crescendo. Then as the extended emotions consumed their energy, the sorrow slid down the back side of the bell curve and the crowd stood worn and fatigued. Their anguish and pain had given way to exhaustion. Bleary eyed and drained, one by one, they walked away from the interred.

It had started to rain about dusk. Most of the mourners had dispersed long ago. The rain was coming down harder now and the flowers that remained on the grave site were quickly matted and splattered with mud from the huge drops. It had been a mass grave, and the rains came down to meld the soil to the coffins and to welcome those inhabitants to their new native residence.

Amjad sat alone in the mud, rain dripping down his face. There was no reason to stay, and yet there was no reason to go. There was no*where* to go. Behind him, in the distance, footsteps sloshed but he did not turn to look. The footsteps came closer but he stared straight ahead. They stopped next to him and a man leaned down to him.

"How do you feel?" the man asked.

Amjad did not reply.

"How do you feel?" he repeated.

Amjad said nothing.

"I think I know how you feel but I want you to tell me how you feel."

Amjad turned his head. "Go away," he said.

The man knelt down, grabbed Amjad by the shoulders, and turned him so they were face to face. Amjad looked at him through bloodshot eyes. The rain that had fallen on his head streaked down his face, tear-like. It wound its way through three days' growth of whiskers until it collected at his chin, then recombined into larger drops before falling to the earth.

"We are the only ones here and I want you to tell me how you feel," the man insisted.

Amjad brushed the man's hands away. He bent his head down and ran his fingers through his wet hair. "How can you say that you know how I feel?" Amjad said quietly.

"Then tell me! Show me!"

Amjad reached down and grabbed a handful of mud and brought it up to shoulder level. He raised his head and steel eyes looked at the stranger. He squeezed his fist and mud oozed through his white fingers. Jaw muscles tightened. "Give me a gun and I'll show you how I feel. Give me a tank and I'll show you how I feel. Teach me to fly a plane and I'll show you how I feel."

"Do you want to do something?" asked the man.

"Yes!" said Amjad.

"Do you understand what I am saying?" the man questioned.

"What do you mean?" asked Amjad.

"I mean, do you want to do something? Something about this?" As he talked, rain that had streaked down his face and collected on his mustache flew off like bits of spittle. "Do you really want to do something to get back at them or would you rather go back to your hospital and do nothing?"

"Yes, I want to do something," answered Amjad. "I want to make them pay. I don't care about anything else. I want to make them pay."

"If you come with me, you cannot go back."

"I don't care."

"I really mean it. You cannot go back. Ever."

"There is nothing to go back to."

The man hesitated for a moment, then put his hand on Amjad's shoulder. "Come with me," he said.

Amjad looked into the man's eyes. As the man furrowed his brow, he smiled a half smile; a smile more of recognition than anything else. A smile that told Amjad that this man had shared the same pain, felt the same anguish and shared the same sense of retribution that Amjad felt. The wind had picked up and now Amjad could feel the raindrops slap against the side of his face. Wreaths of flowers were being blown across the landscape like so many tumbleweeds. Amjad nodded his head and rose to his feet. The two men turned and started walking from the grave site.

There was a flash of light and a loud crack of thunder as the heavens opened up. Amjad stumbled and fell to one knee in the mud. As he raised himself, he turned to look back. White sheets of rain covered the grave site. He stood there, his soaked shirt slapping against his side as the rain pelted his body. The man tugged at his arm. Amjad turned back to him and the two walked away into the darkness.

Chapter Three
Camp L3

"How much farther?" Amjad asked, his voiced raised over the sound of the rotor blades.

Rahin sat against the bulkhead wall in the dark hold of the helicopter, smoke rising from the cigarette dangling from his mouth. He could have been a curiosity in this part of the world. His father was Palestinian, his mother Irish. In this lottery-like jumble of genes, the red hair and blue eyes had won out. But the long shocks of red hair were held in place by a red and white checked headband of the PLO. The eyes stared ahead with the steel blue gaze of a lifetime of hate.

"How much farther?" repeated Amjad, this time a little louder.

Rahin turned toward Amjad with a questioning look.

Amjad left his seat at the side of the helicopter and moved over to sit next to Rahin near the rear bulkhead. "How much farther to the camp?" he repeated.

Rahin brought his left arm up and rotated his wrist. He took a deep drag and the tip of his cigarette glowed in the dark, illuminating the watch. As he looked down to check the time, a piece of ash dropped from his cigarette tip into his lap. He brushed at it with his right hand, then glanced back at his watch.

"Soon," he said. He looked out through the window into the darkness outside the helicopter. "We'll be there soon," the dangling cigarette dancing as he spoke.

Amjad looked forward at the two men seated at the controls in the front of the helicopter, the glowing gauges in front of them casting an eerie pale that separated them from the dark hold where Amjad and Rahin sat. He breathed and took in the smell of bare metal and grease. He glanced around the empty hold in front of them, then back over to Rahin. "Tell me about the camp," he said.

Rahin glanced back at Amjad and shrugged his shoulders. "Sure, why not," he said. "It will still be dark when we get there." He took the cigarette out of his mouth and tapped the end with his right index finger, scattering ashes. "Actually, we started out in Syria. That's where I met Major Brohan." He pointed his cigarette toward one of the men in front, sitting at the controls and flicked more ashes. "We didn't have much support there, so when Major Brohan offered to set us up here in Libya we jumped at the chance."

Rahin reached for the pack of cigarettes in his left shirt pocket. He took the pack and, with two shakes, offered a protruding cigarette to Amjad. Amjad took the cigarette from the pack and brought it to his lips.

"The camp is near Joffra Oasis," said Rahin. "About four hundred kilometers southeast of Tripoli." He offered the lit cigarette to Amjad. Amjad took the cigarette and brought the lit end to the tip of his, took three quick drags, and returned it to Rahin.

"Most of the weapons and munitions are supplied by Major Brohan," continued Rahin. "The camp has five tents. Three are for the men. One is for munitions and one is for communications." He took a deep drag and let the smoke curl slowly out as he continued. "The men are mostly Palestinian. But there are two Germans. They are the explosive experts. There were originally four men to a tent but now the Germans sleep alone."

"Did you lose a couple men?" asked Amjad.

Rahin turned his head abruptly toward Amjad and laughed. "Oh, nothing like that," he said, smiling. "It's just that they smell so bad." He turned his gaze back to the front and nodded his head slowly. "They smell *so* bad," he said with emphasis. "Only Allah knows." He tapped his cigarette and sent more ashes to the floor. "So now there are two tents with five men while the Germans sleep alone."

Amjad smiled slightly, cocking his head toward Rahin. "Couldn't the two men sleep in the communications tent?" he asked.

Rahin shook his head. "That is where Nadia sleeps," he said. "She is our communications officer."

"You have a female in the camp?"

"Yeah, it is Major Brohan's idea. She is Lebanese. When the Israelis invaded Lebanon, they killed Nadia's father and brother. She and her mother became refugees and made it to a refugee camp in Syria. Her mother is quite a beautiful woman, and the commander of the camp took them both to Damascus with him."

Rahin put the cigarette to his mouth, took a drag, and placed it between his forefinger and thumb, European style. He made an "O" with his lips and sent three perfect smoke rings into the dark, empty hold.

"Is that where Major Brohan found her?" asked Amjad.

Rahin continued examining the smoke rings as they drifted toward the ceiling and melted away. He glanced over to Amjad who returned the look.

"Oh. Oh yeah," said Rahin. "That's where the major met her. Apparently she was working in the kitchen during one of the commander's parties when the major spotted her." Rahin flicked more ashes to the floor. "She was quite a bit younger then. Just a kid, really." Another drag and three more perfect smoke rings to the ceiling. "She stayed with him for a while in Tripoli. Until he got tired of her, I guess. Or someone younger came along. Anyway, he sent her out here with the radios." Rahin looked over at Amjad, smiled, and continued. "Major Brohan wants Nadia sleeping alone for a couple of reasons. First, he does not want anyone else using the radios. That way he can keep tabs on us and he does not have to worry about security violations. Also, when he comes at night, he can call her on the radio and have her light the landing flares." He brought both hands up in a questioningly gesture. "But I've got nowhere else to put you. The two tents are full. And I can't have you sleeping with the Germans." He shook his head slowly. "Only Allah knows." He laughed again. "So for the time being, you bunk with Nadia."

"You said there were two reasons," said Amjad.

Rahin shrugged his shoulders. "The major still considers Nadia his property. When he comes to the camp, he likes to pay her a visit."

Amjad shook his head slowly and brought his cigarette to his lips. He took a deep drag and pursed his lips to an imperfect "O" and exhaled slowly. A "Q" or a

"P" or something like an "M" drifted to the middle of the hold. Rahin laughed. "We have much to teach you here," he said.

Amjad broke out into a laugh of his own. He shot his hand out and swiped at the fading letter, dispersing it into the dark. He turned to Rahin still smiling. "So. What's your story?" he asked.

Rahin's smile faded slightly and he turned his gaze to the floor. He took a long drag and the tip of the cigarette glowed brightly. He exhaled through his mouth and nose and shook his head slowly.

"Come now," said Amjad. "You know all about me. Now what's your story."

Rahin listened to the muffled roar of the helicopter engine and the beating of the rotors through the air. This was the first time he had laughed in what seemed a lifetime. And the first time that anyone had asked about that lifetime. He canted his head to the side to look up at Amjad. Amjad raised his eyebrows and shrugged his shoulders in a quizzical fashion. Rahin returned his gaze to the floor, breathed deeply, and took in the smells of the military paint, metal, and grease of the ship. His head started nodding, slowly at first but steady. He brought up his right hand to his face and his forefinger and thumb massaged his chin.

"I was raised in an Israeli prison," he said to the floor, softly.

"Raised in a prison?" repeated Amjad incredulously.

Rahin nodded his head slowly. "Yes. In an Israeli prison," to the floor again. He curled his red hair with his forefinger and turned to Amjad. "You see this red hair and blue eyes," he said through pursed lips. "How do you think they treat young men with red hair and blue eyes in an Israeli prison?"

Amjad recoiled backwards slightly. "But…but how?"

Rahin turned back to the floor. "When I was thirteen"—he rubbed his chin harder—"my father decided that I had become a man. And that my place was with him in the PLO." He shook his head slowly. He straightened up, put his hands behind his head, and stretched his back. He looked up at the ceiling and took a deep breath. "My father and two other men had decided to go by boat to attack Israel. I would come with them." He arched his back for a moment and then bent forward, elbows on his knees. Two sniffs through his nose was almost a chuckle. "It was almost comical. Really." Shaking his head and another nose sniff. "They commandeered a sixteen-foot fishing boat and siphoned gas from a nearby car for extra gas. We left Gaza at midnight figuring about two hours north and take a right would get us to Israel. We could kill as many Israelis as we could find, hop back in the boat and be back before dawn. But just before we got there, the motor sputtered to a stop. We had ran out of gas just a couple of kilometers short of our target. Fortunately we had planned ahead and brought along the extra tank of gas." Rahin was nodding now. "It was then we discovered one of the immutable laws of the universe. That nature favors unexpected flaws." He laughed sardonically. "The car we had siphoned gas from was a diesel. My father must have pulled the starter chord a hundred times. Nothing. So there we sat. All dressed up with no means to go." Now the nodding stopped and Rahin was gazing at the floor again.

"At dawn the Israelis came," he continued softly but paused. His fingers were rubbing his lips. He opened his mouth and clicked his forefinger nail on his front tooth a couple of times. He took in a deep breath, let it out slowly, and continued talking to the floor. "They killed my father and the other two. I was taken prisoner and sent to an Israeli prison where I spent my youth." The fingers came off the lips and the hands opened expressively. He straightened up. "When I got out, I went back to the PLO. But by then they were more interested in reconciliation and compromise than fighting. I made my way to Syria to form our group, met Major Brohan, and you know the rest."

"I'm sorry," said Amjad quietly.

Rahin took a deep drag from his cigarette and blew the smoke towards the ceiling. "Well, we all have our story," he said.

They both sat there, motionless, quiet, for a long two minutes. Finally Rahin took one last drag, exhaled quickly, and threw his cigarette to the floor, scattering sparks. "Fuck it," he said, and stomped it out with his boot heel.

Amjad got up and returned to the side seat of the hold without saying a word, leaving Rahin by himself. Rahin looked out the window at the blackness, not knowing if he was looking at the sky or the desert. He reached for another cigarette. He took the pack halfway out of his shirt pocket, thought better of it, and returned the pack.

He was tired. He leaned his head back against the bulkhead wall. "What's your story?" His mind repeated the question. He knew the dream would come to him. The dream that he had dreamt a thousand times. Or was it ten thousand times. The dream would come whether he was awake or asleep. It didn't matter. "What's your story?" faintly again. He was so tired. He closed his eyes and lowered his head to rest his face on uplifted hands, his elbows resting on his knees. "What's your story," fainter this time. His parted fingers covered his face as his mind drifted back to a boy sitting in the bow of a boat.

It is cold. The thirteen-year-old Rahin peered out through quivering, white fingers; huddled in the bow of the sixteen-foot fishing boat, shivering. Mushta cursed at the engine as he banged on it repeatedly with his rifle butt. He put his rifle down and tried the starting cord again. Nothing. He yanked on it another dozen times, cursing with each pull.

"Use your rifle butts," Mushta urged the others as he tried the rifle as a paddle. The three had their rifles inverted and desperately paddling towards shore. After an hour they lay back against the gunwales, exhausted, seemingly no closer to the shore than when they started. Mushta raised his eyes and looked at his only offspring, sitting in the bow, shivering. With the help of the morning sky, he could see Rahin looking back at him, questioningly. Mushta put his rifle down and moved over to Rahin. He put his hand out and touched Rahin's forehead. Rahin looked up at him and tried to control his shivering.

"Father," Rahin said through chattering teeth. " I am not afr...afraid." Rahin pulled his collar tighter with whitish, shivering hands.

Mushta rubbed his fingers through Rahin's hair and smiled. "You have your mother's hair and eyes, Rahin," he said. "But you have your father's spirit." He nodded his head unabashedly. "I am proud to call you my son."

One of the other men yelled something and pointed toward the north. In the distance a boat was racing toward them. Even before they could determine the size and shape, they knew it was an Israeli patrol boat. Mushta looked back at Amjad.

"I am sorry," he said.

Flashes from the bow of the approaching boat were followed by a double row of splashes in front of their boat.

"Wait," yelled Mushta. "Their machine guns have a greater range than ours. Do nothing until they are within our range."

As the patrol boat approached one thousand meters, the twin barrel 50 caliber machine gun in its bow opened up again. The water in front of the boat danced in a double row as it accepted the lead emissaries.

Mushta looked at the patrol boat and then back at his son. He reached for Rahin's head and pulled it to his chest. "I'm sorry," he repeated. As he felt the soft, adolescent hands touch his, he felt his eyes begin to water and his throat tighten. "It is the will of Allah," he managed to choke out. For a long moment Mushta clutched his only son to his breast. Suddenly he pulled Rahin away and looked him straight in the eyes. "No!" he yelled. "No! By Allah, no!" He picked Rahin up by the shoulders and flung him over the side of the boat, away from the invading craft. He reached down and pulled a seat cushion from beneath his seat and threw it out to Rahin.

Rahin sputtered and coughed. He started to swim back to the boat. Mushta raised his weapon to his shoulders and aimed it at Rahin. Rahin stopped, astonished. As Mushta squeezed the trigger, the water erupted in front of Rahin.

"Swim!" yelled Mushta, "It is Allah's will that you live!"

A wave washed in Rahin's open mouth and he coughed.

"Swim!" yelled Mushta again and released another burst which fell next to Rahin.

Rahin reached for the seat cushion and took one stroke away from the boat. Rahin looked back and saw a smile come over his father's face as his father turned and raised his weapon toward the patrol boat. The other two in the boat rose slowly, deliberately, and placed their weapons to their shoulders as well. Standing shoulder to shoulder all three opened fire as one. As their rounds fell pitifully short, the fifty calibers lit up again. The raining crescendo of bullets ripped through the three and set their bodies dancing like puppets jiggling on the end of a marionette's strings. When the firing stopped, the strings were snipped and the three puppets fell to the bottom of the boat in a heap.

The thirteen year old clutched the seat cushion in the water, coughing and sobbing as the cold water turned from a deep blue to crimson. "Father!" Rahin yelled out, and swam back to the boat. The bullets had ripped the sides open and the boat was lying dead in the water, only the gunwales reaching above the small waves. Rahin grasped the starboard gunwale and looked in. The three men lay floating in the boat, facing up, their arms and legs entangled.

"No!" sobbed Rahin as he reached over the gunwale for his father's hand. Mushta rolled his head to the side, raised it slightly above the water, and opened his eyes to Rahin. He painfully reached out and took Rahin's hand. Blood was running freely from his nose and mouth, his chest awash in red. His hands were cold as he squeezed Rahin's fingers. He coughed blood from his mouth. His face grimaced in pain as his hand clenched hard. "I'm sorry," he managed. His head rolled back into the standing water, his eyes staring blankly toward the morning sky.

"No," cried Rahin, pressing his face hard into the gunwale, squeezing the lifeless hand.

A lifeline splashed in the water next to him. He turned to see the Israeli patrol boat bobbing in the water behind him, the soldiers on board aiming their M-16s and fifty calibers at him. He disengaged his hand from his father's and slid his other hand from the gunwale. He put his hands to his face, his whitish fingers covering his eyes and slipped beneath the cold, crimson waves.

The helicopter slipped through the night desert air. In the cockpit, in the right seat, Major Brohan sat before the faint glow of the gauges. He looked out in the dark for a moment, then returned to the map stretched out on his lap. He pulled out a pen flashlight and traced the path from Jofra Oasis, across the Chad border to Aozi, then to Goura, Quinianga-Kabir, and Madidi. He made some mental notes, turned the flashlight off, and folded the map neatly before putting it in his jacket pocket.

Major Brohan was an intelligence officer in the Libyan army. It had been his idea to bring prospective terrorists to Libya for training. This, in exchange for an occasional excursion into neighboring Chad. It had been a long-standing goal of Libya's leader, Muammar al-Qaddafi, to invade Chad. By sending these units into Chad, he could test Chad's response to the incursions without risking any troops of his own. And, as the terrorists sent in were not Libyan, he could deny all responsibility.

Brohan placed his hands behind his neck and interlocked his fingers, leaning back. He looked through the windshield and examined the reflections of the strobe lights as they flicked on and off and the identification lights as they wandered back and forth aimlessly through the dark. He pulled his left hand away and rotated his wrist to look at his watch. They were nearing the camp. He reached forward, brought a microphone to his lips, and started speaking to a woman sleeping on a cot.

Nadia lay dreaming the dreams of a little girl. A smile on her face, she was back in Lebanon, playing with her brother. There were other children, of course, but she liked playing with her brother the best. Though ten years older, he liked playing with her, too. She remembered his smile. Quick to start, it would spring upon his face like a kitten pouncing on its favorite jiggle-toy. And he loved her. She knew he loved her. She could see it in his eyes; those kind, gentle, caring eyes. Deep set and dark, almost mysterious until you got to know him. She could look into those eyes and know that nothing was wrong, that nothing could harm her. He would take care of her. And he did…until that day. The day they came and took him away. The day they stood him up against a wall and took away his eyes. The day they closed his eyes forever.

But she still owned the memories. To summon them, all she need do was to lie back, close her eyes and the memories would come. He would stand before her with his beautiful eyes open and bright, answering her questions, solving her problems, allaying her fears. And all would be well with the world.

She lay sleeping, revisiting the memories when the chirping of her communications radio resurrected her. She sat up and put on the headphones which announced that Major Brohan would be there shortly with Rahin and a new recruit. Nadia acknowledged the message and put the earphones down. Dressing quickly, she grabbed the flashlight and flares and headed out the tent door. Making her way down the path past the minefield to the landing strip, she lit the flares, sat down, and waited.

Ten minutes later the chopper set down beside the camp, kicking up a cloud of sand beneath its rotor blades. Nadia held a handkerchief to her nose and mouth and turned her head to avoid the dust. As the rotors slowed, Nadia turned back to see Brohan emerging from the helicopter followed first by Rahin and then the new man. Nadia waved the flashlight at their feet. All three men crouched as they walked, following the beam through the dust and didn't stand fully erect until they were all the way to Nadia.

Rahin spoke first. "Nadia, this is Amjad," he said. "He will be sharing the tent with you."

Nadia nodded.

"Amjad is a doctor," Rahin continued. "He also has been to America."

The flares were throwing light about in sprits, but there was still enough illumination to see. Nadia looked up at the new man. He was tall, rather well built for a doctor. He had the Mediterranean jet-black hair which amply covered his head as well as his upper lip. He was lighter skinned with strong, pleasing features. But when she looked in his eyes she jerked back. They were HIS eyes; deep-set black, like two coals set in the face of a freshly made snowman. She had just seen those eyes moments before the radio had wakened her. Her brother's eyes! This man had her brother's eyes! Her eyebrows raised and she swallowed hard. He returned her glance and her faculties momentarily abandoned her.

"Hello," Amjad said. His voice was soft and pleasing. Nadia just stood there.

"Nadia?" said Rahin.

Nadia was back now. "Oh, hello," she said. "Sorry, but I just woke up and I'm afraid I'm still half asleep."

"No problem," said Amjad. "I'd just as soon get to sleep myself."

"Nadia," said Major Brohan as he stepped out from behind the other two. "Show Amjad where he will be quartered. I'm going to talk with Rahin for a while. But I'll be by soon."

Nadia acquiesced and led Amjad off to the communications tent.

"Rahin," Brohan started, "in three days I want you to take your men into Chad. You are to attack a village there. It will not be heavily armed. You can kill as many people as you want. Just pretend they are Israelis. There won't be any danger to you and we will get you out before they can mobilize. We just want to see what their response is. We want to test their defenses."

"But we have no quarrel with Chad," answered Rahin. "Our fight is with the Israelis and the Americans."

"Nonsense," replied Major Brohan. "We will supply you with the ordnance and provide choppers to take you there and back. You'll be in and out in an hour or two."

"But…" said Rahin.

Major Brohan interrupted, putting his arm around Rahin's shoulder. "Look, we have a marriage of convenience. We provide you with a base of operations to train your men, free from international interference. And you must help us find out how our neighbor responds to incursions. When you leave here on your own missions, we don't care where you go or who you kill, but you must help us with our requests."

Rahin pursed his lips, looked past Brohan into the darkness beyond the flares. He took a deep breath and let it out slowly. "Three days will be fine," he said. "Where are we going?"

Brohan turned toward the communications tent and started walking. "The name is not important," he said, tossing his head to one side. "We will fly you there. It will be lightly defended. There is a radar station there that we would like you to take out. Kill as many as you like. We are more interested in their response time."

"Fine," said Rahin.

"I have a map of the area for you," said Major Brohan. "You might as well get acquainted with it."

As they reached the tent, Rahin reached forward and pulled the flap open, but only enough so that if one was to enter, he would have to stoop. Brohan stopped abruptly, cocked his head toward Rahin, and leered. Rahin pulled the flap further out and up, and Brohan strolled through the door into the tent.

The tent was illuminated by a battery powered lamp but its light was dimming. Amjad was already on the cot next to the door while Nadia lay on the cot next to the radio. As Brohan walked passed Nadia's cot, he reached down and slid his hand across her right knee and up her thigh before turning to the table behind the radio. He opened the door of an oil lantern hanging from the center post and fumbled through his pockets for a match. Rahin reached quickly into the box of wooden matches half buried under some papers on the table, lit one, and brought it to the lantern.

"Good," said Brohan as he adjusted the light. "Come over here."

Rahin came up next to Brohan, who was taking a piece of rolled paper from his jacket pocket. "This is a map of Aozi in the Tibesti mountain range just over the Libyan border," he said, placing a yellow stained finger on the paper. "Aozi will be an easy target. It is close to the border. It will be lightly defended and the Tibesti mountain range would stand between it and any reinforcements Chad would care to send. Later strikes to Goura, Qunianga-Kebir, and Madidi will be possible, but this will be a good test." Brohan took out an American cigarette and lit it with a Zippo lighter. He took a big drag and acquainted his lungs with a taste of Virginia before slowly blowing it toward the lantern. "You study this map," he continued. "Become familiar with it. We'll be back in two days."

He had not seen Nadia for a while and although she had been replaced, he still remembered her sweet softness. He looked down at her laying on the cot, her knees up, covers to her chin. He took another drag, inhaled deeply, and let it out slowly. Dropping the cigarette to the floor, he stepped on it, twisting his boot sole into the ground. He walked over to the side of Nadia's cot and held out his hand. Nadia looked up at the nicotine stained fingers but did not move. Brohan beckoned with a nod of his head and his fingers twitched toward his palm. Nadia closed her eyes for a moment, squeezing them shut. Slowly she opened them and saw the extended hand, yellow fingers still twitching, beckoning. She rolled the covers down and sat up, her head bowed, her eyes searching the tent floor. The fingers grabbed her loosely by the arm and helped raise her up. The eyes of Rahin and Amjad followed Major Brohan as he led Nadia through the tent door, into the darkness.

"Time to get up," came a voice from far away.

Amjad rolled over on his cot.

"Time to get up." Again the voice.

Amjad grunted. A hand was on his shoulder and the voice grew louder.

"Get up. Get up." The hand was shaking his shoulder as the cobwebs skittered away to the corners of his mind.

"Wha…what is it?" Amjad managed as he squinted into the new light.

"Time to begin your training. Time to get started." The voice was recognized as Rahin's. Amjad raised his head a bit and slid his arm underneath for support. "What time is it?" he asked.

"Time to get up. Your training starts today. The sun is up and we have lots to do."

Amjad rolled back, rubbed his eyes, and yawned. His shoulder ached from the stiff cot and his hips felt a little numb. He moved his buttocks slightly and the feeling started to return. As he opened his eyes he could see Rahin standing over him dressed in camouflage fatigues, tan T-shirt, and combat boots. A red and white checked headband kept his hair in place—his long, red hair which cascaded to his shoulders in defiance of tradition. An AK47 assault rifle was in his right hand and a munitions belt full of rifle clips was slung over his left shoulder. A pack of cigarettes bulged from under the rolled back sleeve of his T-shirt high on his upper left arm near the shoulder and one could barely make out the trademark, "CAMEL," showing through the thinning threads. Three days' growth of red stubble adorned his lower face, and with a six-inch-bladed knife sheathed at his right side, he was the ultimate warrior.

"Time to get up," Rahin repeated as he kicked at the cot.

Amjad rolled to one side and pushed himself up until he was sitting upright. He bent his head down and ran his fingers through his thick black hair. Rahin reached down and picked up Amjad's clothes and slung them at him. Amjad caught them with one hand as he winced backward. He looked over to the cot next to his and saw Nadia roll over and peer up at them. Rahin unraveled the left sleeve on his T-shirt and peeled out the pack of Camels. Shaking the pack until three cigarettes protruded from the rest, he brought the pack up to his mouth and, with his lips, pulled the nearest one from the pack. He took a book of matches from inside the cellophane wrapping and lit one match. Bringing the match to the cigarette, he drew in deeply, holding the smoke within him for a few seconds before blowing out and extinguishing the match. After replacing the matchbook inside the cellophane wrapping, he quickly re-rolled the pack into the shoulder of his T-shirt.

Amjad had slept in his shorts. By the time Rahin had his second drag from the cigarette, Amjad was fully dressed and standing directly in front of him. Rahin stood with his feet apart and blew his second puff of smoke directly into Amjad's face. Amjad squinted as the smoke rolled past him, burning his eyes. As the smoke cleared, Amjad reached over to Rahin's shoulder, unrolled the sleeve of the T-shirt, and extracted the pack of Camels. He shook the pack until three cigarettes separated themselves from the others and, without looking down, brought the pack up to his lips, securing one cigarette. He stared straight into Rahin's eyes as he pulled the matches from the cellophane wrapping, lit a match, and brought it to the cigarette. Nadia pulled her blanket up to her neck as her knees involuntarily came up. Amjad took a deep drag and held it in for a moment before exhaling directly into Rahin's face. Rahin squinted as the smoke passed. Amjad shook the match out and took another drag.

"Let's do it!" Amjad said as smoke escaped from his mouth and nostrils.

Rahin took another drag and squinted further. As he exhaled, a smile came over his face. The smile turned to a grin, the grin to a laugh. He reached out and put his hand on Amjad's shoulder. "Let's do it," he said. He turned and the two disappeared through the tent door.

Kazi looked down at the three canisters at his feet. Oblivious to the staccato of small arms fire that filled the air of the firing range, he squatted down and brushed the sand away from the drab green metal tubes exposing the LAW ROCKET lettering in military block yellow. The tubes cleaned of sand, his brushes turned to caresses and he patted the drab metal as a child pets a new puppy. These were his weekly allotment: three. And only three. He had argued that since he was the camp's expert in rocketry, he should be allowed a higher figure with which to hone his skills. But Major Brohan had set the limit at three and three would have to do.

Kazi inhaled deeply. The morning desert normally smelled fresh, fresh and clean, before the sun could heat the air and whip it into a dry rain of sand. The desert crickets were finishing their long nightly search for romance and their chirping diminished with the shortening of the shadows. Cacti had taken in what dew was presented to them, and they stood erect, almost barrel chested, fully inflated before the sun took back what the night had given. Normally the morning smelled fresh. Normally. But at the firing range the air was filled with the smell of nitrates from the small-arms fire, the explosives, and soon Kazi's rockets.

Kazi picked up the first rocket and stroked the green metal casing.

"Kazi," came a voice from behind.

Kazi turned casually around to see Rahin and another man walking up the path to the range.

"Kazi," Rahin repeated, and held up his hand as if to wave.

Kazi lowered the canister to his right side and shifted his weight to his left. His left arm came up to his forehead and the sleeve wiped away the perspiration that had formed.

"Good morning," said Kazi as Rahin stopped in front of him. The other man stopped behind Rahin.

"This is Amjad," Rahin said to Kazi. "He is our new recruit."

Amjad stepped around Rahin and held out his right hand. But his last step had kicked sand onto the LAW rockets.

"Watch what the hell you do!" yelled Kazi as he bent down and brushed the sand off his precious tubes.

"Sorry," said Amjad apologetically, lowering his hand to his side.

"Kazi," continued Rahin. " I want you to teach Amjad how to fire your rockets."

Kazi looked at the new man standing beside Rahin. He noticed that the man's skin was lighter than normal for this latitude, the hair, Mediterranean black, and the eyes, the eyes that looked deeply inside when met. Kazi looked away for a minute and then, his confidence reestablished, returned to the man. "What brings you here," he asked.

"Same thing that brings you here, I imagine," returned Amjad.

Kazi shifted his feet and lowered his gaze. "I suppose so," he murmured softly.

"Kazi," said Rahin as he reached back, put his arm around Amjad, and pulled him forward until they were side by side. "I want you to show Amjad here how to fire a rocket. He has much to learn before fly-over time."

Kazi looked skyward, raised his left hand to shield his eyes from the sun and squinted for a moment before returning to earth. He looked back at Amjad. "Yes," he said. "I imagine he has lots to learn." He raised the tube from his side to chest level and held it out in one hand. He cocked his head and rotated the tube slightly like a quizzical majorette twirling her baton in slow motion. "Ever fired a rocket?" he asked.

Amjad stood firmly, feet slightly spread. "No," he answered. "No, I haven't."

Kazi's rotation stopped as his other hand reached out to caress the tube. "They don't give us much here," he said, his voice lowering. "We only get three a week." His voice was now almost a whisper. "Only three a week." He gazed at the weapon and his stare seemed to take him elsewhere.

"Kazi," Rahin interrupted. "Why don't you show him how it works?"

Kazi was back now. He straightened up, taking the rocket in both hands.

"This is a LAW rocket," he said. "LAW stands for light anti-tank weapon. It is American. We have access to some Russian and Chinese rockets, but these are much superior. As you notice, these are about a meter in length, forty-five inches to be exact, and three inches in diameter. It is designed to penetrate three-quarter-inch metal. The Russian and Chinese rockets that we obtained are quite powerful, but are large and cumbersome compared to these. These could be hidden inside a trench coat if need be. The ideal rocket for our use." He adjusted his feet and turned slightly toward the range. "To use the weapon, simply pull this pin in back." He pulled the cotter pin at the rear of the tube and pulled the end cap off and down. "The rear cap will come off exposing the rear tube. Simply extend the tube like this…" He pulled the extension tube out. "And the sights will pop up, front and rear. Pull the safety cotter pin." He pulled the safety pin and put the tube to his shoulder. "All you do now is aim and shoot."

Amjad took a step behind Kazi and leaned to his left to get a better look. As Kazi turned to square with the range, Rahin's left hand shot out, grabbed Amjad's shoulder, and pulled him violently to the right. As Kazi depressed the trigger, a flash of flames and smoke exploded from the back of the tube and filled the space which, only an instant before, had been occupied by Amjad's head. The rocket hurled forward, trailing flame and sparks, until exploding in the middle of a dune, sending showers of sand skyward.

Kazi turned his head around and leaned it on his right shoulder. He cocked his head slightly. "Best not to stand directly behind these when they fire," he said.

Amjad looked over at Rahin and swallowed hard. "Lesson learned," he said.

"We don't have too many of these," Rahin said. "Think you can fire one?"

Amjad brushed the front of his shirt and steadied himself. His hand came up to his mouth and his index finger went roughly through his mustache as he swallowed again. After clearing his throat he said, "Yes, yes, I think I can."

"Good," said Rahin. "We have a lot to do before fly-over time."

"Fly-over time?" questioned Amjad.

"I'll tell you later," answered Rahin. "We still have time for explosives and small arms." He walked past Kazi and gestured to Amjad. "Come with me," he said.

Rahin led Amjad past sprawling bodies firing machine guns into distant dunes. Some were standing and firing. Some were firing from one knee. But most were in the prone position, with bursts of fire exploding from the muzzles in front of them.

"The Germans are at the other end of the firing range," said Rahin. "I like to keep them downwind." He put his right thumb and forefinger up to his nose and squeezed as his face grimaced. "I mean, the *smell*. Only Allah knows." He shook his head slowly. "Only Allah knows."

As they made their way past the small arms fire, Amjad could see the Germans sitting at the end of the line, away from the others. One was sitting on a wooden crate while the other stood beside him, fiddling with something in his hands. As they approached, it became evident why they trained alone. Rahin looked at the blowing sand, noticing the wind coming from a forty-five degree angle to the Germans and positioned himself accordingly.

"This is my friend, Amjad," Rahin started. "He is here to learn all we can teach him." Amjad took a step closer to Rahin.

The German sitting on the crate rose and extended his hand to Amjad. "Ja, das ist gut," he said. "My name is Franz and this," he nodded at the other German, "is Heinrich."

Amjad inhaled slightly and held it as he leaned forward to shake the men's hands. Then he retreated slightly behind Rahin and slowly exhaled.

"We are the explosives experts here," Franz continued. "Do you know anything about explosives?"

Amjad shifted his weight to his left. "I know there are bombs, rockets, and dynamite," he said. "Stuff like that."

"Nein, nein, nein," interrupted Heinrich as he stepped forward, his voice rising as he spoke. *"Das ist nicht richtig. Kommen Sie hier. Ich werde Sie zeigen."* He looked at Amjad's quizzical stare, stepped back a pace, and lowered his voice to normal. "Those are just toys," he continued. He reached down to the crate and grabbed a gray-white glob of putty. "We deal with this." He twisted the piece of putty in two and threw one at Amjad. Amjad, startled, reached up instinctively, and caught it as he stumbled backward.

"What the…" Amjad blurted out.

Franz laughed. "Don't worry," he said. "It is not dangerous. That is the beauty of it. We can mold it or shape it any way we want." He stepped forward and wrested the putty from Amjad's grip. "What we have here is plastic explosive." He held it up in front of his face, admiring it. "The main ingredient," he continued, " is RDX, or cyclonite. This is a hard, white crystalline solid. It has the highest energy yield of any common explosive. By itself it is difficult to shape and is quite sensitive. But when mixed with elatomeric or polymeric binders it becomes as easy to play with as a child's toy."

Heinrich stepped forward, reached out and took the putty from Franz. Franz yielded it begrudgingly and his eyes followed it back to Heinrich's hand where Heinrich recombined it with the other piece.

"Ja, a child's toy," Franz said softly, turning back to Rahin and Amjad. Straightening up he took a deep breath and continued. "Usually it is detonated electrically with detonators. But it would also detonate if you shot it with a bullet. And it is perfect for our needs." Franz's eyes widened a bit. "Here," he said. "Here, I want to show you something." He took a step back and reached down to the table. Picking up the putty, he twisted off a small piece and held it up for Rahin and Amjad to see. "See this?" he asked, showing them a piece the size of his thumb. "Watch this." He reached inside of his pocket and produced a small capsule and placed the capsule in the putty. He turned and walked forty meters into the desert, placed the small piece of putty on the ground and returned to the others. As he reached the wooden crate he stooped down and opened an olive drab backpack. "You watch," he said, his voice rising as he searched the backpack. "Here," he said as he pulled a small, black box from inside the backpack. He twisted a dial on the box and a red light came on. "Watch this now," he said, with noticeable excitement in his voice.

He turned and looked at Heinrich. Heinrich pursed his lips and nodded his head. Franz turned back to Rahin and Amjad. "This is what we can do," he continued. "Let's suppose you want to kill someone." Franz's words were coming faster and his voice a pitch higher. "Let's suppose it was an ambassador." He looked back at Heinrich and winked. Heinrich smiled and nodded, sharing the reenactment. "Suppose you cut the ambassador's phone line and then showed up as a telephone repairman. And while you were alone in his office you took off the phone receiver cap and placed this amount," he raised his thumb up, "of plastic explosive and a small detonator into the receiver and replaced the cap. After you leave, you reconnect the phone wire and call the ambassador. When he answers, you ask for the ambassador." His voice quickened and spittle flew from his mouth. "And when he confirms that he is the ambassador he will have the phone to his ear…" His eyes opened wide and his eyebrows raised as he leaned toward Amjad. "Just push this little button…" His eyes were glazed as he thrust the box forward, toward Amjad. "And BOOM!" Franz depressed the button and the desert behind him exploded with a loud crack. A shower of sand hurled into the air and the wind took it to Rahin, Amjad, Heinrich, and Franz. Three of them ducked as the sand shower fell on them. Franz held firm, his arm still extended toward Amjad as the sand pelted him. He started to laugh. "He has no head!" he yelled, and continued to laugh.

Rahin turned to Amjad. "You get the picture?" he asked.

Amjad peeked from under the arm that he had put up to shield him from the sand shower. "Yeah," he answered. "I get the picture."

Rahin put his arm around Amjad as Amjad turned to go with him.

"Interesting work we do here," said Rahin as they started to walk away from the Germans.

Franz was still pointing the black box at them as if following them with a gun. "He has no head!" he yelled again, and continued laughing.

"Interesting!" echoed Amjad.

The two continued walking until they were back at the range next to a man lying prone, firing his machine gun into cardboard targets in the distance. Rahin stopped and turned to Amjad, sliding his AK47 from his shoulder and held it in front of Amjad.

"What do you know about firearms?" he asked.

Amjad looked down at the weapon and slowly shook his head.

"Not to worry,'" replied Rahin. "We can teach you what you need to know." He held the weapon out in front of Amjad like a soldier presenting arms at an inspection. "This is our main weapon," he continued. "This is the AK47. The rifle was designed by Mikhail Kalashnikov in 1944 or '45. It fires a 7.62 by 39 mm M43 bullet. It has an effective killing range of 350 to 400 meters but it has a somewhat looping trajectory at longer ranges, so you may have to aim a little high. That is why we practice at the range here. This weapon will operate effectively in cold or heat, desert or rain forest. Fully loaded with a thirty-round magazine, it weighs about 5.12 kilograms.

"To load and fire the weapon is very simple." Rahin cradled the stock of the weapon under his right arm next to his chest. "We start with the weapon unloaded," he continued. With his right hand he pushed the magazine release catch in front of the trigger guard and pulled the magazine from the receiver.

"Now the weapon is empty. Never carry a weapon around with a bullet in the firing chamber. Even with the safety on, it is better to not have a bullet in the chamber until you are ready for action." He held the magazine clip up for Amjad to see. "This is the magazine clip," he continued. "It holds thirty rounds. To load the weapon push the selector…" He fingered a metal switch directly above the trigger. "…To the upright position. Insert the magazine into the receiver right in front of the trigger guard. Bring the magazine in at a forward angle inserting the forward end first. Then swing the magazine back and up, pushing it firmly into the housing until the release catch locks here." He pointed to a small latch in front of the trigger guard.

"Hold the rifle by the pistol grip with your right hand and reach over with your left hand and pull the charging handle." He pulled a lever above the magazine with his left hand, his right hand on the pistol grip. "All the way back as far as it will go." He pulled the lever back and released it. "Then release it. Make sure you do not hold it while releasing it. There is a spring and it will release automatically. Push the selector down. The mid-position is automatic and the lowest position is for single shot." He pushed the selector to the mid-position. "Take aim and shoot."

He brought the gun up to his shoulder and pointed it out into the desert, weaving it back and forth in a spraying motion. "When it is empty, the action closes on an empty chamber. Just repeat. Push the magazine release catch here," pointing, "and it will release the magazine. Put in a new magazine, remember to slant it forward, then up and in. Pull the charging handle back and release it. And you are ready to, as the American's say, 'rock and roll.' When you are done, press the magazine release catch and remove the magazine. Pull back the charging handle to eject the bullet in the chamber and push the selector lever to the upper position."

Rahin glanced at his watch. "We've got ten minutes before fly-over time," he said. "Are you ready to 'rock and roll?'"

Amjad reached out and took the AK47 from Rahin. "Yeah, I'm ready," he said. "But what is this fly-over time?"

"Oh," said Rahin looking skyward. "That is the Americans. They have a spy satellite whose orbit goes directly over our camp. The Russians have calculated the orbit and forwarded the information to the Libyans who forward it to us. Since we know the fly-over times, we simply duck inside our tents and the Americans look at canvas and sand." Rahin returned his gaze to Amjad. "We only have ten minutes," he said. "Are you ready?"

Amjad looked skyward for a moment and then out to the cardboard figures in the distance. "The Americans and their technology," he said in disgust. He thought back to a time when the American technology put a plane above Baghdad that no one could see. American technology had created a special bomb. American technology had targeted a special building. With American technology, nothing was supposed to go wrong.

Amjad pushed the selector to the full automatic position, retracted and released the charging handle. He looked out into the sand where the cardboard figures stood. A gust of wind picked up a patch of sand and sent it swirling into a tan spout in front of the figures, momentarily obscuring them. Amjad raised the weapon to his shoulder. The wind calmed and the spout dispersed to the ground leaving a clear path to the target. Amjad took aim and squeezed the trigger.

Two hundred miles above the earth, spy satellite MRT1 drifted eastward toward fifteen degrees east longitude. In ten minutes it would enter the Libyan "window," open its shutters, and take pictures of the tops of tents, vacant vehicles, and the empty, shifting sand of a seemingly deserted terrorist camp. The images would be sent back to earth and make their way to the sixth floor of an office building just outside Washington, D.C., where they would be analyzed and catalogued. The analysts would input them as another dry run for MRT1. But these analysts were less interested in images from MRT1 as they were in images from MRT2; a new spy satellite whose technology far surpassed that of MRT1. A spy satellite whose trajectory, fly-over times, and advanced capabilities were unknown to anyone outside of that six-story office building: not to the Russians, not to the Libyans, and not to the inhabitants of Camp L3.

Chapter Four
Beta

In the deep, black expanse of space, spy satellite MRT2 swept eastward, chasing MRT1 endlessly across the sky. Each day they would rendezvous at 105 degrees east longitude like two lovers locked in a circadian rhythmic tryst. High above Indonesia, MRT2 would catch MRT1, pass it, and circumnavigate the globe twice before catching it again. MRT1's orbit would take it over fifteen degrees east longitude, thirty degrees north latitude, the Libyan "window," at 9:00 A.M., local time, each day. MRT2's passes over the "window" would occur at 3:00 P.M. and 3:00 A.M. each day. Although it was designed to make two passes per day, and one of the passes would be in darkness, the nighttime passes were not wasted.

Both satellites represented the latest generations of spy satellite technology.

A KH-11 class satellite, MRT1 was a marvel of space technology and espionage engineering. With a telescopic focal length of 240 inches and over a billion pixels, its ground resolution was approximately six inches. From two hundred miles above, its eye could read a license number off a Jeep; or better yet, tell which side of a flipped coin, when striking the ground, would be facing up. MRT1 also had four small motors designed to rotate the telescopic camera in synchronization with the orbital speed of the satellite in relation to the earth, allowing the shutter to stay open longer for a more precise image. Using advance active optics it could negate the blurring effects caused by atmospheric distortion. The Itek active-optics equipment aboard the KH-11 would analyze the distortion in front of the aperture and then guide the Perkin-Elmer mirrors in the telescope to adjust for it. And images could be broadcast in "real time." Rather than simply taking still pictures, "real time" capability shows figures in action as the action occurs.

While KH-11 represented the fifth generation of spy satellites, the KH-12 series represented the sixth. MRT2, a KH-12 satellite, possessed all of the capabilities of KH-11 but added one very important feature: the ability to pick up the longer wave infrared emissions from objects. The electromagnetic spectrum is made up of waves. The mid-length waves represent the light that we see. The very short waves are the ultraviolet band. And the very long waves are the infrared band. Heat emits the very long waves of infrared. With the ability to detect IR emissions, one can "see" a warm object against a cool backdrop. While the midrange band of visible light is blocked by certain objects, such as the canvas tops of tents, the long-range band of infrared passes right through: through the tops of tents, through the nighttime sky into endless space.

In the cold 180°K of space, MRT2 would drift high above fifteen degrees east longitude and hungrily drink in the minute amounts of energy appearing from below. Then the images would be converted into digital bits, encrypted, and shot in an electrical stream to a data relay station in a geosynchronous orbit over the United States. From there the bits would be downloaded on a frequency of twenty-one gigahertz to a ground station near White Sands, New Mexico, where they would be distributed to the agency most affected by it. The man most interested by the tiny amounts of energy being emitted from fifteen degrees east longitude and thirty degrees north latitude was an sitting at his desk in a cubicle on the sixth floor of the old CIA building in McLean, Virginia.

Phil Soran sat back in his chair and yawned. *Lemon,* he thought to himself. Phil liked the smell of lemon: so clean, so polished. The cleaning crew would clean the floor every night. But once a week they would scrub and wax it. They would polish it to a nice shine. And they always used polish with the smell of lemon. It made the whole building smell antiseptic. Germs couldn't survive in this building, not with that smell of lemon. Phil looked at the shine on the floor. He looked at the bare, Sheetrocked walls, at the white, suspended pressboard ceiling. The sound-absorbing material on his cubicle wall was the only thing that looked warm. Everything else seemed so cold. He could use flowers. He could use flowers or something else colorful to spruce up his cubicle. A picture would be good. When he arrived two years ago, he had put a picture on his desk. A picture of a girl from back home. But that picture had lasted only a month or so. After it hit the wastebasket it had not been replaced. He would get another picture, he thought. As soon as he got another girl.

Phil was in charge of keeping an eye on Camp L3 for Beta Group. Beta Group is the name given to the counter-intelligence center established by the CIA. Operating from the sixth floor of the old CIA building in McLean, it was established in 1986 by CIA Director William Casey to answer the intelligence directive signed by President Reagan to identify terrorists and respond to any possible threat that they might pose. The better known Delta Force was designed to respond militarily to any kidnapping, hijacking or strike by a terrorist force which was already in progress. Beta was prescribed with the prescient task of knowing when the operations were supposed to happen *before* they happened and then stopping them. Also they were to apprehend any terrorist who had committed crimes against Americans abroad and bring them to America for justice. In keeping with the CIA's charter, their mission was international in scope, leaving the domestic issues for the FBI.

The first director of the counterintelligence center was Dewey Clarridge, who had been responsible for the apprehension, among others, of Fawaz Younis, a Lebanese terrorist who had hijacked a plane at Beirut International Airport. After Clarridge retired, Wes Covington was named the new director of the center. His first request was to the National Reconnaissance Office for the latest in satellite surveillance over the Middle East. From behind the doors of Room 4C-1000 of the Pentagon, the NRO's executive committee, consisting of the deputy secretary of defense, acting as the chairman, the science advisor to the president, and the director of central intelligence had assigned two satellites to Beta Group: a KH-11 satellite, code named MRT1, and later, a more advanced KH-12 satellite, code named MRT2.

MRT1's orbit was quickly discovered and tracked by the Russians, who had given the information to their friends in Libya. The fly-over times were forwarded to the various camps whose inhabitants would simply duck into their tents as the satellite passed over. MRT2 was launched after the breakup of the Soviet Union which no longer had the money or the inclination to follow a satellite that did not directly affect them. So MRT2 would float silently overhead at 3:00 P.M. and 3:00

A.M., its shutters open, drinking in two bands of electromagnetic waves, converting them to digital information, and sending them to a building outside Washington, D.C. A building with white Sheetrocked walls, white suspended ceilings, and lemon-smelling floors. A building where Phil Soran would be waiting.

"Whatcha got?" said John Bolder as he rounded the cubicle wall.

Phil Soran looked up from his terminal and sat back in his chair. "Hey, welcome back. How was vacation?"

"Vacation was great," answered Bolder as he reached in his shirt pocket and brought out a piece of gum, unwrapped it, and stuck it in his mouth. "It was great to get back to Alabama," he continued. "There's nothin' like home." He reached back in his shirt pocket and brought out another piece of gum, unwrapped it, and joined it with the first. "Sweet home Alabama!" He rolled the empty wrapper and threw it in the direction of the wastebasket. But the wadded paper hit the rim and fell to the floor. "Whatcha all been doin'?"

Soran arched his back and reached out his arms to stretch. Stifling a yawn he said, "Looks like we have a new player." He picked up a pencil and pointed the eraser end at the screen. "This is a replay from last week," he continued. The CRT screen was displaying in real time and showing two men talking near the firing range. One man had long, flowing red hair with a red-checked headband and the other boasted jet black hair and a thick Mediterranean mustache. The second man had an AK47 to his shoulder while the first man seemed to be giving instructions.

"The man on the left there," Soran said as he pointed the eraser, "that's Rahin. The one on the right with the AK47 is the new man." Soran drummed the eraser against the screen. We heard from inside that there was a new man. And he's already been logged on to 'Desist.' But here's our first look at him."

Bolder reached into his shirt pocket and extracted a pack of spearmint gum. He tapped it against his open palm until one stick extended from the others and brought it up to Soran. "Spearmint?" he offered.

Soran looked up at Bolder and shook his head. Bolder took out the stick of gum and unwrapped it. Rolling it into a ball, he brought it to his nose and took a whiff before popping it in his mouth. John Bolder had been keeping an eye on camp L1, a Lebanese terrorist camp outside of Ajedabic near the Gulf of Sidra. It had been abandoned after an ill fated strike against Israel had left most of its members dead or captured. Camp L2 was an Irish Republican Army post which, while interesting, posed little threat to the United States. So, after inputting the latest overhead passes into "Desist," the agency's computer system devoted to tracking terrorist organizations, Bolder had come over to assist Soran on Camp L3.

"Well, great," said Bolder. "The more the merrier."

Soran looked up at the clock on the otherwise bare wall. 8:00 A.M. He calculated the seven-hour time difference. "Actually, MRT2 is beginning its 3:00 P.M. pass right about now. Care to look in? In real time?"

"Why, hell yeah," answered Bolder. "It'd be a good way to get back in the swing of things. Some real live action."

Soran punched at his keyboard. The screen went blank for a moment and then came back to life showing a vast expanse of desert. "Any moment now," said Soran. Small dark lines appeared on the screen. "There she is," Soran continued. "Let's see who's home." Soran punched some keys. "Upper quadrant enhanced." Three-fourths of the screen disappeared and the remaining fourth enlarged to fill the screen. "Um, nothing of interest there." He punched more keys and the picture was back to the original position. "Let's look at the lower right quadrant." More keys punched. Three-quarters of the screen disappeared and the remaining fourth enlarged to fill the screen.

"What's that there?" asked Bolder, pointing to the screen.

"Let's see," answered Soran. "Enhance again." Three-fourths of the screen became blank with the remainder enlarged.

"One more time," said Bolder. "I want to get a look at that one." He pointed a pencil at a figure on the screen. Soran enhanced one more time.

"Isn't there a woman in this camp?" asked Bolder.

Soran waited for a moment, studying the figure on the screen. "Yes, there is," he replied.

"Well, that's got to be her," said Bolder. "That's got to be her because I see tits."

Soran enhanced the picture again so that the figure almost filled the screen. He studied the picture. The picture was clear. It definitely was a female. She was walking. Alone at first. Then from off screen, an arm came out from behind her, reaching for her.

Nadia walked purposefully to her tent. From behind a hand reached out and grabbed her by the right shoulder, spinning her around. A man stepped directly in front of her. His worn blue jeans had holes torn in the knees. His dirty T-shirt with a faded Coca-Cola insignia had its sleeves rolled up to the tops of his shoulders, partially contracting the area stained from his armpits. His face showed the pockmarks of raging acne and when he opened his mouth, dark spaces appeared where three teeth should have been. The teeth he had left were covered with gray-green slime which issued a pungent odor when he opened his mouth to speak.

"How come you never speak to me?" he asked in a raspy voice. "You know my name is Kahlil. You know me. Why do you never speak to me?"

Nadia recoiled at the odor and took a step back.

Kahlil waved his hand at her. "You always walk around with your nose in the air and you pretend that we are not even here."

"I don't have time for this," said Nadia as she started to turn.

Kahlil reached out and grabbed her, spinning her around again. "What are you, too good for us?" he said. "Just because Major Brohan thinks you're pretty, you think you are too good for us. Why don't you play with us for a while?" His right hand came up and reached for her chin.

"Leave me alone," said Nadia as she brushed the hand away. "Just leave me alone," she said, and turned to walk away.

Kahlil reached out with both hands and grabbed Nadia's shoulders. "Why you little bitch," he said. He turned her to face him. "Let's take a look at you. Why should Brohan have all the fun?"

He grabbed the front of her shirt and ripped it open to the navel. Nadia threw out her hand and slapped Kahlil on the left cheek. He loosened his grip on her blouse and put his hand up to his cheek. Nadia pulled her blouse back together and started to turn.

"Why you little bitch," said Kahlil as he grabbed her by the shoulder. His right hand hit her high on the cheekbone with enough force to send her sprawling to the ground.

"You little whore. Let's see why the major thinks you're so special." He started unzipping his fly. "I'm going to do you right here," he said as he knelt down next to her. Still dazed by the blow, Nadia instinctively, but slowly, raised her knees.

"Stop it!" came a voice from behind Kahlil. "Stop it right there!"

Kahlil turned around and looked up. A man was standing behind him but the sun was directly behind the man's head. Shards of sunlight glistened about the head, darkening his face. Kahlil squinted for a monument, said a quick "fuck it," then turned back to his prey. Nadia opened her eyes and looked past Kahlil to the man standing in front of the sun.

"Let her go!" It was Amjad's voice.

"Fuck you!" said Kahlil. "This little bitch has been walking around here for weeks." Small bits of spittle were forming on Kahlil's lips as he spoke. "A prize for Major Brohan. The little bitch hit me so now she's going to be mine." He turned back to Nadia, reaching out for her breast.

Amjad's hand reached down and grabbed Kahlil by the back of his shirt, hauling him to his feet. "I said that's enough. Leave the girl alone!"

Kahlil pulled away from Amjad's grasp. "You shouldn't butt in where you don't belong," he yelled as he raised his right fist and hurled it at Amjad's head. But Amjad blocked the blow with his left forearm and sent his right hand, palm open, to the bridge of Kahlil's nose, splitting it. Blood splattered out from the crushed cartilage as Kahlil stood momentarily dazed. Amjad stepped to the side, brought his right foot up, and kicked out, catching Kahlil's right knee on the side of the joint. Kahlil shrieked in pain as the joint buckled, sending him sprawling to the ground. Amjad stood over him for a moment and then turned to Nadia.

"Are you hurt?" he asked as he knelt down to her. Nadia pulled her blouse together and sand fell from her hair as she shook her head. Amjad reached for her. "Let me help you."

"Look out!" cried Nadia, and pointed behind Amjad. Amjad raised up and turned around to see Kahlil kneeling on his good knee. Blood was streaming from his nose and mouth. From beneath a furrowed brow, dark, malevolent eyes glared at Amjad. Amjad looked down and saw a knife in Kahlil's right hand.

Kahlil spit out some blood. "Now you die!" he said, pointing his knife at Amjad.

As Amjad took a step toward him, Kahlil reached down, picked up a handful of sand, and hurled it upward into Amjad's face. Amjad reeled backward a step, throwing his hands to his face. From his kneeling position, Kahlil burst forward with all of the power that his good knee could muster, burying his shoulder into Amjad's abdomen, sending them both sprawling.

Amjad lay on his back fighting to get his breath. The sand was in his eyes and mouth and he coughed. There was pressure on his chest. He opened his eyes and looked upward but the sand and tears blurred his vision. The pressure on his chest was greater. He tried to roll over but couldn't move. He rubbed his eyes and the vision started to come. But time seemed to slow. He was aware of everything that was happening, but everything was happening slowly; as if he were examining reality rather than simply experiencing it.

His hands felt something warm, something warm dripping on them. He turned them over and saw drops of blood on the backs of his hands. He looked up and saw the outline of someone, someone sitting on him. He blinked twice and the vision cleared. A man was sitting on him, straddling his chest with his head bowed. As the head moved upward, Amjad could see Kahlil's face. It was no longer the face of anger. The pain was gone. The eyes were open wide and the brow smoothed. Amjad could see Kahlil smile through crimson teeth. The blood from Kahlil's nose and mouth ran down his chin, dripping on Amjad's chest. He spit blood as he said, "Now you die!" and raised his knife.

But he paused for a moment. As Amjad looked up, Kahlil's face turned back to the pain. But this was a different pain. Kahlil's eyes squinted as his brow furrowed. He brought his lips back exposing gritted teeth. There was real pain in his expression—not the pain of moments ago. Not the pain of a previous blow. But pain that was happening now. Severe pain. Kahlil's head turned slowly to his right and Amjad followed his gaze to his right hand—his hand and the knife. But now there were fingers around Kahlil's right wrist. As the fingers dug into the wrist, the skin around where the fingers pressed was white from the blood being forced elsewhere. Kahlil was still holding the knife, but the grip was loosening. The hand on the wrist gripped tighter, like a vice.

Kahlil let out a low, gurgling sound and squeezed his eyes tightly. He raised his upper lip and hunched his shoulders in pain. The knife tumbled from his hand.

Amjad looked at the fingers holding Kahlil's wrist. His slow-motion gaze followed the hand up the arm and to the shoulder where a pack of Camels showed through a threadbare T-shirt. He followed upward but the man's head was directly in front of the sun, darkening his face. Steams of sunlight flowed from around his head forming a corona, a sunlit halo. As the head moved slightly, Amjad saw a shock of blondish red hair held in place by a red and white checkered headband. Rahin!

Rahin let go of Kahlil's wrist and stepped directly behind him. He put his right hand under Kahlil's chin while his left hand went to the top of Kahlil's head. He snapped his right hand violently up and to the right while at the same time his left hand went down and to the left. There was a loud crack. Amjad looked at Kahlil's face. The pain was gone. The eyes stared forward and a drop of blood dribbled down from his now loosened lips.

Rahin returned Kahlil's head to its original position and repeated the procedure. Once more a loud crack. Rahin lowered Kahlil's lifeless body to the ground and put his right knee into Kahlil's back. He put both hands under Kahlil's chin and pulled back with his hands as he pushed forward with his knee. There were two loud cracks and the head lay limply, unsupported in Rahin's hands. Rahin let go of the head and it fell to the earth, kicking up sand as it landed next to Amjad's face. Lifeless eyes stared at Amjad's car. A crimson bubble formed from the right nostril as a collapsing lung ushered out its final breath.

Amjad was back to real time now. He shuddered for a moment. He had seen death before. He had seen it on the operating table. He had seen it raining from the skies over Baghdad. But he had never seen a man's life taken at the hands of another man; the raw, brutish power. The primordial, beastly act. The original sin.

He shoved the dead face away from him and scrambled to his feet. As he straightened up a queasiness came over him. His skin felt clammy and his hands were cold. Something was moving in his stomach, moving upward. He looked around and saw his tent only a few meters away. As he moved toward the tent, his vision clouded and his steps became painstakingly labored as they shuffled through the sand. He missed the front of the tent and tripped over the guide wire, stumbling to the ground. As he pushed himself upward from the sand, he felt what was in his stomach quickly approaching his throat. He leaned over and let it go.

"Man," said Bolder, sitting on the edge of Soran's desk, unwrapping his third stick of gum. "Did you see what I just saw?"

Soran was sitting back in his chair, his hands resting on the keyboard. He was staring at the screen. The screen that was blank. The screen that just minutes ago had displayed a dance of death from six thousand miles away. And this was not just pictures on a screen. This was real. And although this was displayed in real time, Soran somehow felt that he had watched in slow motion. Time had slowed for him and all he could do was to stare at the blank screen. His hands were cold and his skin felt clammy. From a distance he heard a voice. The voice was familiar but he couldn't quite make it out. The voice seemed to be calling him. "Phil," the voice called. He continued to stare at the screen. "Phil," the voice was closer. Still the stare. His left shoulder was being pressed down. He blinked, shook his head, and he was back in the room.

Bolder took his hand from Phil's shoulder as Phil turned to look at him. "Man, you okay?" Bolder asked.

Soran took a deep breath and put his head backwards, stretching his neck. Pulling his hands from the keyboard, he arched his shoulders and closed his eyes.

"You okay?" Bolder repeated.

Soran opened his eyes and released his breath, slowly, deliberately. Brushing a hand through his hair, he cocked his head and turned to Bolder. "Yeah," he said. "Yeah, I'm okay."

Bolder slipped the fresh stick of gum into his mouth and said, "Man, did you see what I just saw?"

Soran put both hands on the arms of his chair. "Yeah, I saw it."

"Well, scratch one bad guy!" Bolder said laughingly as he slapped his left thigh.

Soran's hands were on the keyboard now. "Yeah," he said. "Scratch one." As he typed, the screen came to life. The words "ROUTING TO DESIST" appeared on the screen and then were gone.

"Jeez, have you ever seen anything like that?" asked Bolder.

Soran shook his head slowly, deliberately. He took a deep breath, held it for a moment, and then let it out slowly. He looked down at his cold hands. Cold hands on the cold keyboard. His eyes followed up his forearms and noticed the normal tan coloring was gone. His throat felt thick and full.

"If you don't feel well, you all know the bathroom's down the hall and to the right," Bolder said jokingly with an Alabama twang.

Soran sat for a moment, pinching the bridge of his nose with his left thumb and forefinger as he squeezed his eyes shut. Opening his eyes, he looked up at Bolder whose broad smile had turned to a quizzical look. He pushed his chair back and stood up. Patting Bolder on the shoulder as he passed, Phil Soran rounded the cubicle wall, walked to the hall, and took a right.

On his way to the communications tent, Rahin examined the events of the previous day. It had come down to a choice, really. Someone was going to die.

That choice had already been made. Made before he got there. Not by him, but by Kahlil. Once the confrontation had escalated, it would not have been a choice of whether someone would die but of which one would die. Blood feuds were an anathema to terrorist camps. Intolerable. The cadre could ill afford to have warring camps within itself. Each one would be looking over his shoulder, keeping an eye on his adversary rather than keeping his mind on his assignment. And the possibility of the feud erupting at an inappropriate moment could place the whole cadre in jeopardy. No, it had not become a question of whether but who. This was Rahin's camp. Now it had become Rahin's time to choose.

Kahlil had not been a bad comrade, a little argumentative at times, vulgar to be sure. He had taken orders fairly well, mastered the AK47, and was tolerated by the other men.

But Amjad was another matter. Here was a man Rahin could identify with: intelligent, successful, a leader of men—a strong man, but deeply sensitive. Rahin had been sensitive once—long ago—before all of the hate. The all-encompassing, overpowering, devouring hate. A hate which fed upon itself and whose appetite seemed to increase in proportion to that which it consumed. Amjad represented what Rahin could have become. Now Amjad would become what Rahin is. It was a simple choice. A quick choice. A deadly choice. The right choice.

Rahin reached for the tent door and pulled the flap slightly open. Nadia was sitting on her cot, facing the door. Amjad was on the floor of the tent, kneeling on a prayer rug, his head bowed to the ground and his Koran laded hands thrust forward in supplication to the east, to Mecca. Rahin slowly closed the tent flap and took a step back. The wind had come up and was swirling the sand around his feet. As he stepped back he looked down at his footprint in the sand. The sole of his boot had five traction bands in a star burst pattern making five indentations in the sand. He stared at it for a moment and remembered the Five Pillars. He had tried to be religious once, a follower of Islam. But the years had been hard on him. He had known the Five Pillars. He had tried. Belief in Allah and Mohammed, his prophet: sure, why not? Pilgrimage to Mecca: he was sure to get around to it. Alms giving to the poor: as soon as he found someone poorer than himself. Fast of Ramadan: ooh, that's a long time to be hungry. Daily prayer: where in the world does the time go?

The wind swirled around Rahin and a few specks of sand hit him in the cheek. He swatted at them like they were insects and looked back at the ground. The swirling sand had filled the boot imprint and nothing remained to show that he or anyone else had been there.

"Thank you for waiting," came a voice.

Startled, Rahin blinked his eyes and looked up. The door flap of the tent was open slightly and he could see Amjad's face illuminated in the light. "What?" responded.

"Thanks for waiting 'til I finished," answered Amjad. "I felt you at the door when you opened it and I appreciate you waiting."

Rahin looked at Amjad in the light and then back down at the sand shifting before his feet. "Ah, no problem," he managed.

Amjad held the door open further and beckoned with his hand. "Would you like to come in?"

Rahin kicked at the sand with his right foot. "Yes," he said. "Yes, I would."

Amjad held the flap open still further and Rahin's shoulder brushed him as he entered the tent. As Amjad walked over and sat on his cot, Rahin motioned to Nadia. "Nadia, I would like to be alone with Amjad for a moment."

Nadia tilted her head and shrugged her shoulders disinterestedly. She rose from her cot, grabbed her jean jacket, and disappeared through the tent door. Rahin walked over to Nadia's cot, pulled it over to next to Amjad, and sat down facing him.

"What happened yesterday was necessary," he started. "But you must learn that here you cannot fight a man halfway. There is no room for civility. When you go up against a man, there is only one outcome."

Amjad pursed his lips and lowered his gaze to the floor.

"Amjad, look at me," said Rahin. Amjad brought his right elbow up to his right knee, while the fingers of his right hand found and massaged his chin. He tilted his head upward until his gaze met Rahin's.

"I know this is all new to you, Amjad," said Rahin. "But you must get used to this now. You must learn. This is your life now."

"I know," Amjad said in a low voice. "And I am willing to learn. I want to learn."

Rahin stuck his dirty fingers in his shirt pocket and retrieved two cigarettes. He pointed them at Amjad. "It's easy here," he said, and put both cigarettes to his lips. He reached back into his shirt pocket and pulled out a pack of matches. Holding the pack in one hand he flipped open the cover and bent one match in half. As his thumb pressed the match head against the strike plate, his fingers rearranged themselves for a better hold on the book. One flick of his thumb and the match burst into flame. As the smell of sulfur filled his nostrils he brought the flame to each cigarette and drew in the smoke. He offered one to Amjad as the smoke, dragon-like, escaped through his nostrils.

"No one is firing back at you," he continued. "And there are no live targets. We are shooting into paper, cardboard, and sand. Later you may be called upon to use your weapon to kill. And it won't be shooting cardboard or blowing up sand. It will be real people. If you are killing someone to defend yourself, you should have no problem." He took another drag from the cigarette and inhaled deeply, held it for a moment, and exhaled. He squinted as he looked through the smoke and into Amjad's eyes. "But you may be called upon to kill someone who you may think of as innocent. It is then that you have to reach down inside of yourself and remember the goal. We are all here because we believe the goal is more important than any innocent life. It is more important than your own life. But there may come a time when you will question yourself. It is that time that you must dig down inside yourself and have a reason to pull the trigger. But you cannot wait 'til the time comes to go searching for the answer. The answer must be with you always. You must be able to reach out and grab it at any time. Do you have the answer now?"

Amjad closed his eyes. His mind looked down to a little girl's red shoe nestled in his hands.

"I will not have a problem," he whispered.

Soran stopped typing and reached for his cup of coffee. John Bolder was standing next to his desk, leaning over.

"Whatcha got?" he asked.

Soran took a gulp of coffee and looked down at the stack of manila folders on his desk. Each folder contained the profile of a terrorist listed in this camp. Information was as complete as possible: probable nationality and age, physical features, right-handed or left-handed, what weapons he trained with, with whom did he train, with whom did he come. Sometimes they got a name. They always tried to get a picture. In the event of interdiction, ID's had to be positive.

"Whadaya think?" asked Bolder with his southern drawl. "Think they're up to somethin'?"

"Well," answered Soran. "Major Brohan has been checking in lately and it wouldn't surprise me if something was afoot."

"What's your best guess?" asked Bolder.

Soran punched a couple numbers on his keyboard and pushed "ENTER." He picked up a pencil and put the eraser to his forehead. "I don't think it's anything in the Middle East," he said. "They just don't seem ready for that yet. And with Brohan popping in like that." He took the pencil from his forehead and drummed the rim of his coffee cup. "You know, the Libyans don't do anything for free. The Palestinians are welcome there, but only for a price, to do something for the Libyans for their favors.

"We've known for some time now that Qaddafi would like to invade Chad. This would be a way for him to gauge their response. I don't think they are ready for the Middle East.

"No, I think it would be something local. I'd think it would be Chad."

Chapter Five
An Offering to the Heavens

"Can't sleep?" came a voice from behind him.

Amjad stood at the door of the tent. The tip of his cigarette glowed as he took another drag. A rope-like spindle of smoke drifted skyward in the cool desert air only to be broken as Amjad exhaled and scattered it into the night.

"Can't sleep?" Nadia repeated.

Amjad turned around and looked at her. She was lying on her side on her cot, her head propped up by her right arm and shoulder. Sharing the tent with Nadia had been a blessing. Amjad had felt that they shared a common thread. Her world had been destroyed by the Israelis, his shattered by the Americans. Yet, awash in the sea of hate, she had possessed a certain gentleness. A member of the cadre, to be sure, but still possessed of the trappings of a woman. And she had seemed to appreciate his presence. She had not said so. Nor had she made any outward signs to that end. But still he had felt a sense of sharing. He would not let her get in his way. He would not be deflected from his course. But, still, it was nice to have a respite from the storm.

"No," he said as he flicked the cigarette into the cool air. He watched it tumble, end over end, until it landed in the sand, scattering its fiery essence into a few small embers that glowed for a moment and then were gone.

"No," he repeated, "Not too sleepy right now."

"Me neither," she added as she pushed her head and shoulders off the cot and supported them with her right elbow. "There's a special place I like to go when I can't sleep. Especially on a calm, beautiful night like this. I know a way through the mine fields and I go there from time to time. It's very peaceful there at night." She raised herself so she was now sitting up. "Not much there, really," she continued. "But I just like the peace and calm. Sometimes I look over the dunes and think I'm sailing on an ocean of sand, just letting the breeze take me where Allah wills."

"Sounds very nice," he said.

Her right hand came up and brushed aside the curl of hair that had fallen on her forehead. "Would you like to go there with me tonight?" she asked.

Amjad looked out the door of the tent into the bright, starry sky, the full moon at center stage. "Yes, I would," he answered.

"Be with you in a minute," she said, and hopped out of the cot. She was wearing panties and a T-shirt that covered her bra. She turned her back to Amjad and pulled off the T-shirt. She grabbed her shirt and put it on, buttoning the buttons carefully. Her pants were quickly on next and she sat back down on the cot putting on her socks and shoes.

"Let's try not to wake the others," she said as she got up and walked through the tent door.

Amjad followed her eastward, past the latrine and the firing range and out into the open desert. They walked for about half an hour until they stood before an enormous dune.

"Well, this is it," she said, bending down to take off her shoes and socks. Amjad quickly followed suit. She dug her toes into the sand. The night air was cooling but the sand still held the warmth from the previous day. She took him by the hand and led him to the top of the dune.

It was just like she said it would be, he thought. It seemed as though they were high atop a ship in an endless sea of sand. The sky was clear and the full moon bathed the landscape with its pale light. She dug her feet into the sand again and felt yesterday's heat. But somehow the warmth seemed to come from the moon and the stars, not the endless miles of sand. They stood there together, the stillness broken occasionally by the searching chirping of a sand cricket.

"This is my special place," she said. "I come here when I want to be alone."

She turned to face him. She looked down at his hands and then took them in hers. Her hands were warm and dry but had a slight tremble. She kept her head down, not ready to look into his eyes. "I like you being here," she started quietly. "Being here with me."

Her thumbs started caressing the backs of his hands. "You are gentle and kind. Not like the others."

His grip grew firmer on her hands and he brought them up to his lips and kissed them. "Look at me," he said.

She raised her head slowly, unsure, but her eyes stopped at shoulder level.

"Look at me," he repeated.

She raised her gaze until she was looking into his deep, black, soothing eyes.

"You are a beautiful woman," he continued, "You are young and full of life. You do not belong here."

Her eyes started to water. "I do not know where to go," she answered.

"Anywhere," he said. "Go anywhere. Here you have no future."

She let go of his hands and flung her arms around his shoulders, her head coming to rest on his chest.

"Take me with you," she said. "Take me away from here."

Amjad put his left arm around her back as his right hand came up and caressed the back of her head. "I cannot do that," he said.

"But…" she started as she pulled her head back.

"No," he interrupted. "I cannot do that. There is something I must do. Something I must do alone."

She looked again into his face. His look was understanding but firm. She put her head back on his chest. "Then," she started but paused for a moment. "Then stay with me until you go," she continued.

He held her firmly for a few seconds and then brought his right hand up to her chin. He raised her head to face his. Her eyes were closed and streaks of tears were making their way down her cheeks. Wiping the tears away with his right hand, he leaned down and softly kissed her eyes. She moaned softly. He tilted her chin up a bit and bent down to place his lips fully on hers. Her moan grew as she pulled her trembling hands to his shoulders. Their mouths were open now and their tongues probing. She was up on her toes as their lips parted and his mouth went down and found her neck, kissing her gently. She gasped for air, grabbed his neck, and held tight.

But he straightened up, grabbed her hands from behind the back of his neck and lowered them to her side. She looked up at him questioningly, but he leaned down and gently kissed her forehead. His hands left hers and reached up to take her shoulders. With gentle pressure he pushed the left shoulder back while the right one came forward. She realized that he wanted her to turn around and she rearranged her footing to accommodate him. After she had turned, he put his right hand on her right shoulder and his left hand on her left shoulder. Squeezing gently he bent down and kissed the side of her neck. She leaned her head back into him and sighed. As his hands went down and found her breasts she caught her breath and moaned again, turning her head to the side. Her hands came up and pushed his hands firmer to her breasts as she arched her back in confirmation. His breath was hot against her skin as his hands quickly undid the buttons of her blouse. Her hands went down to her side as he opened the blouse and slowly slid it over her shoulders and down her arms. His hands went up her arms, over her shoulders, and found her bra-covered breasts again. She moaned again and rolled her head. His hands went up to the straps of the bra and slowly brought them over her shoulders and down her arms to her elbows. The cups were still covering her breasts but he gently tugged at the straps until the cups loosened their grip and slid down over the mounds, exposing them to his view. She bit her lip as he quickly undid the bra clasp and slid the bra and blouse from her arms.

His hands were on her wrists. He felt her trembling as his hands made their way up her arms, past the elbows, and slowly to her shoulders. Gently he pulled her shoulders back, pushing her firm breasts out into the cool desert air. He held her there momentarily as if bathing her bare breasts with moonlight. Then he slowly turned her around until he faced her. Her eyes were open and looking into his, expectantly. He pulled his hands from her shoulders to her breasts and, as he touched the nipples, she quivered as her eyes closed. Slowly he sank to his knees and his hand found her belt and undid it. As he unbuttoned her pants, she opened her eyes and looked down at him but kept her shoulders back as her arms dangled at her side, slightly behind her. He slowly slid her pants down and she quickly stepped out of them. As he pushed gently on the inside of her knees, she adjusted her stance by spreading her legs apart. His hands were on her left thigh, his left hand on the inside, the right one on the outside. He massaged gently upward until he came to her crotch. Sliding his hands over her crotch to her other thigh, he massaged downward. He repeated the process with her right thigh, and as he crossed her crotch he put his hand gently against her crotch and felt the wetness coming through her panties. He finished going down the left thigh and then reached up and slowly pulled her panties down. When they reached her mid-thigh she put her legs together as he slid the panties down and off.

Gentle pressure on the inner thighs and she quickly reassumed the spread position. His hand came up her left thigh again until they reached her crotch. This time he placed his hands very gently on her crotch as he passed to the right upper thigh. When he had completed the right thigh and was up to her crotch, he put his hands next to the crotch, leaned forward and kissed it. The sweet womanly smell reached his nostrils and he pressed his face harder against her. Then he moved back and kissed her inner thighs, his lips retracing the path that his hands had worn before returning to center. With his hands next to her crotch he used his thumbs to pull the labia aside and his mouth moved forward. As his tongue found her clitoris she gasped, widened her stance, and thrust her hips forward. Her hands moved to the back of his head and guided it forward. He moved his tongue in and out, side to side, and in a circular motion, playing a bit with her. He quickly noticed that her left side drew the strongest response. He stroked the left side back and forth, up and down. When it was clear that he needed no further direction, she took her hands from behind his head and brought them to her side, then up to shoulder level and held them there, Christ-like, with palms open. Her head went back as she arched her back, her breasts an offering to the heavens.

His palms felt the top of her thighs stiffen as his thumbs pulled the labia further apart. As his tongue found a faster pace, her breath came in short spurts. She gasped and held her breath as a low moan emerged from deep within her. He felt the warm gush of fluid as her body spasmed with the orgasm. Her lower abdomen was taut and her thighs flexed. Rotating her hips slightly, the low moan continued momentarily and then stopped. She was breathing again.

Amjad's tongue backed away as his thumbs brought the labia back together. He kissed the wet, matted dampness lightly as his lips made their way from the pubic area to her belly. As he raised himself upward, he continued lightly kissing her front, past the belly, beneath each breast, and then to each nipple. Her arms were still outstretched and his hands followed the curve of her back as his lips explored her front. He kissed the base of her neck and below her ears. He found his way past her cheeks and to her closed eyes. After kissing each of her eyes, his hands went out to meet hers and their fingers intertwined. Their hands squeezed as their lips met and parted.

He loosened his grip on her hands and put his arms around her, squeezing her to just short of the breaking point. She moaned a different, pleasing moan as he lowered her down to the sand beneath them. He laid her down and then sat up as he undid his trousers and pulled them down past his buttocks. They quickly went over his knees and past his feet and just as quickly were cast aside onto the sand next to them where they make a little "poof" sound when they landed. Lying back down next to her he raised her head slightly as he slipped his arm under her neck to pillow her head.

She smiled a warm smile. Her left arm was curled under her as her right hand pressed against the hair on his chest. His left hand pushed her hair from her face and stroked the side of her head for a while before venturing to her shoulders and down her back. Back up her back his hand came as he felt her warm breath against his chest. Her breathing was rhythmical and peaceful and belied the tempest she had just passed through. The stars looked down upon these resting lovers and seemed to twinkle their approval.

Amjad's hand was sent back down to the small of her back. He moved it to her side and worked it under her right arm until he found her right breast. He gently massaged it as she moaned softly. His hand moved to her left breast and she pressed harder against his chest. His mouth came down and found her lips again. She opened them and willingly found his tongue. His left hand was back on her right breast again but the massaging was a bit firmer. His breath quickened and their mouths opened more, their tongues entwined. Her breathing was matching his now as he rolled over onto her. He took her arms by the wrists and pushed them into the sand at shoulder level, pinning her to the sand. Her eyes opened widely and she gasped as she felt him enter her. He surged forward and then drew back;

An Offering to the Heavens 57

forward again and back again. Her eyes were still wide open and she found herself joining him in this lover's dance. As her pelvis rocked back and forth she looked up at this big, bold, beautiful man. She gazed at him for a while and then closed her eyes and pushed her head back in the sand.

Suddenly the rocking stopped as Amjad loosened his grip on her left wrist and put his right hand under her neck. He leaned his shoulder down and to the right as he pulled her neck up. As he rolled to the right, her body followed his until she was upright and on top of him. He loosened his grip on her right wrist and, as he adjusted his buttocks in the sand, his hands once again found her breasts. With her knees beside his hips and her hands resting on his shoulders, she was in total control. She rocked up and down, gently at first but eventually the pace quickened, as if her body was trying to keep pace with the increased beating of her heart. Her face felt warm as the blood raced throughout her body. The warmth proceeded downward followed by goose bumps which covered her arms, breasts, and thighs. Her passion had taken over and was controlling her motions. The pace quickened again and her throat tightened, emitting a low uncontrollable moan. Her body became rigid as she felt him ejaculate within her. Her pelvic area spasmed in a tugging sensation as a new flood of fluid was sent forth to meet his ejaculate. She held her breath for what seemed an eternity as the world stopped its rotation to wait for her.

When the world came back into view, her breathing started with a long, slow exhalation as if all the inequities of a sinful world were made whole by that single breath. Her body felt warm in the clean desert air. She uncurled her toes but her arms were still quivering. He reached up, took her shoulders, and lowered her down to him, kissing the perspiration that had formed on her upper lip. Her legs stretched out as she collapsed on top of him, totally spent. Amjad stroked the back of her head and she breathed hot breath on the side of his neck. Amjad looked up as he stroked her. For breathtaking, awe inspiring beauty, the night desert air has no rival. But he was looking past the moon, past the stars; beyond space and time and into eternity.

Chapter Six
Chad

Radio waves travel in straight lines. Not a single straight line but many straight lines, like the pond ripples from a dropped pebble spreading forth in all directions. They are true, raw, pure energy. Unburdened by physical matter they travel from their emitted source at the speed of light and scatter into space. Naked, unprotected, unguarded they spread forth. Unable to cloak themselves from the intruding ear of a collecting antenna, they send their essence to the furthest reaches of the universe. Or to anyone or anything that would listen along the way.

High above the orbits of MRT1 and MRT2, satellites MAGNUM and VORTEX listen in the dark quiet of space. They hold their geosynchronous orbit above the Middle East 22,300 miles above the earth. Their velocity matches the earth's rotation, and their orbital centrifugal force is perfectly matched by earth's gravitational pull. Held in place by a tether of Newtonian physics, perfectly balanced like the immutable scales of theoretical justice, they listen to the radios of the world.

The radio waves are collected, encoded, and transferred to a transmitting antenna which sends them back to earth. Captured and laid bare, they surrender their secrets to strange men in white-walled rooms. Most are perused and discarded. But occasionally, one in their midst catches an eye and makes its way to a computer in Virginia named DESIST.

Waves of airborne sand pelted the tent as the storm played out its fury. The Arabs call them *ghibli,* the dry, desiccating winds of sand and dust that darken the midday sky. Inside the communications tent the oil lantern rocked with the swaying of the center pole, throwing intermittent patterns of light and shadows dancing on the canvas walls. Puffs of fine sand dust would filter through the seams around the tent door and drift aimlessly around the room. The flapping of the walls cast loose collected dust that combined with cigarette smoke floating through the air.

Major Brohan stood at the table by the center post of the communications tent, studying a map. He pulled a pack of cigarettes from his shirt pocket and offered one to Rahin, who was standing next to him. Rahin raised his right hand and showed Major Brohan an already lit cigarette. Major Brohan grunted and brought the pack to his mouth, attached one cigarette to his lips, and pulled it from the pack. As he fumbled for his lighter, Rahin brought a lit match up to the dangling cigarette. Major Brohan turned his head toward Rahin, squinted, then sucked the flame into the head of the cigarette. Rahin lowered the match slowly before bringing it to his lips and blowing it out.

The tip of the cigarette glowed brightly as Major Brohan took the smoke deep into his lungs. As he slowly let it out, he suddenly convulsed in a hacking cough, deep from inside, and bent over, banged his hand against the table. Rahin reached for him, grabbing him by the shoulders.

"Are you all right?" Rahin asked.

Major Brohan, sucking air back into his lungs, held up one hand toward Rahin. He raised himself up and reached for the canteen hanging from the center post. After fumbling to get the cap unscrewed, he raised it to his lips and took a large swallow. He craned his chin up, stretching his neck. Handing the canteen to Rahin, he coughed slightly into his hand. "I'm okay," he said in a raspy voice. "It's just the dust of Ashar."

Rahin screwed the cap back on the canteen and returned it to the center pole. He brushed the front of his shirt with both hands and turned back to the major.

"You'll be going in at 0300 tomorrow," said Brohan. "This ghibli will be over by then. I have two helicopters to take you to here." Brohan pointed his nicotine-stained finger at a point on the map near the Chad border. "It will take about two hours. There the helicopters will be refueled. I will have a fuel truck standing by. You will then take off, cross the border, and head for Aozi. That will take about another hour. You should be getting there about dawn. The target is a radar station. You find the target and destroy it. The helicopters will be standing by to take you home. Any questions?"

Rahin turned over to Amjad lying on his cot. "Amjad," he said. "Come over here. I want you to see this."

Amjad rose from the cot and walked over to the table. Major Brohan was watching Nadia, laying on her cot, and noticed as her gaze followed Amjad cross the room. As Amjad reached the table, Brohan turned to him, raised his eyebrows, and smiled a deep, leering smile, his large white teeth poking out from under his thick, black mustache. "So, you have been busy, my friend," he said.

Amjad cocked his head, furrowed his brow, and with half squinting eyes said, "Pardon me?"

Brohan looked at Nadia and then back at Amjad. He laughed and slapped Amjad on the shoulder. "Ah, never mind," he said, and took a deep drag from his cigarette. He let the smoke escape through his mouth and nostrils as he looked back at Nadia. "It is nothing," he said.

"How heavily is it defended?" interrupted Rahin.

Brohan flicked the ashes from the end of his cigarette. "What?" he said turning back from Nadia.

"How heavily is it defended?" repeated Rahin.

"Oh, ah, very lightly," lied Brohan as he looked back down at the map. He did not know for sure and really did not care. These were not Libyan troops he was sending in. If they made it back, so much the better. But at the very least, the radar station should be taken out and he could gauge the Chad response.

"What kind of terrain?" asked Amjad.

"Hilly," said Brohan. "But that serves our purpose. The hills will hide our helicopters from the radar to get you close enough to approach them by foot. I have brought some C4 and a few LAW rockets. Can you handle them?"

"The Germans will handle the C4, and Kazi will take care of the rockets," said Rahin. "The rest of us will support them."

Brohan lit another American cigarette and watched the smoke curl around his yellow-stained fingers.

"So, you will be ready?" he asked.

"We will be ready," replied Rahin.

A slight breeze curled around Amjad as he sat in the dark near the landing area, awaiting the arrival of the helicopters. The night air was cool and the fury of the recent ghibli, though only hours absent, was just a recent memory. Amjad looked up at the clear, nighttime sky of the desert. Soon he would light the landing flares. Soon. But now he would sit back and watch the nighttime sky, the parade of stellar hosts. The moon, half sheathed in darkness, poked its lighted half out for a look. The stars, the massive accumulation of stars, were so numerous that Amjad wondered if they could outnumber the grains of sand of the endless, shifting desert beneath him. And every few minutes the flashes across the sky, the gifts from the heavens sent to earth, the meteors. These tiny specks of sand and rock passing through eons of time, the whole of their being insignificant compared to the grandeur of the cosmos.

And then the astronomical coincidence of an encounter with an atmosphere of twenty-one percent oxygen. They glow as they come alive. They would shout if they had voices. They would laugh if they had mouths. They would cry if they had tears. They would give all that they have. And they do. After eons and eons of endless drifting, they burst forth in flames as they streak across the sky, their seeming destiny fulfilled, their one meaningful moment in eternity. Then their brash rage of riot that defines their reason for being consumes them. A brief dash across the sky and they are gone.

Amjad picked up a handful of sand and tossed it a few meters in front of him, watching in the starlight the granules disperse on the ground. He wondered when another hand or foot or gust of wind would send this sand aimlessly sprawling along another path, motion without direction, totally dependent on outside forces. Existence without meaning.

He thought back to a time when twisted beams and pulverized concrete had set him adrift in a sea of hate. Taken from him all that he cared for. All that he knew.

Chad 63

And he thought of a land far away where one final act could give meaning to his life, define his existence. He reached down and picked up another handful of sand.

"Amjad," came a voice from behind. His hand closed tighter on the sand.

"Amjad," came the voice again, louder.

He turned and saw Nadia coming down the path to the landing area, flashlight in hand. Amjad looked down at his clenched fist.

"Amjad, they are coming," yelled Nadia. "Light the flares."

Amjad rose to his feet and turned to face Nadia. Her flashlight was searching back and forth like a lighthouse beacon searching for a ship lost at sea. The sound of helicopter rotors grew faintly in the distance.

"Amjad," Nadia yelled again, her flashlight swaying back and forth until it landed and remained fixed on Amjad. "Light the flares. They are coming!"

Amjad stood for a moment, caught in the light, his fist still clenching the sand. Slowly he turned from Nadia's beam toward the darkness of the landing area. His clenched fist relaxed and the sand sifted through his fingers, spilling to the ground. "It is time to go," he said in a quiet whisper. The sound of the rotors was increasing as he pulled a flare from his pocket. Pulling the end cap off and reversing it, he brought the strike plate to the phosphorous fuse at the end of the flare. "Time," he struck the strike plate at the fuse, "to go." The flare burst forth with a blinding brilliance that flooded the landing area. The incandescence of a thousand candles that would rule the night. Until the fiery essence, consuming itself, would be spent. Then fade and surrender to the darkness.

Plumes of dust and sand billowed through the landing area, pushed on by the invading rotors of the helicopters. Rahin turned to the side, slouched a bit, and shielded his eyes in the crook of his left elbow. Although he was somewhat up the path from the landing area, nonetheless he was pelted with the fleeing sand and dust. As the rotors slowed, he raised his eyes above his arm and peered toward the vessels. The lights from the flares danced throughout the dust clouds, illuminating the helicopters which appeared like ghost ships slipping through the fog.

As the clouds settled, Rahin looked incredulously at the machines. These were not the American helicopters that he was expecting. Major Brohin always traveled in American helicopters. But these were Russian; durable to be sure, but smaller than the American helicopters. He turned around to the assembled men behind him. As the men shouldered their packs and weapons, he walked back and picked out two men. Grabbing one by the arm and motioning to the other with his head, he led them a few steps away.

"Look," started Rahin. "These helicopters are not big enough to carry all of us." He cleared his throat. "You two will have to stay back."

One of the men looked over Rahin's shoulder at Nadia, her AK47 at her side.

"What about her?" he asked. "Why is she going?"

Rahin looked over his shoulder at Nadia and then returned to the two men. "It's my decision," he said. "She goes."

"Why is she going while I stay?" the man demanded. "She is a woman, a girl. Can she fight better than me?"

Rahin grabbed the man by the shirt and pulled him closer so they were face to face. "She is our communications officer," Rahin said firmly, his black eyes glaring. "We need her with us and she needs experience in the field. She is going and you are staying."

The man pulled away from Rahin and slung his AK47 over his shoulder.

"But she's a fucking woman," the man repeated.

"Don't argue with me," shouted Rahin. "We don't have time. Go back to your tent."

The man pulled a cigarette out of his left shirt pocket and put it in his mouth. "Fuck it," he said. He lit the cigarette, turned and walked away.

The flight to the refueling station took two hours. The helicopters landed and the cadre disembarked while the helicopters refueled. Rahin pulled Kazi aside.

"Have you ever flown one of these?" asked Rahin, his head motioning toward the helicopters.

Kazi looked strangely at Rahin. "What do you mean?"

"I am familiar with the American helicopters and I think I could fly one in a pinch," answered Rahin. "But these Russian ones…" His voice trailed off and his right hand came up to his chin, massaging his whiskers.

"I want you to watch the pilot," Rahin continued. "I don't trust these Libyans. You go in one helicopter and I'll go in the other. Watch the pilot. See what he does.

Learn what you can. We may have to fly these things out. When we get there, I'm going to leave two men back with the helicopters. We should not need them if it is lightly defended and we arrive unnoticed. If there is trouble, we could use them at the radar station but I'm afraid we would fight our way back and the helicopters would be gone. Leaving two back would at least insure that the helicopters would be there. I don't plan to walk back to our camp."

Once the helicopters were refueled, the men got back in and took off. Rahin sat in the co-pilot's seat next to the pilot, trying to memorize the exact cadence of motions the pilot displayed. All helicopters had to fly the same way, he figured. It was just a matter of figuring out which dial monitored what performance. Which lever or switch performed what function. Fuel mixture, rotor pitch, accelerator, elevator and joystick to control pitch, roll, and yaw. Yes, all helicopters function basically the same. If need be, he could do it.

Rahin leaned back, took a pack of cigarettes from his shouldered sleeve, and extracted a cigarette. He lit it and watched the smoke drift upward for a moment before being caught in the back draft near the ceiling of the craft caused by an ill-fitting side door. He looked at the compass heading: SSE. He looked out through the windshield into the night. He could not make out the horizon in the blackness. But it would be NNW on the way home. He sat back, brought the cigarette to his mouth, and took in the smoke deeply. He held it in while he turned his head around, catching a glimpse of Amjad. Amjad caught Rahin's look and nodded at him. Rahin nodded in response and turned his head back to the black sky in front of him. He relaxed his throat and let the smoke filter through his nostrils and mouth. He watched it linger for a moment, drifting upward before it caught the draft, hurried backwards, and escaped through the crack in the side door.

"Another pitcher?" the waitress asked as she leaned over and pulled the empty pitcher of beer from the table.

Soran looked at Bolder across the table and shrugged his shoulders. Bolder turned to the waitress, pursed his lips, squinted, and canted his head to the left in his best James Dean. "Why, sure thang, perddy lady," he said in his Alabama twang. "What the hell. It's Saturday night."

"You mean, you don't have to get up early tomorrow and go to church?" the waitress said with a wink.

"Sure," answered Bolder. "St. Mattress. The Church of the Presumptuous Assumption." Bolder leaned back in his chair, his left elbow on the chair arm, his left hand rubbing his chin. "I believe God leads by example. 'And on the seventh day he rested.' I believe we should follow his example."

The waitress smiled a pretty smile. A smile Bolder knew was meant more for tips than appreciation. She placed the empty pitcher on her tray. "And that was…" she asked.

"Bud Light," answered Soran looking up momentarily

"Be right back." The waitress turned and headed for the bar.

Bolder watched her as she crossed the room. "I'd like to meet her three stooges tonight," he said.

"What do you mean?" asked Soran.

Bolder reached out and fondled two imaginary breasts in front of him. "You know, Moe, Larry, and, ah…" his right hand went down to fondle an imaginary crotch. "Curly."

Soran laughed into his beer mug.

"Perddy lady," said Bolder as he grabbed another handful of peanuts.

"Yes, she was."

"Still is."

"Yes, she still is."

Bolder cracked a peanut shell and forced it open. "Say," he said. "You're a good looking guy." he popped the peanuts into his mouth. "Why don't you have a steady girl?"

"Oh, I don't know," answered Soran. "Guess I haven't found the right one yet."

"But I know you date a lot of girls." Another peanut shell cracked. "Ain't none of them special?"

Soran cracked a peanut shell and popped the nuts into his mouth. "Yeah," he said. "They're all special. Every girl I go out with is special."

"Ain't that the gospel."

The waitress was back with a new pitcher. "Excuse me," she said smiling at Bolder. *More tips,* thought Bolder. As she bent over to place the pitcher between the two, her blouse flopped open, exposing a generous amount of ample cleavage. *A lot more tips,* thought Bolder as he squashed a peanut between his thumb and forefinger, pulverizing the nuts inside.

"Six-fifty," she said, holding the tray forward.

Bolder shifted through the stack of bills in front of him, extracting a new ten spot with a crease folded neatly down the middle. "Here," he said, tossing the bill on the tray. "Keep it."

"Why, thank you," she said, smiled, and turned away from the table.

"And thank you," said Bolder as he watched her disappear into the crowd.

Bolder looked down at the crushed peanut in his hand and brushed his hands together as if to clean them. "Everyone should have a perddy lady," he said with a sigh.

He looked over at Soran who was already filling his mug with the new offering. "Say, you used to have a picture of a girl on your desk when you first got here." Soran continued to pour. "What happened to her?"

Soran put his mug down and held out the pitcher to Bolder. "More?" he asked.

Bolder raised his mug to meet the offering. "So, what happened to her?" he repeated. "She must have been perddy special to you. You kept her picture on your desk for quite a while after you broke up, as I recall."

Soran finished pouring and put the pitcher back down on the table. "Yeah, she was nice," he said.

"Well, I know she was nice," said Bolder. "What I want to know is, what happened."

"Well, if you must know." Soran grabbed another peanut and pressed it hard between his right thumb and forefinger. "She went and fooled me." The peanut shell cracked, its sides opening up allowing Soran entry to the inner seed. "She ran off with another guy." Soran stroked the inner seed with his thumb. "Never saw it coming. She just kind of went nuts on me. She turned twenty-five and she just went nuts on me. Ya know, I've dated a lot of women and I've noticed that they go through some kind of change when they turn twenty-five."

Bolder brought the beer mug down from his mouth and wiped his lips with the back of his hand. "Don't 'spose any of us men go through any of those changes, do ya?"

"Well, I don't date men so I can't comment on that," answered Soran. "All I know is that they go through some kind of change. For some it may be twenty-four, for others it may be twenty-six. But it usually happens around twenty-five. Something happens to them and they fool ya."

Bolder cracked open a peanut shell and popped the peanut into his mouth. He leaned over the table, reached out and put his hand on Soran's shoulder. "Phil, my friend," he said, "they'll fool ya at any age."

The black of the night had given way to the cool pale of pre-morning. From beyond an azure horizon, the sleepy sun sent forth its golden emissaries to announce its advancing arrival. The air was crisp and clean and lay in wait for the coming of the warming rays. The rays that would end the calm and send the air scurrying to and fro like some ethereal broom sweeping an endless earthen floor.

Rahin looked through the windshield of the helicopter at the changing landscape beneath them. They were now in the foothills of the Tibesti range approaching Aozi, the empty sands of the Sahara behind them. With mountains in the background, the rolling hills were peppered with large rocks and numerous stands of tamarisk, acacia, and cypress trees. Scattered shrubbery dotted the landscape while the tumbleweeds lay in wait for the slightest breeze to send them skittering along their way.

Rahin noticed that the pilot had been following a road. Not directly on top of the road but about one hundred meters to the left, but following it just the same. Rahin put his left hand on the pilot's shoulder and pointed with his right hand down at the road. "Is this the road to Aozi?" he shouted over the noise of the rotors. The pilot nodded. "How much longer?" Rahin asked loudly.

The pilot pointed out the windshield to a clearing ahead. "We are here," he answered.

Spraying up clouds of sand, the helicopters set down softly. After disembarking, Rahin pulled two men aside.

"I want you two to stay here with the helicopters," he said. "It won't take us long, but if there is some trouble, I don't want these two helicopter pilots getting cold feet and taking off without us. I want you to stay in the helicopter the whole time. If they try to leave us, shoot one and keep the other alive until we get back. Got it?"

"Got it," was the response.

Rahin assembled the group. "I'll take the point. Amjad, you stay back with Nadia and the radio. Kazi, you stay back a bit and keep the Germans in the rear. In the name of Allah, you can smell them coming a kilometer away."

They started out. They were about one hundred meters from the road that led to Aozi, but Rahin had decided to parallel the road at this distance just in case it was guarded. His position had put them between the road and the rising sun. They made their way through the brush and rocks, keeping the road in sight, but allowing the natural terrain to give them cover.

When they were a half kilometer from the town, they saw that the road made a left turn and disappeared behind a hill. Rahin signaled for the group to stay there. He motioned for Kazi to come up and join him. Together they went around to the side of the hill furthest from the road and quietly began to climb it. When they were near the summit, Rahin's hand came down on some metallic objects. He stopped and picked one up. Shell casings. Above him, on the ground, were piles of shell casings. Signaling silently to Kazi, he held up the shell casing he had in his hand and pointed to the summit. He put the casing down along with his AK47. He pulled out his knife and held it up, showing it to Kazi. Kazi followed suit. Rahin put the knife between his teeth and continued to inch his way up the hill on all fours.

At the top of the hill was a pile of sandbags, and poking through a slot in the sandbags was the barrel of a fifty-caliber machine gun. Rahin crept up to the side of the sandbags and took the knife out of his mouth. He peered over the top of the sandbags and saw one man in a khaki uniform lying motionless on the ground, curled into the fetal position.

He leaped over the sandbags and pounced on the man. His left hand grasped the man's mouth an instant before his right hand plunged his blade into the left side of the man's neck. The man's eyes startled open as a muffled gurgle came from his mouth. His eyes quickly fixed on a distant focus and Rahin knew he was dead.

Kazi crawled over the side of the sandbags and pointed to the other side of the hill. Rahin crouched over, moved over to the other side of the sandbags, and peered over the top. At the bottom of the hill near the bend in the road stood a French tank. Next to the tank was another pile of sandbags hosting another machine gun. By the sandbags was a large tent.

Fingers of sunlight were now casting long shadows over the distant landscape. No one moved around the tent. Rahin ducked down and leaned back against the sand bags. Realizing that he had just killed the only sentry, he cursed to himself. The radar station was supposed to be lightly defended. But now he had a tank to deal with. He rose to the top of the sandbags again and looked past the tank. He could see the radar station about one hundred meters up the road. The radar station consisted of a large concave dish five meters in diameter next to a command shack which housed the electronics as well as the operators. The complex was surrounded by a wire fence but otherwise seemed unguarded. Rahin stooped down and slid back to Kazi.

"That fucking Brohan," cursed Rahin, his voice slightly above a whisper. "Now we have a fucking tank."

"I can handle it," said Kazi, his eyes widening.

Rahin looked at him. "Can you take it out?"

Kazi slid over to the side of the sandbags closest to the tank and peered over the side. A quick glance and he was back down next to Rahin. "I can't destroy it with my rockets. This tank is too big. But I could get a rocket to the tank's treads. That wouldn't destroy it but it would keep it from pursuing."

"Yeah, but this tank has to have support. That is what the tent is about. We have the element of surprise and I'm sure you could take the tank out. But that would raise the defenders that are here and we would still be one hundred meters from the radar station."

Rahin slid over to the other side of the sandbags and peered over the top. He looked down at the tent, then over to the radar station. Then he slipped down and slid back to Kazi. He looked down pensively and bit his lower lip. "We can still pull this off," he said. "It looks like we just killed the only sentry. Everyone else is still asleep. We can slip by the tank from the other side of the hill, set some delayed fuses, and slip back again before anyone knows what happened."

Kazi nodded. "And I can stay here. I can be your rear guard. If they wake and make a fuss, I can put a rocket in the tank's treads and use this," he patted the fifty-caliber machine gun resting on its tripod next to the sandbags, "on the men."

Rahin looked Kazi in the eye and pursed his lips. He reached over, patted Kazi on the shoulder and nodded. "Let's do it."

Rahin and Kazi made their way down the hill to where the others were waiting. Rahin quickly explained the situation as Kazi gathered his rockets and headed back up the hill. Rahin led the group around the hill into a stand of trees twenty meters from the fence guarding the radar station. The radar station had been placed quite a ways from the town and was on the only road leading to town from that direction. There was a light on in the command shack but no one was guarding the fence. Rahin went back to where the Germans were.

"Can you get me a fifteen minute fuse?" he asked.

"Ja," said one of the Germans.

"Can you rig it so we can have a fifteen-minute fuse but still be able to blow it remotely if we want? Someone is bound to be here soon and I don't want to leave here and have them find it prematurely. Also, we have to slip by that tank again and if we get into a fire fight, I'd like to be able to distract them."

"Ja, das ist no problem."

Rahin took a pair of wire cutters from his bag. "I'll get you in. Then it's up to you," he said.

Rahin traversed the twenty meters to the fence, knelt down, and quickly cut a hole in the fence. He signaled for the Germans. They crossed the road and were within the compound in seconds. Rahin followed them to the station. The Germans put one stick of C4 plastic explosive on each of the three tripods of the disc and another stick on the rear of the shack next to it, housing the electronics. After putting in the detonators, they hooked up the delay switches and electronic receivers.

Just then the door of the command shack opened and out stepped a man in a khaki uniform. He closed the door behind him, stretched his arms, and made a groaning sound. He reached down, unzipped his fly, and began to urinate. Rahin leaped up and grabbed the man by the throat with his left hand while he plunged his knife into the man's lower back, just below the rib cage, piercing his liver and right kidney. The man arched his back, gave a spastic swing with his right arm backward and then went limp.

Just then a second khakied man came through the door with a pistol in his hand. Rahin turned, still holding the dying soldier in his arms, as the second man raised his pistol. Rahin still had his left hand under the chin of the dead man and his right hand on the hilt of the still embedded knife. Using the knife as a handle, he lifted and slung the body of the first soldier at the second. The pistol fired, but the bullet entered the first soldier. Rahin shoved hard forward and the three bodies tumbled through the door and onto the floor inside the shack.

Rahin was on top of the first soldier who, in turn, was on top of the second. The second soldier's arms were pinned under the first soldier. Rahin pulled the knife from the back of the first soldier, raised it, and sent it plunging through the eye socket and into the brain of the second soldier.

Rahin heard a noise at the other end of the shed. He looked up. A third soldier was standing at the other end of the shed holding a pistol in his hand. Youthful marks of post adolescence were on his face and a thin-haired mustache was straining to emerge from his quivering upper lip. His hand was shaking, but he raised the pistol and cocked it. Then he pointed it at Rahin with still shaking hands. Rahin grabbed at the knife but it was stuck in the eye socket. Rahin looked up and saw the young man's shaking finger start to squeeze the trigger. Rahin closed his eyes. The loud report of a gunshot filled the room. Rahin squeezed his eyes, pressed his lips tightly against his teeth, and hunched his shoulders in anticipation of the pain. But there was no pain. He relaxed his shoulders and his eyes blinked. He was still alive.

He must have missed, thought Rahin.

He feverishly tried to pull the knife out of the skull but it wouldn't move. He looked up again at the third soldier. But where there once was a nose was now a gaping bloody hole. The eyes were crossed and slanted upward, the hand still outstretched but the gun was hanging loosely, caught by the index finger stuck in the trigger guard. As the gun slipped from the finger and fell to the floor, the boy slumped to his knees. Then his whole body stiffened and fell forward all at once, his face hitting the floor in front of Rahin, his body kicking up dust from the floor where he fell. Rahin turned around. Amjad was standing at the door, a gun at his side with smoke easing out of its muzzle.

"I told you to stay across the road!" yelled Rahin.

"There are two vehicles coming this way," said Amjad. "I just came to help."

Rahin rose to his feet and brushed himself down. He pushed his way past Amjad, walked crisply through the door and turned the corner of the shed.

"Are you two ready?" he called.

"Just finished," came the reply.

Rahin went back to the front of the shack and looked down the road. There were a Jeep and a truck moving toward them about fifty meters away.

"Let's go!" he commanded.

Hoping to catch the soldiers off guard, they raced to the fence. Rahin held the hole in the fence open as the two Germans and Amjad went through. The Jeep stopped. Then Rahin was through the fence. There was some yelling back at the Jeep as one person got out, put a machine gun to his shoulders, and opened fire. Rocks danced and skipped at Rahin's feet as he dashed across the road to the trees. From the trees, Nadia and the rest of the cadre opened up, strafing the Jeep.

But now soldiers were pouring out of the truck and returning the fire. Rahin went back to the Germans.

"Do you have any more C4 yet?" he yelled.

"Ja," came the reply.

"Can you rig it with a three minute fuse?"

"Ja."

"Then do it! Right here. We'll fall back and when they come in after us, boom! Let me know when you're ready."

"Ready now," the German said as he pulled out a stick of C4 and put in the detonator and the fuse.

"Okay, everyone. Fall back!" Rahin shouted.

Kazi had heard the first gunshot as he was removing the fifty caliber machine gun from its tripod and replacing it on the sandbags facing the tank and tent. He reached for a rocket launcher, removed the holding pin, and extended the tube. The sight popped up and he raised it to his shoulder. He aimed at the front of the tread right under the armor where it was exposed. He took in a deep breath, let it out slowly, and squeezed. He followed the fiery trail to the front sprocket and saw the explosion. There was fire and smoke but he could not be sure. He picked up another rocket and sent another missile to the tread.

Immediately men were springing from the tent, half clothed but shouting wildly. Kazi threw the empty tube down and grabbed the fifty caliber. He swung it around toward the men and opened fire. The sides of the tent popped as the bullets ripped through its walls. From out of the front of the tent a shirtless man stumbled and fell forward to his knees, screaming. His left hand supported his weight while his right hand held something dripping red, protruding from his stomach. The men left standing quickly ducked behind the tank as bullets kicked up sand and ricocheted off the tank with a loud, rapid clanging noise. The tank lurched forward but a pair of cleats had been blown off its right tread and it soon came to a halt, its unfulfilled sprockets clawing the air. Its turret moved back and forth like a wounded animal searching for its tormentor. Then the turret swung around and faced Kazi. Its cannon elevated and Kazi ducked behind the sandbags. The cannon roared, there was a brilliant flash of light, and all was still.

Rahin and his followers rushed by the hill, firing back at their pursuers when they heard a loud explosion. The three minute fuse had worked. Rahin caught up with the two Germans.

"Blow it! Blow it now!" he yelled.

The first German unzipped his bag, fumbled around for a while, and then brought out an electronic box. He pulled out the antenna, flipped a switch to arm it, and pushed the red button. Behind them was a tremendous cacophony of explosions. A huge fireball mushroomed skyward and debris filled the air. Rahin came up behind Nadia.

"Nadia," he called. "Get on the radio and raise the helicopter. Tell them to start their engines!"

Nadia put on the headphones and started talking into the transmitter.

They threaded their way around the hill where Kazi was making his stand by the sandbags. Rahin sent the rest ahead and started up the hill to Kazi. Suddenly the top of the hill exploded. Rahin was sent sprawling. When he came to rest, a hand grabbed his arm. He whirled around. It was Amjad.

"Look!" yelled Amjad. "Look, there's Kazi!"

Kazi was three-fourths of the way up the hill. He was lying in the dirt with his head below his feet. His arms and legs were at odd angles to their joints.

"He's dead," said Rahin.

"We can't be sure," said Amjad.

"He's dead!" yelled Rahin.

Amjad started up the hill. Rahin grabbed him by the arm and brought their faces close.

"He's dead, I tell you!" said Rahin.

Amjad returned the glassy stare. His eyes squinted and his eyebrows firmed. "I'm not leaving him here," said Amjad. He pulled away from Rahin's grasp and started up the hill.

When he reached the body, Rahin was right behind him. Amjad reached down and put his middle finger on Kazi's carotid artery.

"I have a pulse." said Amjad. "He's alive!" He grabbed Kazi by the right shoulder. "Help me with him."

Rahin slung his AK47 around his shoulder and grabbed Kazi by the left shoulder. Amjad looked up. At the top of the hill were three men in khaki uniforms who were now raising their weapons. Behind Amjad and Rahin, an AK47 opened up. Crimson splotches appeared on the khaki uniforms like badly misplaced battle ribbons. The three men fell backward with their now raised weapons firing chaotically into the air as their fingers spasmed on the triggers. Amjad and Rahin turned around to see Nadia lowering an AK47 from her shoulder.

"Let's get out of here!" yelled Rahin.

Rahin and Amjad hoisted Kazi to their shoulders and dragged him down the hill. The sun was fully up now and they could see the path back to the helicopters. Rahin and Amjad adjusted their grip on Kazi, with each throwing one arm around a shoulder and the other under his thigh. They made their way down the path with Nadia taking rear guard.

When they reached the landing zone, the helicopters were fully revved. They carried Kazi to the first helicopter and piled him in. Rahin turned around to look for Nadia. Nadia was running toward the helicopter when the sand around her exploded as bullets strafed her path and she went flying to the ground.

Rahin pulled his AK47 from his shoulder and fired into the grove of trees from where the firing had come. From the bushes, two khaki clad men fell forward to their knees, firing into the ground. Rahin ran over to Nadia and pulled her up. He dragged her to the helicopter and two hands pulled her in. He threw his AK47 in the hold and climbed in. The helicopters lifted off and headed north.

Chapter Seven
"I'll Tell the Director"

Wes Covington turned the corner of the cubicle and put his coffee down on Phil Soran's desk.

"Someone took out a radar station in Chad last night and I wonder if it might have been your boys." he said.

"Wouldn't surprise me a bit," answered Soran. "They certainly seem ready for something. MRT1 flew over a while ago and didn't show much activity. Just a couple guys strolling around. That's kind of odd. Everyone is usually inside for MRT1. MRT2 will begin to pass in…" Phil turned his head and looked at the clock. "Eight minutes. Why don't you stick around and let's take a peek."

John Bolder turned the corner of the cubicle and almost bumped into Covington.

"Sorry, Mr. Covington. Didn't see ya," said Bolder.

"No problem, John," said Covington. "You got something?"

"Yeah, seems our man in Tripoli has been busy. He's been following Major Brohan's driver. It seems this driver has an affinity for the masculine gender. And he likes them young. Well, we were fortunate to get some intimate pix. We confronted him with the pix and while this may play in San Francisco, it ain't going to play in Tripoli and if he wants to keep his pecker, he better sing us a happy tune. Well, we had him singing like a canary in springtime."

Bolder reached into his pocket for a stick of gum and continued.

"We got lots of good stuff on Major Brohan. It's in the file. But I want to bring you up to speed on this new character. Seem's he's from Iraq. Had his whole family killed in that bomb shelter we thought was housing the big wigs. He's a doctor. First name is Amjad but we didn't get a last name. He's been to America and speaks English real good."

"Probably better than you," said Soran as he picked up his cup of coffee.

"Oh, shit," said Bolder. "I'm just a good ol' boy from Alabama, but we sure know how to have fun." He stuck a second piece of gum in his mouth.

"How many pieces do you chew, John?' asked Covington.

"Oh, hell," said Bolder. "Got's to be four or five before you get any flavor."

Bolder rolled the chewing gum paper into a ball between his hands and threw it at the wastebasket but it ricocheted off the rim and fell to the floor.

"Oh, yeah," he continued. "And they're talking nuclear."

"Nuclear?" asked Covington, his interest obviously piqued. "What kind, where, when?"

"Don't know," said Bolder. "But I suspect a nuclear power plant somewhere. Could make a bomb but where would they get the plutonium? And even if they did, how would they get it into the country? No, I suspect it would be a power plant somewhere."

"Yeah, but where?" asked Covington.

"I don't know," said Soran. " But we better have SAS close by just in case."

SAS was the interdiction force for Beta Group. The long arm of Beta Group, they were picked assassins. Although they were hired, trained and paid by the CIA, they were transported by the Navy, assigned to aircraft carriers in different theaters throughout the world. They were usually former special forces personnel who liked their profession a little more than the army could allow. SAS provided a home where they could apply their skills with vigor.

"Don't worry," said Covington. "SAS is in the arena. But we have to have more than this if they are to become a player."

Soran interrupted. "MRT2 is entering the window now. Let's take a look."

All three turned to the video screen. The wide angle lens was first. The screen was white with tiny specks in the upper left quadrant. Soran pressed the keyboard and enhanced the upper left quadrant. The specks were larger now. Again enhanced, the camp was now visible. Outside the camp were two helicopters with men milling around them. The upper left quadrant of the screen was boxed and the close angle lens brought the men closer.

"Good God!" exclaimed Soran. "Looks like we like we caught them coming back. Look! They're fully armed and tired by the way they walk. And here comes stretchers. See them load that guy on a stretcher? They've been in a shoot-out all right! And see that guy leaning over the guy in the stretcher, the guy with the black hair? What am I saying? They all have black hair, but the guy leaning over his face, I bet that's the new guy. What's his name? Amid? Aman?"

"Amjad," said Bolder.

"Yeah, Amjad," continued Soran. "That's got to be Amjad. He's a doctor. He would be looking after his new patient. Hey, Amjad, turn around, you son of a bitch! I want to take your picture. Come on, look up here."

The man holding the rear of Kazi's stretcher stumbled, pitching the stretcher momentarily askew. Amjad turned to look up at the man and barked an order.

"Gotcha!" said Soran as he followed them until they disappeared into the tent.

When it was over, Soran pressed "ENTER," typed "ROUTE TO DESIST," "ENTER" again, and "REWIND."

"John, why don't you help me with this. We need a head count."

"That has to be the group that hit Chad," said Covington. "Can you get confirmation from your source?' he asked Soran.

"Hope so," said Soran. "If these guys are thinking nuclear, they are not going to make too many more practice runs, especially if they picked up casualties here. We could hit them and blame it on Chad for a reprisal raid. No one would be the wiser. Whadaya think, Wes?"

"I'll go talk to the director," said Covington.

"Bring him to my tent," yelled Amjad. "I want him in my tent!"

They carried Kazi's stretcher into Amjad's tent.

"Put him on my cot," said Amjad.

Rahin entered the tent carrying Nadia and put her down on her cot.

"How is Kazi?" asked Rahin, catching his breath.

"He's alive." replied Amjad. "He's got a concussion and possibly some internal bleeding. It would be better to get him to a hospital."

"I'll call Major Brohan," said Rahin.

Kazi groaned. Amjad went over to him. Kazi had bled from his ears, nose, and mouth and now the dried blood had caked pathways leading from their orifices. Amjad took his canteen, poured water on a cloth, and wiped the blood from Kazi's face.

"The bleeding has stopped. That is good," said Amjad. "But it is better that you rest, my friend."

Amjad patted Kazi on the cheek and turned to Nadia. "What happened to her?" he asked Rahin.

Rahin replied, "There are no bullet holes. She must have tripped and hit her head when she fell."

Amjad moved over to her cot and started searching her limbs for broken bones. He took out a flashlight, pulled back an eyelid, and watched the pupil shrink to escape the invading light. He checked the ears and the throat. "I will have to wait 'til she wakes up, but it looks like she just passed out," he said. "She could have hit her head but she will be okay."

"Amjad," Rahin put a hand on Amjad's shoulder, "I would like to thank you for saving my life."

"Thank Allah," said Amjad. "He put me in the right place. I was his instrument. But it was Allah's will that you should be here now, talking to me."

"Allah must be looking out for both of us then," said Rahin. "If he had not sent Nadia with us, we would both be entertaining sand worms."

"It is Allah's will," said Amjad.

Rahin nodded. He looked down at his hands. They were no longer shaking. He felt his mustache with his left hand while his tongue went out and up to taste the salt and the dirt. He looked around the tent and smelled the tangy smell of hot canvas amid the dust. Turning back to Amjad he said, "Sit down, my friend, I would like to talk with you."

They both sat down across the tent from Kazi and Nadia.

"You did well today, my friend," said Rahin. "You fired your weapon at the right time. You did not hesitate. You fought well."

Amjad was looking past Rahin out the door of the tent and into the distance and did not speak. After a moment, Rahin interrupted the silence.

"Amjad?"

Amjad relinquished the horizon and brought his focus back to the ambience. He looked straight into Rahin's eyes.

"Rahin, my friend," he said. "I have learned much. But now I must go. I have no quarrel with Chad, or for that matter, with the Israelis. My quarrel is with the Americans. You have taught me all I need to know. I can gain nothing by staying."

"But why? Where?" asked Rahin.

"To America," came the reply.

"America?" asked Rahin. "Why? What can you do there?"

Amjad put both hands up to his head and pushed his fingers through his jet black hair. "The Americans killed my family and took all that I had. I have made a vow to Allah to make them suffer as I have suffered."

"Do you have a network there?" asked Rahin.

"No."

"Then you know someone who can help you."

"No. I will be alone."

"But what can one man do there?"

"Enough. I know what I can do. And it will be enough."

Rahin put his hand on Amjad's shoulders. "Earlier today you saved my life," he said. "Now you want to go. I do not know what one man can do, alone in a foreign land, but I will not stand in your way. But tell me, my friend, what is it you plan to do? I think you owe me that much."

"You are right," said Amjad, "I do owe you that much."

Rahin took his hands off Amjad's shoulders and leaned back. He took a pack of cigarettes out of his breast pocket and offered one to Amjad. Amjad accepted and brought the offering to his lips as Rahin flicked his lighter. Amjad leaned forward to join the tobacco to the flame. He took a deep draw on the cigarette and let the smoke fill his lungs. He paused for a moment, holding the vapors captive until he finally released them, allowing free access through his nostrils.

"My plan is to make them suffer for a long, long time," Amjad began. "My plan…" he paused. "My plan is to give them nuclear devastation."

Rahin sat upright. His pack of cigarettes slipped from his fingers and dropped to the floor. "How can you do that ?" he asked. "You are just one man. Even if you make the bomb, where will you get the nuclear fuel? Where will you get the plutonium?"

Amjad took another drag from his cigarette, turned to look out the door of the tent and fixed his gaze on the horizon.

"It's already there," he said.

"Another goddamn meeting," Bolder said through the five sticks of chewing gum nesting in his mouth. "You know, most of the time I think they have meetings just to hear themselves talk. Why, once I went to a meeting to discuss why we were having so many meetings."

"Yeah, I know," said Soran as they passed down the corridor and into the doorway of Covington's office. The other members of Beta Group were standing against the walls of the office with their hands in their pockets like recently lost sheep back in the safety of their shepherd. Normally they would be laughing and joking around, but one look at Covington told them that somber was the correct inclination of the day. His face was ashen and his look stern.

"Come in," Covington said.

It was not an invitation. Soran and Bolder slid inside the room with the others. Normally Covington would get up, amble over to the window, and scrutinize the pigeon droppings on the window ledge to add poignancy to his coming dissertation. But now Covington just sat there, his face pale and his hands on the point of trembling.

"We've had a problem," he started. "A terrible problem." He had everyone's attention. "As you know," he continued, "we have been losing an inordinate amount of moles in Eastern Europe and Russia." His voice was quavering now. "An inordinate amount." He paused and looked at the ceiling as if counting the acoustic holes in the ceiling panels. "It appears we have found the cause."

Soran's palms were getting sweaty. He knew what was coming next but couldn't bring himself to believe it. Covington took his eyes from the ceiling panels and lowered his gaze to somewhere in the middle of the room.

He continued. "Gary Eisner has just been arrested for being a spy for the Russians. Most of you know Eisner but for those who don't, let it suffice to say that he had top clearance." His voice raising. "Goddamn it! Top clearance!"

It seemed like whatever air was left in the room had now been sucked out. But it didn't matter. No one in the room was breathing.

"That means that he could have had access to all of your files. We are checking now for computer access to files, but it could take some time. Your mole could be standing in the sunlight. We know of nine operatives in the Eastern Bloc that have been eliminated as a direct result of Eisner. He may have only given the Russians what they were interested in close to home. But if he was spilling all, the Russians could use anything they get for further influences in the Middle East."

Covington looked around the room. His voice was steadier now. His pent-up anger had been released. Color had come back to his cheeks. He got up from his desk and walked to the window to scrutinize the pigeon droppings on the ledge. He was in control again. He continued, "We'll try to get what we can from Eisner, but I'll leave it up to each of you to determine if you have been compromised."

Covington paused again. "Well, that's it for now," he finally said. "We'll let you know anything else that we get."

Soran and Bolder were closest to the door and their positioning was rewarded as they turned and crossed through the doorway into breathable air once again.

"Jesus," Bolder said. "Can you believe it?"

Soran walked straight ahead.

"Can you believe it?" Bolder echoed himself. "Jesus, I can't believe it. I mean, CIA Op who turns. I mean, why?"

"Well, shit, John," said Soran. "Who knows? Could be money. Could be blackmail. Could be a closet gay discovered. Could be a lot of things. Hell, we do it all the time. Why can't they?"

"Yeah, but this is America," countered Bolder. "Hey, we're the good guys!"

"I'd like to think so," answered Soran. "But I guess it's all in the perspective. If everyone thought like us, we'd be out of a job."

They rounded the corner and were soon back to Soran's cubicle. Soran sat down in his chair. Bolder rested himself on the corner of Soran's desk and stuck his sixth piece of gum in his mouth.

"I've never met R1," Soran started. "But I surely would like to some day. But right now I don't know."

He turned on his display unit and noticed the cursor flashing above message waiting. He pushed the message retrieval command and a line of integers appeared on his screen.

"Message from R1," he said as Bolder slid his left cheek off the desk and came around behind Soran's left shoulder. Soran put his hands to the keyboard and printed STORE and DECODE BETA ALPHA and pressed "ENTER." Below the line of integers printed the message, "L3, AMJAD COMING TO USA. PLANNING NUCLEAR REVENGE." Soran pushed print and then typed "R1 STORE." He pushed enter as Bolder reached for another stick of gum.

"So they're comin' here with the nukes," said Bolder.

"Looks that way," said Soran. "And this Amjad character is leading the pack."

Soran leaned back in his chair and brushed his hands through his thick black hair until his fingers, at their journey's end, met at the back of his neck. "Let's see what we have here," he said. "We know that they are coming here with some shenanigans and yet they just finished an incursion into Chad. This is a terrorist outfit with a hard-on for Israel. Their training hasn't been very covert, just a lot of shooting guns and blowing up things. To go nuclear you've got to sneak around a lot. But these guys look like they want to break down the front door."

Soran paused in thought. "Ya know, I'll bet there are only a few that are planning to come here. It wouldn't make sense for all of them to come. But a few highly motivated individuals might make it particularly nasty. Let's put this together and bring it to Covington with a request for SAS. R1's cover may be blown so it's good timing anyway. If need be, we can blame it on Chad for retaliating. They can get R1 out. But they have to be surgical. We need confirmation and pix of all. I want to make sure we get this Amjad character."

Chapter Eight
Seemann

C aptain Gary Conniff liked his tea. Sometimes it was oolong, sometimes Darjeeling, and sometimes orange pekoe. It didn't matter to him as long as it was hot. He had given up on coffee shortly after taking command of the aircraft carrier USS *Eisenhower*. He had been a heavy coffee drinker, starting the day with a cup before breakfast, another after breakfast, and the ever-present cup beside his captain's chair at the helm. But about eleven every day he found himself quite owly. He figured it had to be the caffeine. So he had made the decision to change to something that had a little less caffeine and was a little more gastrointestinally friendly. So he switched to tea. Being in the Mediterranean offered an abundance of tea varieties. But Conniff wasn't too selective. As long as it was hot.

He was sitting in his captain's chair, admiring the steam escaping the grips of a fresh mixture of orange pekoe when a signalman entered the bridge, walked up to the captain and saluted.

"Message form CINCMED, sir," he said. "EYES ONLY"

Conniff raised his hand to his cheek to return the salute and took the envelope from the signalman. He climbed down from his chair and headed for the hatch, tea mug in hand. A midshipman near the hatch barked out, "Captain leaving bridge!" and came to attention as he passed through the hatch.

The tea was still warm when Conniff entered his quarters. He closed the door behind him and secured it. Walking over to his desk, he took one sip of tea and then put the cup and envelope down. He reached over to his safe and bid his fingers do their magic. The door of the safe came open and he pulled out a small code manual. Sitting down he opened the envelope, pulled out the papers from inside and unfolded them.

The first paper was addressed to him. He flipped the code manual to the appropriate code and within minutes he could read the message.

TO: CAPTAIN CONNIFF, USS ENTERPRISE
FROM: CINCMED

PRIORITY ONE EYES ONLY OPERATION SAS
RENDEZVOUS TOMORROW 01:30 HOURS
GULF OF SIDRA
APPROX 32 DEG LAT 17 DEG LON
TWO HELICOPTERS ASSIST SAS
GIVE FOLLOWING PAGE TO SAS

ADMIRAL OCONNOR, CINCMED

He folded the paper and put it on the desk. He looked at the second paper. It was in code assigned to SAS. He pushed the third switch on the intercom, leaned over and said, "Ensign Johnson to captain's quarters."

He leaned back in his chair, raised the cup to his lips and took a sip. Pursing his lips, he spit the tea back into the cup and put the cup down on the desk top hard. The tea was cold.

"Damn!" he said.

"Captain on the bridge!" sounded the room, and people snapped to attention as Captain Conniff passed through the hatch. He raised his hand to his cheek and flicked his fingers as if he was swatting at a slow-moving fly. The men came at ease and the bustle returned to the room. He walked over to the man at a consul and said, "Doug, can you get me to latitude thirty-two longitude seventeen by one-thirty tomorrow?"

Doug punched the coordinates into the computer, pressed a few more keys and the screen came to life. "That's in the Gulf of Sidra, near Libya," said Doug.

"I know that, son," answered Conniff. "Can you get me there?"

More keys punched. "No problem, sir."

"Do it!" said Conniff.

Bob Seemann had just finished his sixtieth push-up and rested before continuing the next forty that would make up his regimen of one hundred. He remembered back to the days when the century mark would be attained without interruption. Those were also the days when the aches came less frequently and disappeared more rapidly. But still his pectorals, deltoids, and triceps make a liar of his DEC sheet which listed his date of birth as 4-23-45. Anyone would guess his age as mid-thirties, the streaks of gray hair being accounted for by prematurity.

He had started his career in the Army Special Forces and served three stints in Vietnam. It became obvious to him that the war had no direction and served no purpose other than killing young men just for the sake of proving that we were capable of having young men killed. There was no apparent reason other than to sustain the momentum that had already been established. The military had been handicapped by the politicians and the politicians had no direction. When the CIA recruiters came, he was ready.

And he was perfect for them. He had been very good at his job but thought of advancement as being mired in bureaucracy. And yet he still maintained Special Forces discipline and would follow orders. An assassin who would patiently lie in wait and then dutifully spring into action when called upon.

When SAS formed, he was the first in line. He had killed a man in Singapore for a political reason he could not understand. Although he never doubted his duty or questioned his orders, he was tired of neutralizing targets to satisfy some bureaucratic whim of political caprice.

But SAS would be different. There he would face a real foe. An adversary worthy of his talents. And increasingly more important to him, an opponent that deserved to die. He headed a unit with nine other men, who, although younger, matched his skill and conviction. They were assigned to the aircraft carrier USS *Eisenhower*. Only the captain knew their mission, and his knowledge was limited. He was only to put them in the proper place at the proper time and to provide any assistance they needed. They did not need much.

Seemann's unit was not assigned any details related to the running of the ship, but they kept themselves busy. Bodies were honed and weapons cleaned daily. The most important task was intelligence. Seemann had been apprised of every viable terrorist camp in his theater of operations. He had detailed maps of each location as well as the strength of each unit. Updates were sent to him as they were warranted. MRT2 had proved invaluable. Its orbit had allowed it to circumnavigate the globe twice in a twenty-four hour period. By day its powerful telescopic lenses would take pictures and identify differences in various facial features. Catalogues were kept and identification was just a matter of detail work.

But at night was when it really worked its magic. The infrared sensors could sense the body heat even through the roofs of the tents. Beta Group knew how many bodies were in each camp and also where they slept. The only place where one could remain undetected was if they were to sleep in one of the vehicles. If there was an interdiction, it would be at night.

MRT2 was also able to map the land mines around the camp. The Libyans had kept the newer, more expensive plastic mines for themselves, while outfitting the terrorists' camps with older, less expensive, more detectable metal mines. Metal retains heat longer than sand. As night came, the sand gave up its heat and the metal mines, lying in their shallow graves, appeared as Christmas ornaments to a heat-loving infrared eye in the sky.

All of this information was forwarded to Seemann who would draw daily coordinates and map strategies to subdue any camp. He was even kept abreast of weather patterns and changes. Nothing was left to chance. When the call came, they would be ready.

Seemann was back in his four point stance, finishing his eighty-seventh push-up when Ensign Johnson came through the hatch.

"Captain wants to see you in his quarters," Ensign Johnson said.

Seemann stopped short of ninety and hopped to his feet.

"Show time," he said as he followed Ensign Johnson through the hatch.

It seemed like the snoring had kept him up half the night. Amjad had been used to sleeping in the communications tent with Nadia. But now he had switched tents with Kazi, and Kazi occupied that quiescent place of rest while he was left to contend with the oscillating decibels of four grown men deep in their somniloquy.

He rose from his cot at first light and rubbed the sleep from his eyes. He slipped on his trousers, grabbed his canteen and walked out the tent door. Around the back of the tent, he opened the canteen and poured half of the contents over his head. The liquid shocked him in the cool morning air. He shook his head and rubbed his hand through wet hair and down over his face. Taking in a half mouthful of water, he swished it around a couple of times and spit it out. He brushed his teeth with his finger and rinsed again. The air was crisp and clean and he took a minute to watch the desert sunrise. The sun had just popped over the horizon and already its rays warmed his skin.

This would be a good day, Amjad thought. He was anxious to see his new patients. It had been a long time since Amjad had patients. That part of him was a world away. He had been a doctor, a healer. But now he had touched the dark side. He had destroyed life, perhaps an innocent life. He had tasted blood. He had known it could come to this. And he knew it could still go beyond. It mattered. It still mattered. But it mattered less now than it did before. He faintly heard the whispering voices carried on the wind. The calling from a thousand centuries ago, calling him back, back to a time long forgotten in a land he no longer knew. But he could not go back. Ever. He knew that. But he still remembered. The calling faded and was gone.

He walked back into the tent, put his canteen down, and grabbed his shirt. He went out the door of the tent and grabbed a lung full of early morning air.

Yes, it would be good to have patients again, he thought to himself, and walked over to the communications tent.

Seemann was up on deck when the sun rose. He was deploying the dish antenna of his portable fax machine. During the night MRT2 had flown over camp L3 and taken infrared pictures of the camp and forwarded them back to Beta Group. Beta Group would analyze the pictures, photocopy the results and fax them to a telecommunications satellite on a geocentric orbit above the North American continent. That satellite would forward the information to another satellite in a geocentric orbit over the Middle East which would relay it down to anyone on Earth with the proper code. Seemann had the proper code.

Seemann could get up-to-date information instantaneously. He had the present weather conditions over the target. He knew where all the land mines were hidden. He knew the number of bodies that slept in each tent. With this information he could determine by which direction to approach the camp and how to deploy his men. Normally, by the time they reached the target the information would be hours old. Seemann wanted more current information. He would get it. His fax was portable.

The mission was designed to place them at the jump off point at 1:30 A.M., allowing one and one half hours flying time to reach the target and set up the fax. MRT2 would be over the target at 3:00 A.M., take the pictures, and forward them to Beta Group, which would fax them back to Seemann. He would have infrared pictures of the killing ground within five minutes. This would be the first time that a fax machine went to war.

Amjad opened the door of the communications tent. Kazi was lying on his back and the rhythmical pattern of his breathing signaled an unencumbered sleep. Amjad turned to Nadia who had rolled over on her side and was looking up at him.

"Good morning," he said, walking over to the chair beside her cot and sitting down. "How are you feeling?"

"Fine. I feel fine," she answered. "Little touch of a headache but I'll be fine."

"Let me look at you," he said. He reached over and pulled a flashlight from the table next to the cot and, raising her eyelid, flashed the light across her pupil.

"What happened?" she asked.

He opened her mouth and sent the light down her throat. "Say ahh," he said. The "ahh" was returned.

"I'm not sure," he said, turning her head, brushing aside her hair, and shining the light into her ear. "I think you might have stumbled and hit your head," he said.

His hands probed her head for lumps.

"Can't find any bruises or lumps, but that doesn't mean anything. How are your arms and legs?"

"Fine. No problems."

"You'll be okay," he said.

Amjad looked into her big brown eyes. He reached out and touched her long brown hair, twirling it slightly between his fingers. He brought a few strands of hair toward the front of her face before letting go, brushing her cheek softly with the back of his knuckles. My, she was beautiful, he thought. Beauty had been absent from his life for so long. A seeming lifetime. And now she had entered his life.

He felt something stir within him. He felt his throat tighten. He tried to look away but he could not bring his eyes to leave her. She returned his gaze, reached out, and touched his arm with a caress that took him back to a time when the bed was soft, the sheets smelled fresh and he was in the arms of someone he loved.

Kazi stirred in the cot across the room.

The spell broken, Amjad said, "Nadia…"

There was a pause.

"Nadia," he continued, "I want to thank you for saving my life."

"I did what had to be done," she responded, brushing her hair from the side of her face. "I did not want them to take you away. I like you being here with me."

Amjad pressed her hand, searching for the words. He turned his eyes from her for a moment and then came back.

"Nadia…I…" The words were not coming easily. He remembered his sacred vow to Allah. There were things to be done, things he had to do.

"Nadia, I must go soon," he said, finally.

Her gaze caught his again and she pressed his arm tighter.

"But why, why must you go?" she asked. Her eyes searching his, questioning.

He pulled his arm back and broke the gaze. "I just have to," he said. "There are things that must be done."

She grabbed his arm again. "I know you have been hurt and you are filled with anger. But these feelings will pass. You need time. Everything will pass. You just need time."

Amjad looked down at this lovely creature and felt her warm hand on his arm. But then he stiffened his resolve and said, "No, Nadia."

She sat up in her cot and threw her arms around him, her face pressing into his chest. He brought his hand up and stroked the back of her head. She pulled her head back and looked up. Up into her brother's eyes. "Please, please don't go. Don't leave me," she said, her eyes welling with tears. He gently pushed her head onto his chest. Warm tears soaked through his shirt and he pressed harder, feeling her warm breath on his chest. Again his throat tightened, tears welling in his eyes. His lower lip quivered for a moment but he clenched his teeth. He had found this love, this light in the very heart of darkness. How could he leave her now? But what of his vow? His vow to Allah?

"I love you, Amjad," she cried into his shirt, her voice cracking. She was crying now, but his chest muffled the sobs. He closed his eyes hard, squeezing them, as if by doing so he could shut out the world and stop himself from doing what he knew he must do. His arms closed tighter on her, his left arm around her shoulders and his right pressing her head to his bosom. Slowly he loosened his hold.

"Nadia, I must go," he said.

Nadia held him for some time but finally, slowly released her grip. She looked pleadingly into his eyes. Amjad's eyes were bloodshot with tears, but filled with resolve. She leaned forward, kissed him on the forehead, and then sat back.

"Are you sure?" she asked.

"I am sure," he replied.

She took her gaze from his and wiped the tears from her cheeks, sniffling. She raised herself off the cot, grabbed the canteen, and walked through the door of the tent.

Amjad sat for a few minutes entertaining the floor with his gaze. It had all been so clear to him before. But now questions clouded his thoughts. The questions, ushered in on waves of emotions. Should he take her with him? Could he start over again? Could he bear to leave her behind? He needed time. Oh, yes, time: nature's own physician, healing the scars of yesterday. He would stay one more day. Another day and his head would clear and he could think again. He took a deep breath, held it in for a moment and let it out slowly.

Getting up slowly, he grabbed the chair, and carried it over to Kazi. Placing the chair next to the cot, he sat down, took out his flashlight, and reached for one of Kazi's eyelids. Suddenly Kazi's hand shot out and grabbed Amjad's left arm.

Kazi tried to raise himself but could only get his head slightly off the cot. As Kazi pulled on Amjad's sleeve, he opened his mouth as if to speak, and Amjad bent closer.

"She's a spy," Kazi said in a raspy voice no louder than a whisper.

Amjad blinked.

"She's a spy," Kazi repeated. "I heard her last night. She thought I was asleep but I heard her on the radio." He coughed.

"You must have been dreaming," said Amjad. "Hallucination." Amjad loosened his grip on Kazi's shoulders. "You had a concussion," he said. "You will dream of lots of things."

"I heard her," Kazi protested with a thick tongue. "I woke up briefly and I heard her. I heard her on the radio. She was saying that you were going to America with a nuclear device."

Amjad sat back, startled. His brow furrowed and he bit his lower lip. His right elbow came to his right knee and he rested his chin between his right forefinger and thumb, working them back and forth. *Could it be true?* he thought to himself, looking back at Kazi. Kazi had raised himself up on his elbows, his eyes open wide, his head nodding slowly, assuredly. Amjad straightened up and turned to look at the cot where minutes ago he had just held her in his arms and gazed into her eyes. Crossing his arms across his chest, he brought his right hand up, pensively stroking his mustache. He leaned back against the chair and thought to himself. Surely Kazi wouldn't have hallucinated something that he had actually said. He put his mind back to yesterday. He was talking with Rahin. Kazi was passed out, as was Nadia. Or was she? He had felt no signs of injury on her; no bumps, no bruises. Could it be she was lying in bed and listening while he told Rahin of his plans? And then passed it along to...

Amjad's blood went cold. His hands were clammy. He raised them to the top of his head and, interlocking the fingers, pressed them down. His eyelids closed and he pressed them tighter. "If she is a spy," he thought, "then for whom is she spying. Major Brohan? Why? He knows all about it. The Israelis, or worse, the Americans?" He took a deep breath and let it out slowly. He clenched his teeth as he opened his eyes. It would be tonight.

He moved back to Kazi and finished his exam. Kazi's concussion would resolve itself in time. He would have Kazi transferred to Rahin's tent today and tonight he would reclaim his own cot. Tonight he would stay with Nadia.

Chapter Nine
Showtime

The nine other men in Seemann's command had gathered in his quarters. He had copied the latest faxes from MRT2 and had given them to his men. There were two photos for each man. One was a daylight photo showing the camp and the other was an infrared photo showing where the mine fields lay, where the men slept and where the vehicles were parked.

Seemann spoke: "Gentlemen, we will be approaching from the northwest. Here!" He pointed to a spot on the daylight photo. "And here." He pointed to a spot on the infrared photo. Memorize these positions. "We will be jumping off at 0130 hours with a ninety-minute flight. We should be next to the target at 0300. I'll have the fax set up and we should have fresh pix within five minutes. Shouldn't be any surprises. Body count will be determined by fresh infrared pix. But we'll need to check the vehicles. If someone slept in a vehicle, it's the only place the eye in the sky won't see. There is one woman in the camp. Her name in Nadia. We think she sleeps here." He pointed to the communications tent. "She is the only 'friendly' in the camp. She is to be taken alive and brought back with us. The others are to be terminated with extreme prejudice. Do I make myself clear?"

The room was filled with aye ayes, yeahs, sures, you-bets, and one fuckin'-A. Seemann continued, "Okay, saddle up. We'll meet up top at 0100."

"How do you think it will go?" asked Bolder.

"Like clockwork," said Soran. He examined the metaphor. It *would* be like clockwork. A precision timepiece. All the parts were in perfect running order. He had set the hands, wound the spring, and released the running mechanism. From now on the machine had a timetable of its own. There would be no stopping it. The results were predestined. He looked at the clock. Eight o'clock—three o'clock Libyan time. In perhaps fifteen minutes thirteen men would be dead.

"Wanna watch?" asked Bolder, sticking another piece of gum in his mouth. Soran thought of thirteen men, killed in their sleep. He looked at the clock again. 8:01.

"No," he said. "It's been a long day. I think I'll catch the highlights in the morning."

"Yeah, me too," said Bolder. "Buy you a beer?"

Soran looked at the clock. 8:02.

"Yeah, I could use a beer," he said, and flicked his computer screen off.

Amjad put his left hand on Nadia's mouth and grabbed her left shoulder with his right hand. Nadia woke up with a start. Her big brown eyes searched wildly around until they found Amjad's. A look of questioning fright came over her face.

"Nadia," Amjad said, and took his hand away from her mouth.

"Nadia, I am going now."

Nadia threw her arms around his neck and pulled herself up to him.

"Nadia," he grabbed her arms and lowered her down on the cot.

"Nadia, I know you are a spy," he said. "Please do not deny it. I just want to know why."

She looked up at him questioningly.

"Nadia, I know you are. I will be gone soon. I just want to know why. After what the Israelis did to your family."

She looked frightenedly toward the door of the tent and then around the room. She looked back at him. Her eyes started watering and her lower lip quivered. She threw herself at his chest and clutched his shirt, holding him closely. Tears were running down her cheeks as she started to cry.

"It was not the Israelis," she sobbed. "It was the Palestinians. It was the PLO." Nadia shook her head and let the curls drop to her shoulders. "My father and brother were drafted into the PLO. During the Lebanese uprising they refused to fight. The PLO put them up against the wall and shot them. They said it would be an example to others."

Nadia sniffled and slid her hand across her cheek in a futile attempt to stem the flow of tears.

"They shot them because they refused to fight," she repeated, clutching his shirt to bring him closer. "They killed my father and brother." She looked up at him, her eyes red with tears. "Don't you understand," she said as she cried. "They killed my father and my brother and made my mother a whore." She lowered her gaze and placed her head back on his chest. "So I work for the Americans," she said, her voice cracking.

Amjad picked her up in his arms, her head resting under his chin. He thought back to a time long past when the smell of a woman's hair made him smile and a soft body close to his made him feel more of a man than at any other time. He closed his eyes and there was the red shoe. And the Americans. The Americans who had taken everything that he had ever loved.

And then came the rage. The rage that closed in on him from the four corners of the tent. Closed in on him like a burning cloud with the sickening smell of scarlet nausea. The powerful, consuming, controlling rage that closed on him like a fist, squeezing him until his skin tingled from his shoulders to the top of his scalp. He closed his eyes harder, squeezing them until his eyeballs hurt. Everything was scarlet. The red shoe that his mind held in his hands. Scarlet. The color of blood that he had spilled. Scarlet. The rivers and streams of innocent blood that ran from the rubble of a bombed out shelter. The roof of his mouth felt thick and dull. He swallowed hard. Pursing his lips he breathed in deeply as his nostrils flared. Clenching his fists until the knuckles turned white, he gnashed his teeth until his flexed jaw muscles pushed out the back of his cheeks. The rage.

His right hand reached down and pulled the knife from the sheath in his belt. She was weeping now as his left hand pulled her head to his chest. The tears that had soaked through his shirt felt warm against his skin and her breath was hot against his chest. He pulled her even closer as he raised the knife. He closed his eyes tightly, squeezing out a tear that ran slowly down his cheek, hesitated for a moment on his chin before falling softly on her hair. He clenched his jaw as he plunged the knife deeply into her neck. She lunged and twisted and pushed as the scarlet effluence from the ruptured arteries seemed to cover the tent. With one final push she shoved her head back and looked up at Amjad. Her eyes were open wide with a questioning gaze. Her mouth was trying to find words but she could only spit out the blood that had invaded the crimson orifice. Then, quietly, the gurgling stopped, her arms went limp, and her eyes fixed their focus far off in the distance. Amjad laid her slowly back down on the cot. He pulled the knife from her neck, brought a blanket up to her chest, and laid his hand on her eyes to close them.

Mark Lee was the second one out of the helicopter behind Seemann. He was the sniper. In his right hand he held a .223 caliber M-16 equipped with a Sonic III sound suppressor. The standard handle sighting bar had been removed and in its place were mounting brackets for a Starlight IV generation night scope. The night scope had been equipped with a quick lock scope ring of his own design. He had spent weeks in the ship's machine shop perfecting it. Ordinary scopes can be bumped and misaligned in transit. But he had invented a quick lock scope ring that allowed the scope to be transported separately from the rifle and yet quickly mounted and perfectly aligned when needed.

The mounting brackets had two slots, each with concave sides to accept an O-ring configuration. The scope rings had mounts that fit into the slots. But rather than O-rings, the base of the slots were equipped with ball bearings that expanded outward when the locking mechanism was screwed downward. The ball bearings would allow for telltale debris such as sand finding its way into the slots. Rather than fight it, the ball bearings would simply push it aside. Once locked down, the scope would be perfectly aligned as before. Mark would be applying for a patent on the scope rings when he returned to the States.

But still, it's hard to align a scope properly aboard an aircraft carrier. There is seldom a day without wind, and the steady motion of the ship can throw the sighting off. But Mark was only half of the sniper team.

G. Weatherman was the third person off the helicopter. He was Mark's spotter. As Mark knelt down to affix the scope to the rifle, Weatherman put one end of a tape on a spike near Mark's feet and ran toward a sand dune in the direction of the camp, stopping when the tape ended. The tape measured fifty meters. Weatherman stuck a pole into the sand at the end of the tape. On top of the pole was a cardboard target three feet in diameter. It was white with a three-inch black bull's eye.

Seemann had figured that they could get within fifty meters of the camp undetected. If everyone was asleep, they could proceed unencumbered. But if someone was up having a smoke or taking a piss, he would have to be taken out. Silently. Lee figured it would be a fifty-meter hit.

Lee had aligned the scope on the ship, but since they had to wait for Seemann to get the fax, they would have time to adjust the scope in conditions ambient to the target area.

Weatherman stepped back from the target. Lee raised the rifle to his shoulder and peered into the green fluorescence of the night vision scope. As his eyes adjusted, he placed the cross hairs on the bull's eye, let out his breath, and squeezed the trigger.

Thit. The rifle kicked slightly.

Weatherman went over to the target and put his finger to the hole. Six inches down and to the left of center. Lee set horizontal and vertical adjustments two clicks each, and put the rifle to his shoulder again.

Thit.

Weatherman approached the target and put his finger to a hole directly three inches to the right of center. Lee adjusted his horizontal one click.

Thit.

Weatherman did not have to show Lee the hole. Directly in the cross hairs was a small circle of light emanating from the middle of a dark, three-inch circle.

Lee released the clip, ejected the bullet from the chamber and flicked on the safety. He put the clip in his left breast pocket, and pulled another clip from his right pocket.

He blew on the top of the clip and inserted it into the rifle. The original clip contained normal .223-caliber forty-grain bullets. But the new clip would yield a special offering. The bullets were forty-grain .223 caliber, but the projectile was of a unique design. The lead was hollow point, to be sure. But hollow points can lose some accuracy even at close range. So the projectile had a polycarbonate ballistic tip which served two purposes: first, the ballistic shaping would allow for true flight with extreme accuracy. Second, upon hitting the target the polycarbonate tip would be forced back into the hollow tipped head, expanding the projectile with such force that the projectile would literally explode. If aimed at flesh and bone, the hydrostatic shock of a 3,500-feet-per-second impact would leave precious little for the coroner. Mark flicked off the safety, turned to Seemann, and nodded.

There were three vehicles just outside the camp parked three abreast near the road leading to Jofra. Amjad slowly opened the hood of the truck. His flashlight found the coil wire. He yanked it out and threw it under the truck. He checked the gas gauges of the two Jeeps and flashed his light on the keys of the Jeep with the most gas.

He pulled the hood up on the second Jeep and tore out its coil wire, throwing it under the truck as well. As he jumped into the first Jeep, he pumped the gas pedal twice. Upon turning the key, the engine came to life. He put it in first gear, gunned the engine, and started down the road to Jofra.

Rahin woke with a start at the sound of the engine starting. Mohammed, who had been sleeping next to him, was sitting up on his cot. Rahin signaled for Mohammed to follow him and they opened the tent door.

"Mohammed," Rahin whispered. "I'll go check the vehicles. You go check the rear of the camp."

Mohammed nodded, turned, and walked west. Rahin put his knife in his belt, grabbed his AK47, and headed for the vehicles. There were only two vehicles when he got there and they both had their hoods up. Rahin quickly saw that they were both missing coil wires. He flashed his light around, trying to spot where they would have been thrown. He finally squatted down and flashed the light under the truck. There were the coil wires. He turned the light off, leaned his gun up against the fender, and crawled under the truck.

The fax was coming over as the men gathered around Seemann. As soon as the paper cleared the cartridge Seemann held it up and put a light on it.

"Here's where we will be coming in from," he pointed with his pencil. "Mind these mines here. Should be a path right here," again pointing. "This pix is five or ten minutes old," he continued. "Looks like they are all snug in their beds. And this here. This is the communications tent." He paused. "Well, looky here," pointing to two bodies huddled together. This is where our gal is supposed to be. Looks like she has a night visitor. Be careful she doesn't get hit. Now I want clean hits and good pix. We have to I.D. all these pricks. If you get separated, use your crickets. One click for inquiry and two for response. I'll make my way around to the other side of the camp where the vehicles are. There is always a possibility someone is sleeping in the cab and our photo didn't pick him up. Then I can come in from the other side so no one gets out."

He turned his head around to see each man was ready. "Okay," he said. "Clean hits and good pix. Let's go!"

It took them fifteen minutes to get to the last sand dune before the camp. As they reached the top, Seemann signaled for them to stop. He motioned for Lee to come up. Lee crouched down and came up to where Seemann was now lying. Seemann pointed toward the camp. In front of the last tent a man was standing, AK47 in hand, peering into the dark. Seemann pointed to his own head. Lee pushed up his night vision glasses as the night scope would tell him all he needed to know. He took the covers off the scope and raised his rifle to his shoulder.

The man's head came into focus. He was right at fifty yards. Lee put the cross hairs in the man's ear, let out his breath, and squeezed.

Thit.

The man's head exploded like a ripe watermelon hitting the pavement.

Good luck on that ID, Lee thought.

Seemann signaled the others to come up. He pointed to himself with one hand and made a circling motion with his other hand. Then he held up three fingers. He would circle around to the other side of the camp. They would give him three minutes. He held his right thumb up. They all returned the sign.

Rahin reached the coil wire when he heard footsteps. The footsteps came from the side of the truck where he had left his weapon. In the distance he heard the faint sounds of thit, thit, thit, thit, thit. From under the truck, he saw boots approach, then stop at the truck. He reached down, pulled the knife from his belt, and slowly, quietly crawled away from the boots and out from beneath the truck. He looked back at the boots. The feet of the man had been facing the cab of the truck but now turned to face the Jeep. Rahin crept around the front of the truck. The man had been leaning over, looking into the Jeep. As Seemann straightened up, Rahin reached around and grabbed the top of Seemann's helmet with his left hand and jerked his head back. His right hand brought the knife over the right shoulder, around the front of the neck to start on the left side. But the chin strap was in the way. The knife sliced through the chin strap and took off the lower half of Seemann's left ear. But as the chin strap released, the helmet flew off Seemann's head and Rahin tumbled back against the truck.

Seemann turned around and instinctively put his left hand up to his ear, his M-16 hanging loosely from his right hand. Rahin kicked out, sending Seemann's gun flying to meet the sand. Rahin lunged at Seemann, his knife held high. Seemann caught Rahin's wrist as the knife was two inches from his face. For seconds they both stood there straining like two Titans in mortal combat. Suddenly Seemann pirouetted on his left foot, thrusting his right hip into Rahin. Seemann bent over and pulled as Rahin tumbled over his shoulder, and they both fell to the ground. Seemann twisted Rahin's wrist and pried the knife from his hand. He lifted the knife and plunged it deep into Rahin's chest.

Seemann fell on top of him, exhausted. He lay there for a few seconds. The "thit, thit, thits" were getting closer. Then footsteps and a cricket's click. Breathing hard he reached in his pocket, pulled out his cricket clicker, and gave two clicks. His left hand reached up and felt what was left of his left ear.

"I'm getting too old for this shit," he said to himself.

In the cold darkness of space, MRT2 floated ethereally on its endless journey eastward. It had been busy the last twenty minutes since its shutters opened, upon entering the orbital window over Libya. Minute amounts of heat were detected by its super sensitive infrared sensors. The data was changed to a digital format and sent home to Mother Earth where it was further analyzed and digested.

Throughout most of the window, the heat sources had been steady. Suddenly, tiny pin pricks of heat were registered on the sensor film and were gone. MRT2 closed its shutters and passed out of the Libyan window.

Chapter Ten
"Tell Him Amjad Mustafa Is Here"

*C**lockwork,* Soran thought to himself as he perused the pictures. Thirteen kills with no reported casualties to SAS. All of the terrorists were identifiable except for the one with his head blown off. By process of elimination they could figure out which one he was. But they still missed one man.

"Good shoot?" asked Bolder as he entered Soran's cubicle.

"Yeah, great," said Soran as he picked up his coffee cup.

"Here take a look." He handed Bolder the folder with the pictures. Bolder put his Diet Coke on Soran's desk as he opened the folder. Bolder didn't drink coffee anymore but had switched to Diet Coke for his morning caffeine fix. He said that the cola products were more compatible with his chewing gum.

"Holy shit!" Bolder exclaimed. "What happened to this guy?"

"Hollow point at about fifty yards I would guess," said Soran.

"Man I'm staying away from that shooter."

"Good plan," said Soran.

Bolder thumbed through the pictures until he came to Nadia. "Is this our good guy?" he asked.

"Yeah, she didn't make it," returned Soran. "As far as I can tell she was zapped before we got there. Her body was still warm and the blood had not fully coagulated. They brought the body back and we'll know more info later."

Soran handed him another folder.

"Look at this," he said. "This is the infrared pix just before the hit. There are two bodies together on the communications tent. That's where we found our gal. We have the positions of everyone before the hit and SAS has given us the positions after the hit. Eleven died in their cots. 'No Head' was found on the west side of the camp, and this fella," he pointed to Rahin's picture, "was on the east side next to the vehicles. And look here. There are three vehicles before the hit and apparently only two after. We are missing one man and one vehicle."

Bolder unwrapped his second Juicy Fruit of the day and said, "I'd say we have one son of a bitch sitting in a Jeep in the middle of the desert who's luckier than Lawrence of Arabia."

Soran took another sip of coffee.

"Want me to help you with the I.D.s ?" asked Bolder.

"In a minute," said Soran. "I want to stay with these for a while. MRT1 should be transmitting now. Why don't you go and check that out."

Bolder picked up his Diet Coke. "I'll check it out. Be back in a few," he said, and disappeared around the corner.

Soran spread out the thirteen pictures in front of him. The pictures faxed back from SAS were clear enough for identification. They could easily be matched up with information supplied by MRT1 and MRT2. Soran just sat and looked at the pictures. Just hours ago these men had been alive. And now they were dead. And it all started with a request by him. It's easy to put in an order for a hit. Seeing the results of what you started is the hard part.

Soran reached for his coffee cup and felt that it had gone cold. He picked his cup up and headed for the coffee room. Once there he poured the cold coffee into the sink and put his cup down. His hands were not dirty but he washed them anyway. He refilled his cup and headed back to his cubicle.

"I am here to see Major Brohan," said Amjad as he brushed his forearm across his brow.

The two men just stood there nervously pointing their rifles at him.

"I am here to see Major Brohan," Amjad repeated. As he lowered his forearm he noticed blood on his sleeve. A lot of blood. He looked down at his shirt and realized that his entire right side was covered with dried blood. He had brought some of Nadia with him to Tripoli.

No wonder these guards are nervous, he thought to himself. How often do they see a man in blood stained clothes at this hour of the morning seeking an audience with their Major Brohan?

"Look," he said. "I know this looks weird."

"Raise your hands!" demanded the first guard.

"Look," said Amjad.

"Raise your hands or I shoot!" ordered the first guard again, poking his gun toward Amjad's face.

Amjad slowly raised his arms.

"Turn around!"

Amjad obeyed.

The first soldier put the muzzle of his rifle into Amjad's right ear while the second soldier patted Amjad down.

"No weapon," said the second soldier.

"What do you want?" asked the first soldier.

Amjad started to lower his arms.

"Keep your arms up!" demanded the first soldier.

Amjad raised his arms again.

"I'm here to see Major Brohan. I have to see Major Brohan," said Amjad.

"Why do you want to see him?"

"Just tell him Amjad Mustafa is here. Tell him Doctor Amjad Mustafa from Iraq is here."

The first soldier nodded his head at the second soldier who turned, walked down a hallway, and disappeared behind a door.

"Look," said Amjad. "You know I am unarmed. You have a gun. Can I please lower my arms?"

"Keep your arms raised or I shoot!"

After a few minutes the door at the other end of the hall opened and Major Brohan came out followed by the second soldier. Brohan was dressed in pajama bottoms and a smoking jacket open to the waist whose belt he was quickly tying. He appeared to be wearing a black T-shirt under the smoking jacket but as he approached, it became evident that it was black, curly hair matting his bare chest. He raised his arms.

"Amjad, my good friend," he called.

The first soldier backed away and lowered his weapon. He snapped to attention and saluted. Brohan ignored him, looking straight ahead at Amjad.

"Amjad," he said again.

Amjad lowered his arms. Brohan stopped in his tracks and stared at his blood-soaked guest.

"What in the name of Allah happened to you?" he asked.

"There was some business that I had to take care of at the camp," answered Amjad. "Can we go somewhere to talk?"

"Of course, my friend."

Brohan put his arm around Amjad and led him down the hallway. When they entered the bedroom, two nubile young girls were lying naked on the bed. Brohan turned to Amjad and pointed to the girls.

"Would you like one of these, my friend?" he asked as a lecherous smile came over his face.

"No, no thank you," said Amjad. "I need to talk with you."

Brohan walked over to the bed, leaned over, and slapped each girl on the rear.

"Come on now you two," he said. "Get out of here."

The two girls each grabbed a sheet to cover themselves and, giggling, they disappeared through the door.

Brohan went over to the window and pulled the drapes open. Sunlight flooded the room. He took in a large breath of air and stretched his arms skyward. He turned around, slapped his belly, and said, "Now, what can I do for you?"

"How did we do?" asked Wes Covington. "Did we get our source out?"

Covington normally did not make precipitous inquiries but rather waited until the complete report hit his desk. But since the discovery of Eisner turning double and selling in-house secrets to the Russians, he had become a man on edge. Nine agents had been known to be executed by the Eastern Bloc. He was hoping to keep the body count to single digits.

"No," said Soran. "We missed it by maybe fifteen minutes. Can you believe it? Fifteen minutes."

He picked up a file and opened it.

"Her name was Nadia," he continued. "She had been with us for..."

"Save it for the report," interrupted Covington. "Just tell me how it went down."

Soran put the file back down and picked up the photograph.

"Well, like I said," Soran continued, "MRT2 took this infrared pix just as our guys were waiting to go in."

He handed the photograph to Covington. "You can see everyone is in the right place. There are two people together in the communications tent. One of them has to be Nadia; the other, her killer."

Soran took a pencil and tapped it on his desk. "It sure would have been great to get a moving picture so we could actually have seen what went on. But from MRT2's altitude we can't do that with infrared and get a clean picture. We're dealing with minute amounts of energy being detected at great distances so we have to take stills and leave the shutter open for two to five minutes, depending on how clear images you want."

He took a sip of coffee and continued to drum with the pencil. "We prefer our images pristine so we leave the shutter open for five minutes. We miss direct action but at 3:00 A.M. how much action do you expect?"

Covington looked down at the photo. "Jesus," he said. "You mean we were right there waiting to go in when she got hit?"

"Looks that way," said Soran.

"God, I can't believe it. I just can't believe it," said Covington, as he realized his personal count had reached double digits.

"We don't even know who did it," continued Soran. "But we think it was this Amjad character. He slept in the tent with her and everyone else is accounted for on this photo."

"Those fucking Russians," said Covington.

"Probably," said Soran. "But what I can't figure out is, why did Amjad kill her and why at three in the morning?"

He stopped drumming and put the pencil up to his forehead. "If the Russians tipped our friend, you'd think it would be their leader, Rahin. He would probably do it in front of the other men. Even if he assigned Amjad to do it, why three in the morning?" Soran pressed the pencil eraser harder into his forehead. "It just doesn't make any sense."

"You say we missed this Amjad fella?" asked Covington.

"Think so," said Soran. "I'm doing the ID matchups now but one vehicle is gone and one man is missing. My first guess is Amjad. I'll have the matchups complete soon."

"But why would he split?" asked Covington.

"Why wouldn't Rahin be there to witness the hit?" countered Soran.

"Well, find out and put it in the report," said Covington. "And I want that report yesterday!"

"You bet," said Soran as Covington turned and left.

Soran picked up Amjad's file and drummed on it with the pencil.

"Something tells me we haven't seen the last of you, you son of a bitch," Soran said to himself softly.

Amjad had told Major Brohan the details of the previous night. That he had found out that Nadia was a spy and the stains on his shirt were hers. He told him that he could not stay at the camp because his quest may have been compromised. He told a very interested Brohan of his plans for revenge against the United States. And that he had to go now but he needed Brohan's help.

"Are you sure you can do this by yourself?" asked Brohan.

"There is no other way," answered Amjad. "But I do need your help."

Brohan did not think Amjad's plan would work but if Amjad wanted to do battle with the "Great Satan," Brohan would hold his coat.

"What help do you require?"

"I need you to get me to Rome. You can get me a diplomatic passport and a visa. That would get me to Rome."

Brohan thought for a moment.

"Yes, yes, I could arrange that. When would you like to go?"

"As soon as possible."

"Good. I'll check on the passport, visa, and flight schedules. In the meantime why don't you get cleaned up. You look a mess."

"Thank you. That would be nice. Also a change of clothes and a business suit."

He put his thumb and forefinger to the bridge of his nose and closed his eyes hard, remembering his fatigue. "Oh, yes," he said. "And I'll need to visit your pharmacy."

Brohan took a pack of American cigarettes from the table, took one out, and offered another to Amjad. Amjad accepted and Brohan put a flame to both. He took a deep drag and put his arm around Amjad as they walked to the door.

"Still, too bad about Nadia," he said. "She was one of my favorites."

Chapter Eleven
On to Rome

Except for No Head, the hits were clean. SAS had been trained to kill with body shots. After completion of the objective, each terrorist's picture was taken. The mission included termination and identification. A file could be set up for each one. With its infrared capabilities MRT2 could keep a count on the number of bodies. Both MRT1 and MRT2 had been able to obtain photos of each of the camp's occupants. With their sources in Tripoli and the input from Nadia, camp L3 had been well inventoried and tended to by Beta Group. Now Soran and Bolder were matching up the portraits in death to the prior composites.

"It's Amjad, all right," said Soran.

"Yup," said Bolder, lifting his can of Diet Coke.

Soran leaned back in his chair and put his feet up on his desk. "Let's piece this all together now," he said. "From the pre-raid pix we know that all are there and Amjad killed Nadia."

He brought his cup of coffee to his mouth and warmed his lips. "Why?" he continued. "We don't rightly know. Could be the Russians. But I discount that. Rahin was the leader and he would have had a hand in it. My guess is that Amjad somehow found out and thought his plans compromised. So he kills Nadia and sets out for parts unknown. We know from the report that the two remaining vehicles had been tampered with so apparently he did not want anyone following him."

Bolder entered the conversation. "Could be he just got scared and ran off."

"No, I don't think so," replied Soran. "He pulled the plug on the other two vehicles so he wouldn't be followed. That's not the act of a scared person. No, our man has real cunning."

"What about Rahin and No Head?" asked Bolder.

"Rahin and No Head are awakened by the Jeep. Rahin goes to the front of the camp while No Head checks out the rear. We zap No Head and Rahin. The rest are on their cots." Soran brought his feet down from the desk and picked up Amjad's file. "We know from our source in Tripoli that Amjad has some nuclear thoughts with America in mind." Soran looked down at the composite. "No, this man is not scared. This man is on a mission, and we'd better find him."

Amjad was over the Mediterranean passing through ten thousand feet. As the seat belt sign was turned off, he unbuckled his belt, reached below the seat in front of him, and pulled out his carry-on bag. He checked the contents again; one change of clothes, one toiletry bag, one diplomatic passport to Rome, and one medical bag.

Brohan had been curious as to why Amjad would want to bring a doctor's bag but he did not ask. He also did not ask about the vial inside the bag. The vial that contained the prescription that Amjad had filled before he left. A prescription that Amjad had said was absolutely vital to his trip.

Amjad closed the carry-on bag and replaced it beneath the seat. He pushed the button on his armrest and reclined his seat. He put his head back, closed his eyes, and nodded off to sleep.

Covington paced the room in front of the huge windows that faced the courtyard. He had his pipe in his hand to show that he was back in control. He did not smoke, and the pipe had not seen tobacco since his yearly check-up seven years ago. Dr. Bjork, the company doctor, had shown him some interesting photographs of what nicotine and tar could do to lips and tongues after continuous exposure. He had discovered that he really didn't need tobacco. The unladen pipe would give him the oral gratification that he needed. There was also the feeling of control. When he had his pipe he was in total control. He tapped the pipe with the palm of his hand.

"Unfortunate we missed this Amjad fellow," he said to the window. Soran and Bolder squirmed a little in their chairs in front of Covington's desk. "Just dumb luck," he continued, as he turned around to face them. "You know, I just don't like dumb luck."

Bolder searched his empty shirt pocket and remembered that he had left his gum back on Soran's desk. Covington circled around to the back of his desk and sat down in his chair.

"Still," he continued, "we got the rest of them and none of our guys got hit."

"Except for Nadia," said Soran.

Covington put the pipe to his mouth. "Yes," he said. "Too bad."

He took the pipe out of his mouth and pointed it at Soran. "That's why I don't like dumb luck," he said. He put the pipe back in his mouth, picked up a folder from his desk and opened it. "So," he continued, "you think this Amjad fellow is coming to America and poses some kind of nuclear threat." He looked over his glasses at Soran. "I don't see any mention of a network here."

"I believe he is acting alone," said Soran.

"Alone?" questioned Covington. "What kind of threat could he be alone?"

"Well," said Soran. "We don't know that." He sat up in his chair. "He may have a network here but I don't see that in his actions."

"How so?" asked Covington.

"Well," continued Soran. "It's the way he left camp. Killing Nadia and then slipping away so that no one could follow him. If he had a network here, the camp would have to be part of it. He wouldn't just slip off in the middle of the night." He put his arms against the armrest and entwined his fingers. "No," he said, "I believe he is alone."

"What can he do by himself?" asked Covington.

"We don't know that," answered Soran. "The first thing we have to do is find out who he really is."

"How do you know he is a nuclear threat?" posed Covington.

"We got it from two sources," answered Soran. "Our man in Tripoli and Nadia."

"Our man in Tripoli?" asked Covington.

"Yes. This Major Brohan is very high up in the Libyan Army. In intelligence. We were able to turn his driver. Appears the driver likes young boys. We caught him in a compromising position, and since they don't look kindly to that sort of entertainment in that part of the world, he was more than willing to help us out. He had driven Amjad and Brohan to the major's place and overheard Amjad talking about nuclear devastation to the United States. He didn't catch the whole conversation but that's the drift he got. And then our last contact with Nadia. She had overheard Amjad telling Rahin the same thing."

"So you take him seriously?" asked Covington.

"Well," said Soran, "we got thirteen dead ones and one live one. Yes, sir, I do take him seriously."

Covington put the pipe in his mouth, put his hands behind his neck, and leaned back in his chair. "Well," he said, "he's alone in Libya. Apart from the members of the camp he only knows one man: Major Brohan." He took the pipe out of his mouth. "When's the last time you talked with the driver?"

"Higher, Daddy, higher," Fatima cried with delight. "Push me higher."

When the swing came back, Amjad obediently pushed harder and sent Fatima two-thirds of the way to the top of the swing set.

"Push me higher, Daddy," Fatima implored. Amjad pushed even harder. "Give me an under, Daddy," she said.

When the swing came back to him, Amjad dutifully grabbed Fatima's seat, ran with it under the swing set, and sent it soaring until it reached the height of the support pole.

He turned to see his daughter. She was dressed in a pink dress and was wearing the red shoes he had brought from America. She was also wearing a white bonnet. She had never worn a bonnet before, but she was wearing one now. He looked below the bonnet but he could not see her face. The swing went back until it reached the extent of the back arc and came forward again. He looked through the mist. He could see her dress, her shoes, and her bonnet, but he could not see her face.

"Carry me on your shoulders, Daddy," the voice said. He stopped the swing and lifted the girl to his shoulders. "Run, Daddy, run" came the voice. Amjad started to run.

"Faster, Daddy, faster." With his hands over her ankles he picked up the pace. "Faster, Daddy. Run faster." Amjad was running but now the grade had increased and he was running uphill. "Please, Daddy, go faster." He kept running but the faster he ran the steeper the hill became. His heart was racing and his legs were burning. He gasped for air as his lungs seemed ready to burst. When his body would no longer obey his mind he collapsed to his knees.

"Daddy, I'm fading." Amjad gripped harder. "Daddy, I'm fading." The voice was distant now. The weight was off his shoulders and his right hand was empty. His left hand still held the girl's ankle joint above the red shoe. He slowly brought his left hand forward. In his hand was the red shoe, the ankle, and the leg which ended in a bloody stump. The leg and ankle faded until Amjad had only the red shoe in his hand. He sat back and stared at the red shoe.

His left shoulder now hurt. Something was pressing on his left shoulder. It was pressing harder. It hurt. So much pressure. Why wouldn't it stop?

"Stop!" Amjad yelled but the pressure was harder on his shoulder and now it was shaking him. "Stop!" Amjad yelled and started to cry.

"Excuse me, sir," the flight attendant said as she shook the man's left shoulder. "Excuse me, sir," she said louder, and continued the shaking.

Amjad opened his eyes and peered forward. Someone was shaking his left shoulder. He looked up at the flight attendant.

"Excuse me, sir. I'm sorry to wake you but you were asleep," she apologized. "We'll be landing soon and the captain has turned on the seat belt sign. Would you please fasten your seat belt and return your seat back to its upright position?"

"Wha...," Amjad blinked his eyes. "Where are we?"

"In fifteen minutes we'll be in Rome."

Covington was shuffling through his papers. "Amazing how much paperwork to close down one camp," he said to himself. They had matched up all the terrorists with positive IDs. All of them except No Head, and they were sure who he was by process of elimination. The report from SAS had come in and the tactics could be studied and critiqued for further missions.

The logistics from the aircraft carrier, the weapons used, the satellite feedback from before and after, the intelligence that had given them reason to interdict all amounted to vast amounts of paperwork. And Covington had the final approval. But when the paperwork was done there would be one less camp to worry about. L2 had gone down previously and now L3 could be closed. MRT1 and MRT2 would have to be retasked to a wider view to follow another camp if and when it sprang up. "Still all this paperwork."

"Got a minute?" Soran's head poked around the corner.

"Yeah," said Covington. "What the hell, I need a break."

Soran crossed the room and sat down on the chair in front of Covington's desk. "This just came in. We checked with Major Brohan's driver and, sure enough, our man Amjad made it to Tripoli."

"No surprise there," said Covington.

"Yeah, but get this," continued Soran. "The driver drove Amjad to Tripoli International Airport and let him off at the Libyan Arab Airlines counter. The only luggage he had was a carry-on bag. The driver stuck around long enough to see him check in to a flight to Rome."

"Rome?" Asked Covington. "Curious. I would have thought Athens."

"Why there, sir?"

"Sloppy airport security. Sloppiest in the free world. Any scumbag can get into Athens and then from there get to almost anywhere." Covington stuck his pipe in his mouth. "Rome, eh."

"Well, said Soran. "There must be something special about Rome. I don't know. Maybe he likes fountains."

Covington looked over his glasses at Soran. Soran sat up in his chair and cleared his throat. "Can't we contact Rome and have them pick him up?" he asked.

Covington sat back in his chair. "We could, I suppose, but what good would that do? What could we hold him on?"

"He killed Nadia." said Soran.

"We've got no proof. We've got no jurisdiction. And the only evidence we have is top secret espionage. I could just hear it in the courtroom. 'Well, your Honor. We happen to find Nadia's body while we were killing all the bad guys.'" Covington put his pipe down. "No I don't think that would fly." He got up and walked over to the window. "How old is this info?"

"We just got it, sir."

"No, I mean what time did Amjad get on the plane."

Soran looked at his watch and did some mental calculations. "That would be about five hours ago."

"Shit!" said Covington. "He's been in Rome for a couple hours now. He probably is on his next flight already."

Soran interrupted. "But what if he only had a ticket to Rome? They couldn't have had time to book a flight all the way through to America. He may have just gone to Rome and tried to get a flight to America from there."

"That means we may still have time," said Covington, his voice rising. "I'll call our friends in Rome."

Lisa Jean Reganetti was approaching the end of her shift behind the KLM counter. She had been checking on arrivals on her computer terminal when the command shift key stuck. She knocked on it twice with the third nail on her left hand. On the third try she knocked harder, and the nail that she had just spent 1500 lira to have affixed to her digit went sailing skyward. She lurched for it but it glanced off her right hand and fell to the floor. With a mild curse she bent over to pick it up.

"Excuse me," came a voice from in front of the counter.

Lisa Jean came up from the floor to face the man but dropped the nail again. This time she trapped it between her right hand and right thigh. She picked it out with her left hand and brought it safely to rest on the counter.

"May I...may I help you, sir?" came from her blushing face.

"Yes," the man said. "Do you have a flight to Minneapolis, Minnesota, USA?"

Lisa Jean pushed the nail over to the side of the counter and sort of patted it to make it stay.

"Let me see," she said as she went back to her keyboard. After a few entries she said, "Yes, we have a flight. Flight 350. There is a stopover in Amsterdam and then connects with Northwest Airlines flight 55 to Minneapolis."

She punched more numbers. "I'm sorry, but that flight is booked. Would you like me to put you on the waiting list?"

"Once it leaves Amsterdam is it nonstop to Minneapolis?"

She punched more keys. "Yes it is but, as I said, that flight is booked."

"Yes, yes, I know," the man said. "What gate is it at and what time does it leave?"

"Gate 43B at 11:53 P.M., but, as I said, that flight is full."

Amjad turned away from the counter, clutched his carry-on bag, and walked toward the B concourse.

Soran was sitting back in his chair with his feet up on his desk thinking about Rome. "What could one man do?" he said to the cubicle walls. Soran did his best thinking out loud. While thinking out loud greatly improved his cognitive powers, it often proved detrimental.

A philosophy professor at North Dakota State University had overheard Soran's ruminations during an exam on Immanuel Kant and mistook his machinations for passing on information to his neighbor and almost expelled him for cheating. The Dean looked favorably on Soran's syllogism: that, A, no person in the entire university understood anything about Kant and that, B, he was a person attending the university, ergo, C, he knew nothing about Kant. And by this declension, he could not pass any information on Kant to anyone.

Soran went on to graduate with honors, in spite of a D in philosophy.

"What could one man do?" he repeated. "Is he by himself or does he have a network? If it's nuclear, where would he get the nuclear fuel? Anyone can build a bomb, but you have to have the fuel for it to work. Pretty hard to smuggle it in the country. Pretty hard to get at the stuff that's already here. Maybe he's going to blow up a nuclear power plant. It's a long way to come for that. We've got those guarded pretty well for one man to attack. What the hell is this guy up to?"

Covington rounded the corner of the cubicle and sat on the edge of Soran's desk. "There is one thing we didn't think of," he said. "What if he has a network in Rome?" He paused for a moment. "What is it? The Red Army or something?

"No, the Red Army faction is the old Baader-Meinhof gang," said Soran. "But they were up in Germany and were pretty well decimated in the late '70s." Soran reached for his coffee. "You're probably thinking of the Red Brigade."

"Yeah, yeah, that's it," said Covington. "They still have a hard-on for America."

"Well," said Soran, "that's a possibility. But I think we should follow the man." Soran took a sip of coffee then put his cup down on the desk again.

"What do we really know about this guy?" asked Covington.

"Well," said Soran, picking up a note pad and pen, "not much. From the driver we know that he is from Iraq and his name is Amjad. We never got a last name. Maybe everyone gives up their last name when they become a terrorist. Maybe it's like a rite or something. It's like circumcision. When you become a terrorist you lose a little part of yourself."

"Yeah, right," said Covington. "What else?"

"Well, he's apparently a doctor and he has been to the good old U.S. of A."

"Is that it?" asked Covington. "Anything else?"

"Just that he's got a weak backhand."

Soran's humor was lost on Covington.

"Let's go with what we've got," he said. "He's a doctor who has been to America. He's an Iraqi so I don't suppose it wasn't a pleasure trip. But you know, medicine isn't very political." He put his pipe in his mouth. "Let's suppose he was here to learn something. Maybe some new surgical technique. Get Bolder and the two of you check with the AMA and see which universities and hospitals invite doctors from the Middle East to teach them techniques of any kind. Then check with the university or hospital that does and find out if there were any doctors with the first name Amjad or anyone else from Iraq. I'll start checking with immigration to see if we can track down visas issued to Iraqis. I'll also check with our boys in Rome to see what the Red Brigade is up to."

Covington took his pipe out of his mouth, patted it in his hand, turned, and walked away. Soran took his feet off his desk and picked up the phone. He dialed extension 453 and waited a few seconds until he heard the familiar click.

"Bolder, get your ass in here. We've got work to do."

Amjad put his carry-on bag on the conveyor belt and walked through the security gate. He waited patiently as the conveyor belt stopped to allow the woman to peruse the scope. Being satisfied that the stethoscope was not a weapon, she turned the conveyor belt back on and Amjad collected his bag.

Flight 350 would be one of the last to leave the airport that night and B concourse seemed almost deserted. Amjad walked to gate 43B and observed that the

Boeing 747 was at the gate but only about half of the passengers were there. Amjad turned and walked back to the bathroom that he had passed. He walked in and observed a row of faucets. Behind the faucets was a wall that hid the urinals. Behind the urinals was a wall that separated the urinals from the toilets. Amjad walked back to the row of toilets. Each stall had a door that was raised about one foot off the floor and went up to a height three feet from the ceiling. Amjad bent down to see if any of the stalls were being used. Satisfied that the stalls were empty, he walked down to the last stall and opened it. He looked inside for a minute and made a mental note. He closed the door, walked back outside, and headed back to gate 43B.

"Whatcha got for me?" Bolder peeked his head around Soran's cubicle.

"We're after Amjad," returned Soran.

"Hot damn!" exclaimed Bolder, and unwrapped a piece of gum. "The fox is loose again. Saddle up your horses gentlemen and I'll go get the hounds." The stick of gum disappeared in the flapping mouth.

Soran pushed back his chair and got up. He picked up a computer graphic composite of Amjad and pinned it on the push pin pad above his desk. MRT2 had gotten a picture of two-thirds of his face when Amjad was carrying Kazi to his tent after the raid in Chad. Prior to that MRT2 had only been able to get the top of his head when he was at the firing range. The computer assimilated the information available and came up with a composite of what Amjad should look like.

"Now, that's our man." said Soran, "We know he's a doctor from Iraq." Up went two pieces of paper to be pinned on the board. "Doctor" and "Iraq." Soran continued. "We know he's looking for something nuclear but we don't know what. We know he was here before. My guess is to learn some surgical technique or something. Covington is checking immigration for visas from Iraq."

Soran sat down. "We've got to check with the AMA to see what hospitals and universities welcome guests from the Middle East." Soran crumpled up a piece of paper in his hand. "I'll take hospitals," he said. "You take universities." He threw the crumpled paper at the picture on the pinboard and looked at the clock which read three o'clock. "Let's get on it. We don't have much time."

Chapter Twelve
"Thank You, Florence"

Gerald Spaulding had spent a wonderful week in Italy. He felt that he owed himself a trip like this. Since the break-up with his lover he had been despondent and unresponsive. His friends had told him "Get away for a while. Go to Europe. Have an adventure."

Spaulding's choice of Italy had been a good one. There was Rome, of course, and Venice. But Spaulding had particularly liked Florence. The amber colors of the weathered sandstone and terra-cotta gave the city a tawny tinge that seemed to exude warmth. The architecture was a combination of Romanesque, Gothic, and Renaissance which not only awed but inspired. For this, after all, was the birthplace of the Renaissance. There were treasures to be found in the museums. The chiseled, gilded, and frescoed ceilings of the great halls in Palazzo Vecchio, Palazzo Pitti, and Palazzo Strozzi left him awe inspired and somehow helped to fill the void that he had left back home.

He had wished that his itinerary had taken him to Florence first so that he could have altered his plans and stayed there the whole week rather than the two days the itinerary had allotted him. He had heard the phrase "See Venice and die." But now he was stirred to think "'See Florence and live!" This cradle of the Renaissance had been his rebirth. He had not met anyone in particular and the traveling alone had, at times, made him lonely, but he had wanted it that way. Now the history, architecture, and beauty of Florence had brought him back to full bloom. He had regained what was lost and was ready to live again.

Amjad was sitting in the outermost row of gate 43B. He peered over his magazine as future passengers strolled by. He lowered his magazine as a man in a brown sport coat approached him. The man had on a tan turtleneck sweater with a rainbow neck chain and a rainbow triangle lapel pin. The man smiled at Amjad and turned to go to his seat. Out of the side pocket of the man's jacket Amjad noticed an airline boarding pass. It said KLM flight 350, Gate 43B.

Soran had been looking up at Amjad's picture for some time. "Who are you?" he asked. "Where are you going and why are you so pissed off?"

His phone buzzed. He turned and brought it up to his ear. "Soran," he said.

"Yeah, what ya got?" It was Bolder's voice.

"Not much. How about you?"

"Well there's only three hospitals that hosted Iraqis to learn new procedures. Johns Hopkins, Stanford, and the University of Minnesota."

Soran was silent.

"Minnesota," said Bolder. "Isn't that where you're from?"

Soran paused and looked up at Amjad's picture. "Yeah," he said, and hung up the receiver.

Amjad was standing across from the man in the turtleneck. Spaulding looked up at Amjad and smiled. Amjad lowered his magazine, walked over to Spaulding, and sat down.

"Where are you from?" Amjad asked.

"Minneapolis, Minnesota," Spaulding returned. "And you?"

Amjad paused. "Egypt. I am an Egyptian."

He pulled his carry-on bag to his lap. "I am going to your country to learn some medical procedures. I'm a doctor."

"How wonderful. Where are you going?"

"The University of Minnesota."

"My God. That's in Minneapolis where I live." Spaulding's eyes were shining now.

"Yes," continued Amjad. "I have been there before."

"Well, that's wonderful. I hope you like it there."

"Yes, I like it every much. Some day I might just stay there."

"Wonderful"

"How about you? What do you do in Minneapolis?"

"Oh well, I'm an actor. An actor and an artist."

"Have I seen you in anything before?"

"Well, I've just done some things locally. I used to be a computer programmer but I tried out for Shakespearean summer stock and just loved it. I decided that that is the place for me. Too many computer programmers anyway."

"Were you in Italy to find work?"

"No. Just a vacation. I had some problems at home, but that's all gone now. I'm all refreshed and ready to go again."

He squirmed a little in his seat.

"I couldn't help notice your lapel pin, "Amjad said. "What does it signify?"

Spaulding squirmed a little more but then regained his composure and looked Amjad squarely in the eye.

"Sexual preference," he said.

Amjad looked back at Spaulding, smiled, and said, "You know, I've always believed that variety is the spice of life."

Spaulding smiled, somewhat relieved. He lowered his glance and then remembered Florence. He looked back up at Amjad.

"Have you ever heard of the mile high club?" he asked.

"The mile high club?"

Spaulding's confidence was growing. "Yes. That's where you have sex above 5,200 feet." He paused. "Oh, that's right. You probably use the metric system. Oh, let's see, 1,760 yards equals..."

"Sixteen twenty-five meters." Amjad laughed. "But I get the picture."

Spaulding waited for a reply. "Well, have you?" he asked.

"Have I?" Amjad repeated. He looked around the almost empty concourse and laughed. Then he looked back at Spaulding.

"Usually I can't wait that long," he said.

Spaulding's eyes opened.

Amjad looked around the concourse and then back to Spaulding again.

"I think I would like to go to the bathroom," he said.

Spaulding felt a tingling.

"Would you like some company?" he asked.

"Yes," said Amjad. "Yes, I would like that very much."

Spaulding followed Amjad out of Gate 43B and toward the men's room. His eyes turned skyward. "Thank you, Florence!" he whispered.

Bolder's cubicle was the same size as Soran's, but with his housekeeping it seemed smaller. He had files strewn about his desk amidst the empty gum wrappers. The push pin pad contained another composite of Amjad, but this one had a wad of Juicy Fruit stuck to its nose. Soran turned the corner and stood by Bolder's desk.

"How'd ya do?" he asked.

Bolder blew a quick bubble then retracted the gum into his mouth. "Well, the business offices of Johns Hopkins and the University of Minnesota are closed. I did get a hold of Stanford but they have no record of an Amjad from Iraq or anywhere else." Bolder looked at his computer. "Then I got on the Internet and sent a memo to the University of Minnesota and Johns Hopkins that we had to get some info, stat. Matter of national emergency and all that stuff. Thinking maybe I'll get lucky."

Bolder clicked his gum. "Then I get this memo from this hacker that says he can access the U of Minnesota. So I tell him I need to know if there was a guest of the University of Minnesota from Iraq named Amjad. The guy writes back and says he will check and let me know."

Bolder tapped his desk with his pen. "Just think," he continued, "We've got this hacker probably breaking into confidential records to try to help with a national emergency. Sort of gets you right here, doesn't it?" He held his hand to his heart.

"Right," said Soran.

"And guess what this guy's handle is?" said Bolder.

"I can't wait."

Bolder paused for effect. "Risky."

On Bolder's computer screen a cursor was flashing. "Looks like something in my mailbox," said Bolder. "Let's take a look."

Bolder punched some keys and his screen came to life.

To: The Hound
Amjad Mustafa from Iraq attended University of Minnesota July 1990 to observe kidney transplants. Host surgeon: Dr. Bellingham. Piece of cake.
—Risky

Amjad led Spaulding into the men's room and observed that it was empty. They walked past the row of sinks and past the urinals. When they reached the stalls Amjad bent over to look under the doors. A quick glance confirmed that they were alone. Amjad got back up and led Spaulding down to the end of the stalls. Amjad put his hand on Spaulding's shoulders and smiled. Spaulding returned the smile and put his hands on Amjad's hips. Amjad leaned over and kissed Spaulding fully on the lips. Their mouths opened and Amjad sent his tongue deeply into Spaulding's mouth. He pulled Spaulding closer and sent his left hand down to rub Spaulding's thigh. Spaulding groaned and returned the favor by fondling Amjad's genitals.

Amjad pulled his head back and said, "Do me first."

Spaulding looked around. Amjad opened the stall door and they went inside. Amjad closed the door behind them and locked it. He put down his travel bag as Spaulding knelt before him. Spaulding's hands nervously fought with Amjad's belt. Having finally mastered it he unbuttoned the pants button and unzipped the fly. He pulled Amjad's pants down to his knees and quickly followed with the briefs. He started fondling Amjad's penis but it remained flaccid.

Spaulding looked up at Amjad. "Don't I excite you?" he said.

"Perhaps if you turned your head this way," Amjad said, and put his left hand on the back of Spaulding's head. He placed his right hand under Spaulding's jaw and with a violent twist pulled his left hand down and to the left while his right hand forced Spaulding's head up and to the right.

Amjad heard a thick crack. He brought Spaulding's head back to the original position and repeated the maneuver, only this time more violently. Another crack.

Amjad took Spaulding by the shoulders, lifted him up, turned him around, and laid him face down on the toilet seat. He pulled up his briefs and pants and buckled his belt. He bent down and placed his hands on Spaulding's forehead while his knee went into Spaulding's back. As he pulled hard onto the forehead, his knee pushed deep into the back. Two loud cracks and the head was limp in his hands. Amjad lifted the body up, turned it around, and set it on the toilet seat. He pulled the airline ticket and boarding pass from the brown pocket. Reaching into the pants, he pulled out Spaulding's passport and wallet. After taking out the cash, credit cards, and driver's license, he threw the empty wallet on the floor. He opened the stall door and kicked his carry-on bag out of the stall. He closed the door and locked it. Lifting himself to the top of the door he swung his legs over and fell to the other side. He picked up his carry-on bag, looked at the ticket and boarding pass, and headed for gate 43B.

Chapter Thirteen
"Sometimes You Just Get Lucky"

Soran and Bolder rounded the corner of the corridor leading to Covington's office. Their pace and bounce was that of two schoolchildren heading for the playground. They reached Covington's door to see him sitting in his chair with his feet up on his desk looking out his window. They had never seen Covington in such a relaxed manner before. The tobaccoless pipe was in his mouth as he drummed a pencil on his desk. Soran cleared his throat. Covington's feet slipped quickly and smoothly off his desk and he swirled his chair like a dancer doing a pirouette.

"Got a name for you, sir," said Soran.

"Good," said Covington. "Very good. What have you got?"

"Amjad Mustafa," put in Bolder.

Soran and Bolder crossed the room and sat in front of Covington.

Bolder continued. "Looks like Amjad spent some time at the University of Minnesota hospitals studying transplant techniques."

Covington took his pipe from his mouth.

"University of Minnesota," he said. "Isn't that in…Minneapolis?"

"Yes," said Soran.

Covington peered over his glasses at Soran. "Isn't that where you're from, son?"

"Yes, it is," answered Soran.

Covington turned back to the window. "Minnesota, huh? What the hell is there?"

"Whole lot of lakes," answered Soran.

Covington turned back to Soran. "Well, I doubt if he's going there to fish," he said.

"Yes sir," said Soran. "Actually that may not be his target at all. It's just where he stayed in America."

"I agree," said Covington. "That is not a very tantalizing target. Certainly wouldn't have the impact of a New York or Los Angeles. But still, it's a place he is familiar with." He pounded the pipe in his hand.

"So what's there besides lakes?"

"Well," Soran pondered for a moment. "There's agriculture, of course, and the industry is pretty well diversified."

"But what could be a target there?" asked Covington. "Power plants. Do they have any nuclear power plants?"

"Yeah, a couple," said Soran. "But ya know, there are a couple companies with defense contracts that have been pretty visible of late."

"Tell me," said Covington.

"Well," said Soran. "I was just thinking that this guy is from Iraq, right? And he's pissed off, right? Well, I figure it's probably because he lost someone in the war. In Minneapolis, Alliant makes munitions and Honeywell makes guidance systems. There have been a lot of protesters, peaceniks, you know, picketers, at Honeywell and he could have picked that up on the news while he was here. Maybe a guided bomb killed someone and he's back for revenge."

He looked at Bolder. "I don't know," he continued, "I'm just looking for different scenarios."

Covington patted the pipe in his hand. "Well, anything's possible with this clown. But I like the power plants. Make more of a splash, ya know. And I lean more toward New York or L.A. Anyway, once he steps foot in the good old U.S. of A., he's out of our jurisdiction. I'll call the FBI and give them what we've got. But first I'll call our friends in Rome. Maybe they can head this guy off at the airport."

Franco Alberti had just finished cleaning the woman's bathroom on B concourse. Since the airport was nearly empty he had hoped to clean the bathrooms and go home early. But he now had to go back to the men's room. He had cleaned it all before he cleaned the women's bathroom. All, that is, except the last stall which he could tell was occupied. Anyone else would probably have just gone home but Franco was proud of his work. His mother had always told him "It's not what you do, it's how you do it." And he trudged back into the men's bathroom to clean that last stall. He pushed his cart to the end of the stall and found the last door locked. He bent down and observed the same pair of legs with the trousers down to the ankles that had been there before. He paused for a moment, listening. Hearing nothing he knocked on the stall door.

"*Scusi,*" he said. "*Come sta?*"

Nothing.

"*Scusi, Signore,*" he said louder. "*Vorrei pulire la toilette, per favore.*"

Again nothing.

He pulled his cart next to the door, climbed up, and peered over.

"*Santa Maria!*" he yelled as he crawled down off the cart.

Georgio La Scalla had been working late that night. He would be getting home around 10:30 or 11:00 P.M. Usually when he got home that late it was because he had stopped off to see his mistress after work. He could have used the excuse of working late to explain his late arrival, but his wife never asked and, what's more, never cared. The fact that she was well taken care of was enough for her. That his sexual pleasures were taken out on someone else was a bonus.

Georgio had used the afternoon hours for his amorous tête-à-tête. A bundle of freshly cut flowers and a bottle of vino had put his lover in a mood to push his paperwork back to midnight. But after two hours, his urges and his palate sated, he ambled back to his office at the Carabinieri, the national police force. An official at the National Central Bureau of Interpol had called him and asked if he would help an American from the CIA. It seemed that the CIA had a terrorist on the loose who might be at the airport in Rome. Since the NCB did not have the resources for an immediate interdiction he was hoping that Georgio would help. His men were already in Rome and could be sent to the airport in time to "catch a thief," so to speak.

He was told that a Wes Covington from the CIA would be calling him and any help he could give would be greatly appreciated. Georgio knew that one can never have too many friends in this business and cheerfully acquiesced.

When Covington called, he explained that a terrorist named Amjad Mustafa was believed to be in Rome and probably at the Rome airport. Although he could have come to Italy to join up with some terrorist organization, it was thought that he was just passing through on his way to America. Covington could fax his composite and hoped Georgio could get some men, go to the airport, and arrest Amjad.

Georgio inquired as to what crime this Amjad had committed in Italy. The somewhat taken aback Covington explained that there was none. When asked what crime was committed in America once again the answer was in the negative. Georgio explained that in Italy he could not arrest someone for landing and taking off again. So a compromise was reached where he would send some men armed with the composite to find this Amjad if he was still there and surreptitiously find out what flight he was on. Then he would pass this information back to Covington to do with as he pleased.

Pleasantries were exchanged and within fifteen minutes he had his fax. Georgio reached for his phone and then looked at his clock. The last flights would be taking off before he could muster his men. He reasoned that if Amjad was on a flight tonight he would be gone by the time they got there. If he had missed a flight he would still be there in the morning. Georgio put the receiver down, laid the fax on his desk, and headed home for dinner.

Since the acquisition of Northwest Airlines by KLM Airlines, the entire system had prided itself on on-time flights. Flight 350 from Rome to Amsterdam was no exception. Upon arrival to Amsterdam, Amjad easily found his way from the KLM arrival gate to the Northwest departing gate. But once there he found the counter unattended. The flight had a three and a half hour layover, so there would be no one at the counter for at least an hour and a half. Amjad walked into the bathroom and splashed water on his face. He walked back to the row of toilet stalls and stood for a moment. He shook his head and walked back to the departing gate.

There had been one man assigned to each concourse. Armed with a composite of Amjad they were to sweep the concourse from rear to front and if no contact was made, they would post themselves by the security points. If contact was made, their instructions were to simply follow Amjad and report back on which flight he took.

Bruno Mocelli approached the security area and showed the guard his credentials. The security guard informed him that there was some commotion at the men's room on this concourse and since he was with the Carabinieri perhaps he should take a look. He ran back to the men's room and found two airport employees just outside, bent slightly over and holding their stomachs. Bruno walked inside, just missing a man on his knees, retching. Bruno stepped across the vomit and walked to the row of toilet stalls. Two security guards were standing in front of the last stall just staring. Bruno walked back to the last stall and looked in. He caught his breath as his knees became weak. Something knotted in his stomach. He turned away, bent over, and sent his breakfast splattering on his shoes.

Amjad awoke with a start. He had not meant to fall asleep. He had just closed his eyes for a minute and...

He blinked and shook his head to clear the cobwebs. Looking at his watch he found that the flight was still an hour away. But now the check-in counter was manned by two Northwest Airlines personnel. The man was busy helping an oriental family with their schedule. The woman was at the keyboard of the computer. Amjad got up, walked over to her and handed her his ticket. She took it and punched in some numbers.

"Well, Mr. Spaulding," she said. "Your luggage has been checked through to Minneapolis. I'll have the seating up in a minute."

She paused to let the machine catch up with her. "Ah, there we go," she said. "Would you like an aisle or a window?"

"Aisle," he said.

"Let's see. 30C." She punched it in and waited. The computer clicked a few times and ejected a piece of paper. She took his ticket and put it in a folder. She put the piece of paper in the slot of the folder and handed it to Amjad. "Here's your ticket and boarding pass. We'll start boarding about a half hour before take off. Have a nice flight, Mr. Spaulding."

Amjad nodded and went back to his seat.

He had always wanted a sports car and now he had it. Yes, this was the car he had dreamed of. Fuel injected, turbo charged, and a horsepower to weight ratio that made the tachometer red line easily reachable with the slightest touch of his foot. Fire engine red, or as he called it "arrest me red." For out here in the country roads there were no speed limits for him. Out here the laws no longer applied to him. The wind whistled through his hair, but aviator shades protected his eyes from the bright sunlight. He reached over and patted the hand of the woman in the passenger seat. She respondingly took a hold of his hand. He looked up at her face. She truly was the woman of his dreams. He had wanted her all his life and now he had her. As he looked into her dancing blue eyes, darkness came over them. He turned to look ahead. They had entered a tunnel. But there was no light ahead. He stepped on the accelerator. Faintly a pin prick of light appeared.

"The end. The end of the tunnel," he said aloud.

The point of light grew as the tach needle crossed the red line. He shifted into the last gear. The light grew larger until they broke through the end of the tunnel and were again awash in brilliant sunshine. He squeezed her hand and shouted, "We made it!"

"Yes we did, son," came the reply.

He turned to see his mother sitting next to him. "Wha..." he stammered.

There was a ringing.

"What..." he again managed.

Another ring.

"Aren't you going to answer it?" she asked.

"Wait, I ah..."

Another ring.

"The car phone. Aren't you going to answer the car phone?" she repeated, and put his hand on the receiver. He lifted the receiver off its cradle.

"Hello," he said.

Another ring.

"Hello, hello."

Covington awoke with a start. His hand was behind his neck and he felt the sheets covered with perspiration. He turned his head and with half opened eyes he read 2:04 A.M. on the luminous dial of his bedroom clock.

Ring. The phone rang again.

He reached over, lifted the receiver, and brought it to his ear.

"Hello," he managed.

"I'm looking for Wes Covington," came the voice at the other end of the line.

"Um, uh," Covington groped. "This is Wes Covington."

"Wes, sorry to wake you at this hour but this is Georgio La Scalla from the Carabinieri in Rome. You asked me to look into a situation for you yesterday, and frankly," he paused, "there has been a development."

Covington sat up in bed.

"The phone number you gave me yesterday. Is it secure?" asked La Scalla.

"Yes."

"How long will it take you to get there?"

Covington looked at the clock.

"Half an hour."

"Good, I'll call you then."

"Right," said Covington as he hung up the phone.

Amjad made it to seat 30C and put his carry-on bag on his lap. He would keep it there until the passengers around him were seated. Then he would stow it under the seat in front of him, providing him with easy access. He leaned back and closed his eyes for a moment.

"Excuse me," came a voice next to him.

He looked up. There was an overweight man in a blue blazer and white shirt hovering over him.

"Excuse me," he repeated. "I believe you have my seat."

Amjad's heart quickened as he reached for his boarding pass. He checked the pass, which said 30C, and looked at his seat number, 30C.

"See," the man said as he showed his boarding pass. "I believe that is my seat."

Amjad looked at the man's pass and felt blood flow freely back into his veins.

"You have 30B," said Amjad. "I am sitting in 30C. Here is your seat next to me."

The man looked at his boarding pass and then glanced at the seat number. "Oh, my God, I'm sorry," he blurted out embarrassingly. "Oh, my God, I'm so embarrassed."

He took a handkerchief and wiped his brow. "See," he continued. "I'm used to flying on a smaller plane and usually 30B would be on the aisle. So I just assumed. I mean..."

"That's quite all right," said Amjad reassuringly.

As the man swung his carry-on bag up to the storage bin, his belly rolled over his belt and the stretch caused the lowest button on his shirt to come undone, exposing his hairy belly button. With the top storage bin secured, Amjad noticed that the man was ready to descend to his seat. Amjad slid over his armrest and stood in the aisle as the man wiggled his way past Amjad and plopped down in his seat.

"Lepster," he said. "The name's J.A. Lepster." He shoved a large hand for Amjad to shake. Amjad accepted the offering and sat back down.

"Hell of a way to get acquainted," said Lepster. "I truly am sorry." He wiped his sweaty brow again.

"No problem," said Amjad.

"I sell insurance back home," said Lepster. He reached into his coat pocket, pulled out his business card, and offered it to Amjad. "I figure were going to be together for a long time so we might just as well get acquainted. Now what did you say your name was?"

"Spaulding," said Amjad. "Gerald Spaulding."

"Hang on a second," said Covington. "I'll put you on the speaker phone." Covington pushed a button and put the receiver down on its cradle.

"There. Can you hear me okay?

"Sounds like you're in a cave," answered Georgio. "But it's okay."

"I've got a couple of my colleagues here," said Covington, "and I'd like them to listen too."

Soran and Bolder sat up in their chairs and inched closer to the desk.

"Fine," said Georgio.

"Well," said Covington. "What cha got?"

"Well," said Georgio. "We weren't able to catch this Amjad fellow for you, but there was a murder in Terminal One last night. Poor chap was apparently going to the bathroom and had his head practically torn clean off. I mean there's nothing holding it on but soft tissue. It just dangles there. I've never seen anything quite like it."

Bolder looked at Soran, opened his mouth and put his finger in his mouth, faking a gag.

"Anyway," Georgio continued. "This chap's got no ID, no passport, no airline ticket, nothing. His wallet was stripped and lying nearby. But most of these wallets have a secret compartment, you know, an extra flap that is hard to see unless you know what to look for. Some people just put extra money on them, some just mementos...you know. Well, this one had one too. Only it held what looks like a love letter. We don't have the envelope and there's no address. It's to Gerald from John. I suppose this poor chap is the Gerald. It's written in English and this guy is dressed like an American, so my first guess is that he's American. The only reference to anything identifiable is this passage where John says he really liked Gerald's portrayal of Aumerle in *Richard II* at the Guthrie. I'm wondering if this 'Guthrie' rings a bell."

"My God," exclaimed Soran leaning forward. "That's the Guthrie Theater! That's the Guthrie Theater in Minneapolis."

"Bingo!" said Bolder.

"Great work, Georgio!" said Covington as he leaned closer to the speaker. "So it looks like this Gerald whoever was going to Minneapolis. He goes in to take a crap and Amjad takes his cash, tickets, passport, and almost his head."

Again Bolder opened his mouth and stuck his finger in.

"At least we have to assume it's Amjad," said Covington. "Can you determine time of death?"

"Too soon for an exact time." replied Georgio. "But we figure around ten last night, give or take."

"This happened in, what, Terminal One?" asked Covington.

"Yes, Terminal One," replied Georgio.

"Can you find out which flights left late last night, say, after 10:00 P.M.? Especially one that connects to Minneapolis?"

"Wait a minute," interrupted Soran raising his voice to the speakerphone. "If we know the destination is Minneapolis, we may be able to work backwards. I grew up in Minneapolis, and the only airline that has a hub there is Northwest Airlines. If I were taking a flight from Minneapolis to Rome I would probably start with Northwest and connect in Europe with whoever. If we could find out who Northwest normally connects with, that could be the airline we're looking for."

The speakerphone crackled. "KLM has a working relationship with Northwest. I'm sure of it."

"Can you tell me," asked Covington, "if KLM had a late flight out of Terminal One last night and check where it landed? Then see if there is a connecting flight on Northwest."

"Yes," came the reply. "I can get that in about two minutes. Shall I call you back?"

"Hell no! Leave this line open!"

"Okay. Hang on."

Soran felt his neck tingle. "You know what this means, don't you," he said. "Not only are we going to find out what flight he's coming in on but now we have a reason to pick him up. The murder of Gerald baby."

Soran gave Bolder a high five.

"God, I can't believe we're going to wrap this baby up," said Bolder. "This calls for a Spearmint." He pulled a pack from his shirt pocket and offered a stick to Soran.

The speaker cracked, "Are you there?"

"Yea, we're here."

"KLM flight 350 left Rome last night as 11:53 P.M. Arrived an Amsterdam at 2:30 A.M. Northwest connecting flight 55 left Amsterdam at 7:00 A.M. our time and is due in Minneapolis at 9:15 A.M. Looks like he's in the air and he's coming your way."

"So, do you live in Minnesota?" asked J. A. Lepster, a broad smile emerging from his round face.

Amjad had his mind elsewhere, but he finally realized he had been asked a question. "What?" he asked.

"I asked if you live in Minnesota."

"Oh, yes," said Amjad. "Yes, I do."

"Do you live in the city or one of the suburbs?"

"Oh," Amjad paused. "I stay at the University of Minnesota Hospital. I'm a doctor there."

"Wonderful work they do there." Lepster put his seat back and pulled his tray down. "What brings you to Rome?"

"Oh, well, I…I attended a seminar. Quite boring really. But it was fun to see the sights. How about you?"

"Oh, me? Well, I've got a daughter living in Rome. Can you believe it?"

Lepster pulled out a pack of cards from his coat picket. "Wanna play some gin or something?"

"No thanks," said Amjad.

"Okay, fine," said Lepster. "I'll play some solitaire," as he started dealing out the cards.

"Yeah, we had a lot of problems with that girl. A lot of problems. When she was younger, I mean. Probably took too much after her dad." He chuckled. "Ah, but she turned out all right though. Went to college and got her degree and then got her masters. Now she's in Rome working for the United Nations. Can you believe that?"

"That's amazing," said Amjad.

"You're damn right that's amazing," said Lepster. "I was one inch away from throwing her out in the street, and now look at her. I'm damn proud of that girl."

"I'm glad for you," said Amjad.

"Well, thank you, sir," said Lepster as he sat back in his seat and gazed at the roof of the plane. "Sometimes you just get lucky."

Amjad opened his carry-on bag and searched until he found the container that held the special prescription from Tripoli. Satisfied, he zipped the bag closed, replaced it under the seat in front of him, and leaned back.

"Yes," he answered. "Sometimes you just get lucky."

The phone rang once before Livingston answered it. As regional director of the FBI, he would occasionally get calls in the middle of the night. But even in his deepest sleep the phone never reached the second ring.

"Yes," he said as he turned on the light.

"Barry," the voice said. "I hate to wake you in the middle of the night. This is Covington from the CIA."

Livingston sat up in bed and turned on the light. His wife mumbled something incoherently and rolled over on her side.

"We've got a live one," the voice continued. "He's in bound and you know we can't operate internally so I was hoping you'd help me out."

Livingston grabbed a pad and pen from the bedside table. "Bad guy?" he asked.

"The baddest," came the voice.

"Okay," he jotted down numbers from one to five. "Who, what, where, when, and why."

"Amjad Mustafa," came the voice again. "Terrorist from Iraq via Libya. Coming to Minneapolis, Northwest flight 55 from Rome via Amsterdam. Arriving 9:15 A.M. We have him planning terrorist action in U.S.A. Cannot prove yet. But we also believe he killed a man in Rome. Anyway we want him picked up. Pick him up on a murder charge. We'll clear the rest later."

"Description?" came Livingston.

"I'll fax you his composite. Got a number?"

The man in seat 30C watched the fat American play solitaire. He wondered why a man playing by himself would cheat at the game. He pushed the button on the armrest, leaned back, and thought of the time he had spent in America. The country was powerful but it had no character. He admired its freedom, but its freedom had no discipline. It had been founded by statesmen but now was led by politicians. Rather than leading the country, the politicians tested the political wind and devoted their entire time to being reelected. Its system of laws was not based on a systematic, immutable, constant ideal of justice such as the Koran, the Bible, or even the code of Hammurabi.

Through self-serving manipulation and indefensible acceptance of legal loopholes, the system had long since given up any hope of obtaining justice in lieu of the self-perpetuation of the system itself. The strength of this country, he thought, was not in its national character, but in its vast natural resources. A country with proper probity of character once defeated can, like the phoenix, rise again. But a country without strength of character, once smitten, would fall like a house of cards. In the short time that Amjad had stayed there, he felt that America was squandering its resources. He felt that they were reckless with the land and had given in to short-range solutions to long-range problems.

He remembered back to the time when he was with a group of foreign physicians touring the Minnesota capitol in St. Paul. He had inadvertently stumbled onto a meeting between owners of a nuclear power plant and the protesters who were demonstrating against the storage of nuclear waste. The power company had sought to have the spent reactor rods stored close to the reactor and on land, which would make the operation economically feasible. The land that they had chosen was an island in the middle of the Mississippi River.

The protesters had argued that if anything happened to the storage containers, hundreds of thousands of gallons of radioactively contaminated waste could be washed into the Mississippi River. And, once in, there was absolutely nothing anyone could do to stop it. They argued that this was not just a Minnesota problem, but that this river nourished the continent. Nuclear waste is not something that would biodegrade. This nuclear waste would stay dangerous to man for somewhere between twenty thousand and fifty thousand years. They argued that if this nuclear waste found its way into the river in sufficient quantity, it would be a catastrophe greater than the compilation of all of the hurricanes and all of the earthquakes that this country had experienced in all of its history.

But the owners of the power plant had assured them that the storage containers would be safe. The containers would be constructed with double walls so that even if one leaked, the other would prevent further damage. But most important to them was the fact that this was the only financially practical location and if they could not build here, they would have to shut down. And if they shut down, people would lose jobs.

Eventually the jobs won the day and the storage containers with their double walls were built on an island in the Mississippi River.

Amjad watched the fat man put down a king. The next card was a jack. The fat man shuffled through the deck to find a queen. Amjad thought of the double-walled containers in the middle of the Mississippi River. At the headwaters of the continent. He thought back to the time the night skies over Baghdad were lit up and two guided bombs were sent from the black heavens. One bomb had created a hole for the second bomb to pass through. The second bomb had taken everything that Amjad had loved and lived for. And he remembered back to the day he had put his loved ones in the ground and waited in the mud until footsteps sloshing in the rain had come to lead him away.

Chapter Fourteen
No Respect

Monty "Buzz" Todt sat in his government-issue Ford sedan in the driveway of Kent Mariska's house. He would rather have been in his Mazerati sports car, but the FBI frowned on the use of anything but government-issue sedans while on company time. He had honked twice but the house was still dark. It was not uncommon for Kent to oversleep. In fact, it was sort of his trademark. Buzz realized that continued honking at this hour of the morning stood more chance of waking the neighbors than waking Kent. He had called Kent thirty minutes ago. Buzz thought, he's probably in the shower. Buzz turned the lights of the sedan off but kept the motor running as he got out and walked to the front door. He knocked on the door. Nothing. He knocked harder. Still nothing. He tried the door handle. It clicked open. He let himself in and called out Kent's name. He walked to the bedroom and repeated Kent's name. There was a shuffling inside the bedroom and Kent appeared at the bedroom door.

"Ah shit," said Kent. "Man, I'm sorry, man." He was dressed in boxer shorts. His hair was messy and his eyes bloodshot. Unshaven, he could have been the poster boy for No Doze.

"Jeez," he continued, "when you called, I got up and answered it in the kitchen so I wouldn't wake Robyn. I just went back and lay down for a second. I must have fallen back to sleep."

"Hey, we gotta go." said Buzz. "There's a bad guy coming in on a plane and we gotta meet him."

"What time is it?" asked Kent.

"We've got a couple hours," answered Buzz. "But we gotta get going."

"Okay, just let me hop in the shower real quick." He grabbed a towel. "I'll dress in the car."

Kent headed for the bathroom and Buzz went back to the dining room. He noted that in the kitchen the wall phone receiver was hanging loose by the cord. He remembered that when he called Kent, Kent had answered but then had gone to another phone to take some notes. Buzz walked over to the phone and put the receiver back on the cradle. He walked back around the kitchen corner and found a Colt nine-millimeter automatic two inches from his nose.

"Hold it right there'" came a man's voice.

"What the..." was all Buzz could muster.

"Hold it right there!"

"This is the Burnsville Police," the man said.

"Jeez..." said Buzz.

"Put your hands in the air."

"But you don't understand."

"I said, put your hands in the air."

Buzz raised his hands

"Turn around," came the voice.

Buzz turned away from the man.

"Put your hands against the wall and spread 'em."

Buzz assumed the position. He felt something cold and hard at the base of his skull. A hand was patting his body.

"Got a gun, Jim," came the voice as the hand found Buzz's government issue Colt nine millimeter.

"Jim, get over to the other side and cuff him."

The other man walked around Buzz and put a handcuff on Buzz's right wrist.

"Hey, guys," said Buzz, "this is a mistake."

"Quiet!" said the man.

The second man brought Buzz's hand down behind him and fastened the handcuff to his other wrist.

"Jim," said the first man quietly, "you stay with this one and I'll check the rest of the house."

Buzz turned around and looked at the two policemen standing next to him. As the first policeman started walking to the bedroom, Kent appeared wearing only a towel around his waist.

"Hold it right there," said the policeman.

Kent stopped suddenly. As he raised his hands in startled supplication, the knot from his towel released and the towel fell, exposing his manhood.

"I suppose you want to frisk him, too," said Buzz.

"What the hell's going on here?" asked Kent.

"Burnsville Police," came the voice. "What's your name?"

"Kent. Kent Mariska."

"Your burglar alarm went off and we got the call. What's your password?"

"Oh," stammered Kent trying to clear his head, "Oh, oh yeah. 13-14-358."

The first officer looked at the second one.

"That's the code," he said.

"Who's this guy?" he pointed to Buzz.

"He's okay. He's a friend."

The first officer lowered his gun.

"Apparently," the officer explained, "someone set off your alarm." He looked at the front door. "It must have gone off when the front door was opened and no one turned off the alarm. Your security company got the alarm and tried to call you but the line was busy. Couldn't call a neighbor at this time of the morning, so we got the call. When we got here, there was a car with its lights out and its motor running so we naturally thought..."

"That's fine." interrupted Buzz. "That's just fine. We know you're just doing your duty. And we appreciate that. But I was just wondering...if it wouldn't be too much trouble for you to," his voice raising, "take these fucking cuffs off me!"

Words were scarce on the drive to Minneapolis St. Paul International Airport. Buzz parked the car in the hourly rate lot and they proceeded to the terminal.

"What's the flight number?" asked Kent.

"Northwest 55," answered Buzz. "Due in at 9:15."

Kent looked at his watch. "We'll be there in plenty of time," he said. "Man, we've got two hours. Let's go grab some breakfast."

"That little incident sort of took away my appetite," said Buzz. "I don't know which is worse; having a gun at the base of my skull or you with your hands up and having to look at your dick. With that sight in mind, I probably won't eat for a week."

"You should see it when it's angry," said Kent.

"Make that a month," answered Buzz.

When they arrived at the gold concourse, Buzz looked up at the arrivals monitor.

After a moment a puzzled look came over his face.

"What the hell?" he said.

"What's that?" asked Kent.

Buzz looked again, confirming that it was a Northwest monitor.

"There's no flight 55," he said.

"What do you mean there's no flight 55?" asked Kent.

"Look for yourself."

Kent studied the monitor. "Maybe we got the flight wrong," he said.

Buzz pulled a piece of paper from his pocket. "No," he said. "Flight 55, 9:15 from Rome via Amsterdam."

"Holy smokes. We better check this out," said Kent.

They hurried over to the Northwest Airlines ticket counters. Each ticket counter was occupied and the corrals were filling. They walked to the nearest ticket counter. It was occupied by a little old lady hunched over in her half fur coat. She was checking her luggage and was putting her Pomeranian in a flight kennel at the counter.

As they approached the counter, both Buzz and Kent took out their identification badges. They flanked the old lady as each put their identification on the counter.

"Excuse me, miss," Buzz told the agent. "We're with the FBI."

He looked at the old lady. "Excuse me, ma'am."

He turned back to the agent. "This is official government business. We need to know when flight 55 is coming in."

The old lady grabbed Buzz's coat. "I'll F your BI young man," she said in a crackling voice. "I was here first and it's hard enough for me to part with my baby here," she patted the kennel, "without you barging in here." She pulled on his jacket sleeve with her other hand. "If you had any manners you'd let me finish before you butt in."

"Actually," the agent said, "it probably would be faster just to take care of her first. My terminal is locked up with her boarding information. I'm just about done. It will only take a minute."

Buzz looked at Kent who mirrored the deer-caught-in-the-headlights look.

"What the hell," said Buzz as he slumped his shoulders. "Go ahead."

"No respect, I tell ya," said Kent in his best Rodney Dangerfield, grabbing the knot of his tie.

The little old lady was processed in less than two minutes, and with one last kiss to her baby and two scowls at Buzz and Kent, she was off.

"Thank you for waiting." said the receptionist. "Now, what can I help you with?

"We were supposed to meet a flight," said Buzz. "But I looked at your arrivals monitor and it's not there."

"That's odd," she said. "What flight is it?"

"Flight 55," said Buzz.

The agent punched at her computer. She paused. "It's not here," she said. "When does it get in?"

"Nine-fifteen," said Buzz, "from Rome."

"From Rome?" she asked.

"Yes, from Rome."

"Is this the first stop in the United States?" she asked.

"I...I think so," he answered.

She punched some more numbers. "Ah, yes. Here it is. It's a direct nonstop flight from Amsterdam due in at, ah, 9:15 all right."

"Well, what's the gate number?"

She continued. "Your party must have taken a flight from Rome to Amsterdam and then from Amsterdam to here."

"Right,' said Buzz. "Now, what's the gate number?"

"Well, since this is the first stop in the U.S., they have to go through customs. It's due in at 9:15 all right, but it's due in at the Hubert Humphrey Memorial Terminal." She looked at them. "I'm afraid you're at the wrong terminal."

Buzz looked at Kent and Kent looked back at Buzz. Once again, deer in the headlights.

The drive to the Hubert Humphrey Memorial Terminal did not take long. Buzz pulled up to the front door and put the car in park.

"Kent," he said, "would you do me a favor?"

"Sure," said Kent.

"Would you go into here and check to see if we have the right goddamn terminal?" he asked. "I'll stay here and keep the engine running in case we have to go to Cleveland."

Kent got out of the car and walked into the terminal. A glance at the arrivals monitor confirmed that flight 55 from Amsterdam was due in at 9:15 A.M. at gate three and was on time. Kent walked back to the car, opened the door, and poked his head in.

"Right terminal," he said. "Plane's on time." He paused for a moment. "Ya know, we still got an hour and a half before the plane gets in. It ain't gettin' in early. Even if it does we can catch him at customs. All they have here is a buffet with doughnuts and coffee. What say we get a real breakfast?"

Buzz had intended to catch a breakfast at one of the restaurants at the Minneapolis St. Paul International Airport while waiting for the flight to get in. Then he remembered back to when he had taken a chartered flight from the Humphrey Terminal. He remembered back to the choice of stale doughnut and staler doughnut. He remembered the coffee tasting better from the machine.

"I never like to catch bad guys on an empty stomach," he said. "Get in."

Chapter Fifteen
"No Problem at All"

The fact that Lisa Mercer was six months pregnant did not stop her from continuing to work as a flight attendant. She had started to show so much that, when meeting someone in the aisle, turning sideways held no advantage. At some other service position, her plight could have been turned into an economic advantage. But for waitresses of the sky, tipping is not an option.

She enjoyed her work. She would have enjoyed any work. She had been brought up with a Scandinavian work ethic. She truly believed, as "Desiderata" had proclaimed: her work was a "real possession in the changing fortunes of time."

But still it would be nice to take some time off when her little bundle of joy arrived. She had thought about taking six weeks off and coming back as a reservations agent with the airlines. This would avail her as to not having to spend so much time away from her baby. She had even toyed with the idea of taking a leave of absence for a year or so. But they had just bought a new home and then there was the car payment. Six weeks looked like a good compromise. She had not yet talked to the airline about her plans but would do so before her next flight.

"I can never sleep on these flights," said Lepster, "so I play solitaire the whole trip. Sure gets boring. Sure you wouldn't want to play a card game?"

"No thanks," said Amjad. "I don't play cards."

"Too bad," said Lepster putting his cards down. "This coffee helps keep me going but it sure goes through me. Probably should have an aisle seat." He put his tray up, moved in his seat, and offered his coffee cup to Amjad. "Would you mind holding this till I get back?"

Amjad took the cup and raised up out of his seat. He looked around. The rest of the plane was dark and it seemed like everyone else was asleep. Lepster wiggled out of his seat and headed for the bathroom. Amjad sat back down and looked around again. No one had been disturbed. He put Lepster's tray back down and lay the coffee cup on the tray. He pulled his bag from under the seat and searched for the vial. Having found it he took one last look around. Satisfied, he opened the vial and poured half of its contents into the coffee cup, replaced the vial, and waited.

It did not take long for Lepster to saunter back from the bathroom. Amjad picked up the cup, closed the tray, and hopped out of his seat. Lepster squeezed back into his seat and put the tray back down. Amjad returned the cup to the tray and sat down.

Lepster took out his deck of cards and began dealing again. He reached for the cup, brought it to his lips, and took a sip.

"Damn," he said. "If there's one thing in this world I hate, it's cold coffee." He put the cup down and pushed the cabin attendant button.

Lisa Mercer was leaning back in her seat. She had felt the baby's feet make its journey across her tummy. What a wonderful feeling. To be able to give life. To be able to feel it grow inside of you. She had had an ultrasound but had not asked to know the sex. But she bet it was a girl. And she bet it would look like her.

The hailing light interrupted her daydreams. She got up from her seat and wandered back to row 30.

"Can I help you?" she asked.

"Yes, " said Lepster. "My coffee's gone cold. Could you warm it up?"

Lisa reached for the cup. "Why don't I get you a fresh cup?" she asked.

"Oh, that would be great," said Lepster as he handed her the cup.

Amjad's heart sank as Lisa took the cup and walked back to her station. Amjad reached down into his bag, palmed the vial, and enclosed it in his fist.

"That sounds good," he said to Lepster. " I could use a cup myself."

He got up and walked past the rows of dozing heads until he reached the attendant's station. Lisa had poured the coffee out of the cup and was refilling it.

"That sounds pretty good," he said. "I'll have a cup too,"

"Fine," said Lisa as she took another cup from the shelf.

"You know," said Amjad pointing at her protruding stomach, "a woman in your condition should stay off her feet."

"It's really no problem," said Lisa as she poured the second cup.

"Really," said Amjad. "Why don't you just sit down. I'll take these cups back."

"Would you?" Lisa asked as she handed Amjad the cups.

"No problem," he said.

As she turned to sit down, Amjad turned his back to her and put the cups on the counter. He opened the vial and poured its contents into one of the cups.

"No problem at all," he said as he picked up the cups and headed back to seat 30C.

Soran awoke and raised his head to look at his clock. It was still an hour before the alarm was to make its scheduled announcement. He laid his head back on the pillow and stared at the ceiling. Thirteen faces came to him. He knew he had been right, but he was still responsible for thirteen bodies in the ground. He had done his job. He had done what he was paid to do. And he was convinced that it was the right thing to do. He probably had saved a countless number of lives. Innocent lives. It was a good trade, he told himself. He'd do it again, he told himself.

But what about Amjad, he thought. This mystery man who had eluded the Beta Team. Resourceful enough to get a passport and visa to get into Rome on short notice. Crafty enough to get a on a plane bound for America. This was not your run-of-the-mill, garden-variety terrorist. This was a man of skill. Of intelligence. Did he have a network helping him? That didn't seem likely. If he was alone, what could he do? What could one man do?

He knew it was something nuclear. He had gotten that from two sources. But what? For a bomb he would need a network already in place here. He could probably build a bomb, but he could not easily obtain the atomic fuel. Without the atomic fuel it's just one very big firecracker. The only other explanation was a nuclear power plant. There certainly were plenty of them around. They were not heavily defended but were designed to shut down if anything were to go wrong. He could do damage to a power plant and perhaps cause some collateral damage to the nearby area. He could cause more damage blowing up an electrical relay station. And for the greatest effect, he would choose New York, Philadelphia, or Los Angeles. Why Minnesota? What could one man do in Minnesota? It didn't matter, Soran thought. Amjad was confined to a plane with only one destination. And two armed FBI agents would be there to meet him. Soon all his questions would be answered.

Chapter Sixteen
Entry

The first pain hit him like a shard of glass piercing his chest. He pushed back against his seat and held his breath. He reached out and clenched the armrests. His palms were sweating and his skin felt clammy. Another shot to his chest and Lepster yelled, "My God!" out loud. A few of the dozing heads shook off their cobwebs and turned to look.

"My God!" Lepster yelled again as a third thunderbolt dove deep into his chest. He gasped for breath and pulled his numbing arms up as his hands clawed desperately at his collar. Overhead lights flicked on as more heads turned. He grappled with his collar with his right hand while his left hand shot out as if to clutch the air. He tried to speak but only gurgles came out. As he put his head back against the headrest, his eyes went up and back into his skull and he collapsed against Amjad. More lights flicked on. Amjad pushed Lepster back and raised the armrest, then lowered Lepster toward him. He slipped out from underneath the big man and grabbed him under the arms. He pulled him into the aisle and laid him down. As he bent over the man he tore off his tie. He ripped open his shirt, leaned down, and put his ear to the man's chest.

"Everything is fine," came a voice. "It's okay. Really. Just stay in your seats." Lisa Mercer appeared next to Amjad.

"What's the matter?" she asked.

"This man has had a heart attack," said Amjad as he grabbed his carry-on bag and pulled it from under the seat.

"Please tell the pilot or the co-pilot to get back here right now!" he commanded. He opened his bag and pulled out the stethoscope.

"But I..." Lisa stammered.

Amjad stood up, stethoscope in hand, and put his hands on Lisa's shoulders.

"Bring me the pilot or the co-pilot right now! Or this man will die!"

Lisa took two steps back, looked down at the body in the aisle, turned, and headed for the cockpit. Amjad bent back down and leaned over the man. He held the chest-piece diaphragm of the stethoscope in his left hand while his right hand disconnected the rubber tubing from the hosel of the chest piece. He held the end of the rubber tubing next to the disconnected chest piece, closed his hand, and waited.

"What's the matter?" What's going on?" co-pilot Unger asked as he peered over Amjad.

"This man has had a heart attack," said Amjad. "His heart has stopped." Amjad continued to press at intervals on Lepster's chest. "I'm a doctor. I'm doing CPR," he continued, "but right now, this man's heart has stopped."

He put the stethoscope to his ears and placed the chest piece on Lepster's chest. He held the chest piece on the chest and took off the headset.

"Here," he said, offering the headset to Unger while keeping the chest piece on the chest. "You listen."

Unger bent down and put the headset on. He listened for a moment.

"Nothing," he said.

"But we can't quit trying," said Amjad pulling the headset from Unger. He raised Lepster's head and pushed the jaw up. He pinched the nose and blew into the gaping mouth five times. He put the head back down and started pumping the chest again.

Unger turned to talk to Mercer.

"There's not much we can do," he said. "We have to..."

"Wait a minute!" yelled Amjad as he bent over and put his ear on the bare chest. With his hands hidden under his chest he reconnected the rubber tube to the hosel of the chest piece.

"I think we've got something!" he said.

Unger turned back to him.

Amjad put the stethoscope to his ears and placed the now working chestpiece on the bare chest.

"Yes!" he said. "Yes, we have something. He's alive again!"

He took off the headset and offered it to Unger. Unger put it on and listened. He looked up at Amjad.

"My God!" he said. "I can't believe it! I just can't believe it! You've just brought a man back to life!"

He turned to Lisa. "I mean you see this on TV and all but..."

Amjad interrupted. "He is alive for now. But if we don't get him to a hospital within thirty minutes, he will die."

Unger stared at Amjad. "Well," he said hesitantly. "We'll be in Minneapolis in..." he looked at his watch, "...in about two hours."

"In two hours this man will be dead," said Amjad. "We have to get this plane down now!"

"But..." Unger stammered. "But I...I don't have the authority."

"Then take me to someone who has!" commanded Amjad.

Captain Dunn was doing routine maintenance checks when Unger stepped into the cockpit.

"We've got an emergency," said Unger nervously. "I mean we have a medical emergency."

"What is it?" asked Dunn.

"It's the damnedest thing," said Unger. "A passenger had a heart attack and actually died. I mean, I heard with my own two ears. This man was dead." He took a deep breath. "But then this man..." he stepped aside to reveal Amjad. "This man used CPR and brought him back. I mean, I've seen it before on TV and such but..."

"Captain," Amjad interrupted stepping forward. "We have to get this plane down now!"

Dunn looked over at the flight engineer. "We'll be in Minneapolis in about two hours," he said firmly.

"We don't have two hours!" said Amjad. "If we don't get down in thirty minutes that man will be dead!"

Captain Dunn looked back at his flight engineer.

"Well, I don't know," he uttered.

"Captain," Amjad stepped closer, his hand on the stethoscope around his neck. "I am a doctor. I have just brought that man back to life. It is my professional medical opinion that this man has to be treated within thirty minutes or he will die. If you do not do everything you can to save him," he paused and moved closer, "I, and the courts, will hold this airline and you personally responsible."

Dunn stared at Amjad for a few seconds and then picked up his flight schedule. He turned to his flight engineer.

"Roger," he said. "How soon can we get to O'Hare?"

The flight engineer punched a few buttons on his computer.

"I'd say... about twenty to twenty-five minutes," Roger replied.

Chuck Woodson loved chess so much that Janice had bought him a hand-held computer chess board for his birthday. This was with full knowledge that once the monster was loose, she might not have an extended conversation with him for the next two years. But she loved him enough and cast fate to the wind.

Gerald had called in sick and they were waiting for a replacement to fulfill the full complement of their paramedic team when the call came.

"Smith Three, Smith three," the speaker crackled.

Janice picked up the mike. "This is Smith Three."

"Smith Three. We've got a coronary at O'Hare," came the speaker. "Inbound plane. Gate 43."

"Roger that," said Janice. "But we're down one man. We're awaiting the replacement.

"Can't wait. All other units are occupied. You'll have to wing it."

"Roger. O'Hare. Gate 43. Over." Janice turned to Chuck, "You want to drive?"

Chuck had just entered into a Nimzo Indian Defense and was matching white move for move.

"No thanks, hon," he said. "Why don't you drive."

Janice started the engine, turned on the emergency lights, and two thirds of the paramedical team headed for O'Hare.

Chuck and Janice arrived at gate 43 just as the plane met the docking gate. They were met by John Chancellor, assistant head of airport security for Terminal One.

"Looks like we got a sick cowboy," said Chancellor through a thick walrus mustache. His badge sat atop an enormous chest and, when he smiled, his teeth showed the yellow stains of chewing tobacco.

"Guess so," said Chuck as the door of the plane opened.

Chuck and Janice rushed in and made their way to row 30.

"What do we have here?" asked Chuck as he knelt down over the big man sprawled on the floor.

"Heart attack," said Unger.

Chuck started taking vital signs.

"Damnedest thing I ever saw," said Unger. "This man was dead. I mean, really dead. I heard it with my own ears." He pulled on Amjad's stethoscope still hanging around its owner's neck.

"And this man," Unger continued grabbing Amjad by the shoulder, "brought him back."

Chuck looked up at Amjad. "Good work," he said.

"Thank you," said Amjad. " Looks like he's got a chance."

Chuck took the pulse with his rubber-gloved hand.

"Yes, he does," offered Chuck.

Amjad held out his stethoscope. "Would you like to use this?" he said.

"No thanks," said Chuck. "We've got what we need."

He turned to Janice. "Go get the gurney, please," he said.

Janice turned toward the front of the plane.

"No, wait," said Chuck. "The gurney probably won't fit in these aisles. Bring the stretcher."

Janice nodded and headed for the door. Chuck stood up and turned to Amjad.

"You a doctor?" he asked.

"Yes, I am," replied Amjad. "As the co-pilot said, this man's heart stopped and I brought him back. I sort of consider him my patient."

"I can see why," said Chuck.

"I would like to stay with him until he stabilizes," said Amjad. "We've been through quite a bit together."

"Well," said Chuck as Janice arrived with the stretcher, "there are regulations..."

"Janice," said Chuck as he grabbed the stretcher. "I'll take the head. Why don't you go down by his feet."

Janice stepped over the big man's chest and arrived at his feet. Chuck set the stretcher down beside Lepster.

"Maybe you can help me tilt him up while we slide the stretcher underneath him," he said.

Chuck and Janice pushed Lepster over on his side while Chuck managed to slide the stretcher beneath him.

"Okay," said Chuck. "Let's center him."

They pulled his shoulders and hips as he grudgingly slid to the center of the stretcher.

"Okay, let's go," said Chuck as he lifted his end of the stretcher. It was an impossible task from the beginning and Janice knew it as soon as she saw the man. Her 120 pounds were full of vitality and spirit, but her half of the stretcher would exceed her own weight. She pulled hard but knew there was no hope.

"Let me help with that," said Amjad as he stepped over the man's chest and picked up the abandoned south end of the stretcher.

"I don't know," said Chuck hesitantly. "Our insurance doesn't allow..."

"Goddamn it man!" snapped Amjad. "This man is dying and you're talking about insurance. Now pick up your end and let's get this man off the plane!"

Chuck lifted the north end of the stretcher. They made their way to the plane door and heaved Lepster on to the gurney. They started to roll the gurney up the ramp.

"Wait a minute!" Chancellor yelled, running over and putting his arm on Amjad's shoulder. "You can't get off that plane," he said.

Amjad turned to look Chancellor in the eye.

"Look," he said, "This man has died. I just brought him back to life. I am his doctor." He fingered his still-adorned stethoscope. "I will not leave my patient until he is at the hospital and stabilized."

Unger burst forward.

"That's right," he said. "I witnessed the whole thing. I mean this man was dead," he pointed to Lepster. "I heard it with my own ears. He had no pulse. His heart had stopped. And this man," he put his hand on Amjad's shoulder, "brought him back to life." He looked at Chancellor's badge.

"It's the damnedest thing I ever saw. I mean, he really brought this man back to life. I mean, you see it on TV and such but it really happened here and I saw it."

Chuck pulled on the gurney.

"We gotta go," he said.

Amjad grabbed the gurney and held it in place.

"Look," he said to Chancellor. "This is my patient and I'm going to stay with him." He reached in his coat pocket.

"Look," he said. "Here is my passport."

He handed it to Chancellor.

"You keep it," he said. "I can't get into the country without it. I'll get this man to the hospital, see that he's stabilized, and get right back here."

"Actually," Chuck interrupted. "We're down one man and we could use the help."

Chancellor stood there holding Amjad's passport.

"But really," said Chuck. "We have to go now or this man may die."

Chancellor stood for a moment. "Okay," he said. "Get going."

Chuck and Amjad pushed the gurney up the ramp.

"But remember," yelled Chancellor, waving a small blue booklet. "I've got your passport!"

"Can't beat Perkins," said Kent.

Buzz nodded.

"The food at the main terminal isn't bad," continued Kent. "But the Humphrey terminal. Forget it!"

The government-issue sedan headed down 34th Avenue and turned into the Humphrey Terminal driveway.

"Why don't I let you out here," said Buzz, "and I'll go park the car." Buzz pulled over to the curb and let Kent out. Kent put his arms up, bent his shoulders back, and stretched, taking in the fresh morning air. Such a beautiful time of the day, he thought as he walked through the terminal doors. He headed over to gate 3 and looked up at the arrivals monitor. An entry in the middle was flashing:

"Northwest 55 Amsterdam DELAYED."

"So." said Chuck. "Where do you practice?"

Amjad turned away from the man on the gurney. "Oh," he said. "University of Minnesota Hospital. Transplant division."

"Well," said Chuck. "That was really something back there."

"Yes," said Amjad looking at the monitors.

Chuck followed Amjad's eyes to the monitors. "Seems to have stabilized" he said.

"Yes," said Amjad leaning back. "It is good. Still, I feel very close to this man."

He patted Lepster's hand. "I feel he opened up a whole new world for me. I feel that he put me in a place that I would not have gotten to without him."

"I know what you mean," said Chuck. "Saving a life can change a man."

Janice swung the ambulance into the emergency room driveway and stopped. Chuck opened the rear door and jumped out. He pulled the gurney out and set the legs in place. Amjad jumped out and helped Chuck push the gurney through the emergency room door.

"Where is the bathroom?" asked Amjad.

"Down the hall and to the left," answered Chuck.

"I've got to make a stop," said Amjad. "You'll be in the ER?"

"You bet," said Chuck.

Amjad took a couple steps down the hall, stopped and turned back to Chuck.

"As soon as I'm sure he will be okay, I'd like to get back to the airport," he said. "Could you give me a lift?"

"I could arrange that," said Chuck.

Amjad turned and disappeared down the corridor.

John Chancellor held the blue passport in his right hand and patted it against the palm of his left hand.

"Well," he said to himself. "I'm not going to wait around here forever. If he's not here by the end of my shift I'll just leave it at the gate and if he doesn't find it, it will just be his tough luck."

"John Chancellor," his radio crackled. "Code 2."

Chancellor pulled out his radio and switched to channel 2. "This is Chancellor."

"John," came the radio, "the FBI is on the phone and they want to talk to the head of security. Johnson is out so I thought you should take the call."

"Right," said Chancellor. "I'm at gate 43. Can you connect me there?"

"Will do," squawked the radio.

Chancellor sauntered over to counter 43. "FBI," he said as he fingered his mustache. "Bet they've heard of me and wanna offer me a job."

As the phone rang he picked it up. "Hello."

"Who is this?" asked the voice.

"This is assistant head of security for Terminal One. The name's Chancellor, John Chancellor."

"You had a plane land there," came the voice. "A medical emergency. Northwest flight 55."

"Yes," said Chancellor. "I handled it myself."

"Is the plane still there?"

"No. It just left."

"Did anyone get off?"

"Well, yes. The man had a heart attack. Can't have a heart attack and stay on the plane. This guy died on the plane but was lucky enough to have a doctor on board who knew what he was doing and brought him back to life."

"Did anyone else get off?"

"No," he paused. "Except for the doctor, of course. But he ain't goin' nowhere. I got his passport right here."

"What is his name?"

Chancellor opened the passport. "Spaulding," he said. "Gerald Spaulding." Chancellor peered closer at the passport. "No, wait," he said. "Wait. This ain't the guy."

"What?" came the voice.

"No, the picture," said Chancellor. "The picture in the passport. This ain't the guy who got off the plane!"

Chuck was watching the monitors. Lepster's pulse was weak and his blood pressure was low, but all of the vital signs were steady. Looks like the fat man will make it, he thought. He would wait around for the miracle worker and give him a lift back to the airport. In the meantime he would get back to his Nimzo Indian defense. As he headed out of the ER, Paul Robson pushed the door open and brushed past him. Robson stopped and turned to Chuck.

"You!" Robson demanded authoritatively. "Wait here."

Chuck observed the badge on Robson's lapel that identified him as head of hospital security. Robson went over to the first nurse.

"Which one of these came in from the airport?" he asked.

She pointed to stall three. Robson walked over to stall three and said, "Who brought this man here?"

The doctor lowered his glasses to assess the person making this demand.

"I did," Chuck interrupted.

Robson turned to Chuck. "Did someone else come with you?" Robson demanded.

"Yes," said Chuck, "There was this doctor from the plane…"

"Where is he?" Robson snapped.

"Why, he went to the bathroom," Chuck pointed to the corridor. "But he's coming back."

Two other members of hospital security came through the ER door.

"You!" Robson said to the first one. "You stay here with this man," pointing to Chuck

"You!" he said to the second. "Come with me."

The two rushed through the ER door and down the hallway. When they reached the bathroom, they stopped while Robson pulled out his revolver. Robson signaled that he would be first to go in and proceeded through the door.

The sinks and urinals were abandoned, but the first of two toilet stalls had its door closed. Robson looked beneath the door. Shoes and trousers. He stood in front of the door. He pulled his gun up to waist level and raised his right foot. His foot hit the door with such force that it tore the slide lock from its mountings. The door swung open and crashed against the side wall.

The fourteen-year-old on the stool looked up with startled eyes as he gazed at the barrel of the thirty-eight. His mouth dropped open and a double wad of chewing gum fell to the floor. A Batman comic book dropped from his hand and a stream of urine was missing the bowl lid and wetting his dropped trousers.

"Shit!" said Robson, and moved to the second stall. Empty. He turned and rushed through the bathroom door and out into the corridor. He looked one way and then the other. The corridor was empty. He put his revolver in its holster, picked up his radio, and brought it to his mouth.

"He's gone," he said.

Chapter Seventeen
"Better Buckle Your Seat Belt"

H e's gone?" yelled Soran. "What in the hell do you mean, he's gone!"
Covington put his unladen pipe in his mouth.
"They missed him," he said. "They just missed him."

"How in the hell could they miss him?" asked Soran. "They had his composite. They had the flight. The flight only lands at one place."

Covington took the pipe out of his mouth and turned to the window. "Not this one."

"What do you mean?" asked Soran.

"He diverted the plane," said Covington. "He made them stop in Chicago."

"Stop in Chicago? What did he do, pull the cord?"

"No, some kind of medical emergency. He had them stop in Chicago to let off a passenger who allegedly had a heart attack. He got off with him."

"You've got to be kiddin'. Wasn't the crew of the airplane alerted to let the FBI know if there was a deviation in the flight plan?"

"That would be standard procedure. But something went wrong here. The FBI guys at the airport checked in all right, but then couldn't be found for about an hour. That's when this whole thing went down."

"So they couldn't get the word and pass it on to Chicago to hold the plane and passengers."

"That's the way it looks."

"Well, where the hell were those guys?"

"Don't know. My guess is that they either went out for breakfast or they were taking the world's longest dump. It might as well be the latter, cause they're in the shit house now."

"Son of a bitch."

"Well, looks like you called this one wrong. It wasn't Minneapolis after all."

"What do you mean?"

"Well, hell. He's in Chicago. If he wanted to be in Minneapolis he'd have gone to Minneapolis."

"Not necessarily. To go straight through to Minneapolis, he'd have to go through customs. My guess is he may have a passport but doesn't have a visa. He's coming from Libya and I can't imagine that we'd be giving out too many visas to Libya. No, my guess is he just wanted to get into the country without going through customs. He's been to Minneapolis before so he knows that the flight is nonstop from Amsterdam. All he has to do is create a medical diversion. He's a doctor so that should be a no-brainer. Once he creates the diversion, he forces the plane to land anywhere. And in the confusion he slips away. So now he's entered the United States and could go anywhere."

"Where do you think he will go?"

"I don't know. Maybe the East Coast. More people there, so he could create more havoc. He could stay in Chicago. But my guess is Minnesota."

"Why the hell Minnesota?"

"He's been there. He knows the territory. He is familiar with it. My guess is he saw something when he was there. Something that intrigued him. Something that he thought he could do alone."

"Well, it's not our problem anymore."

"What do you mean, it's not our problem?"

"He's in the United States now, remember. We don't operate in the United States. It's up to the FBI now."

"But there's got to be something we can do. They've screwed it up once and they'll screw it up again. There's got to be a way we can do something. There's got to be a way."

"It's out of our hands." Covington put the pipe back in his mouth, swiveled his chair, and looked out the window.

"They sent us to the wrong goddamn airport. Can you believe it? The wrong goddamn airport."

Lawrence Malcolm, Midwest Division Manager of the FBI, was having a bad day.

"Minneapolis? An international terrorist is coming to town and they send us to Minneapolis? What's he going to do, blow up a snowman or go fishing?"

He pulled his hands through his thinning, graying hair and walked over to the map of the United States.

"Well," he said. "What do you think he'll do? Stay put or head east?"

Special Agent Lyle Peters got up from his chair and headed over to the map. "CIA thinks it still may be Minneapolis," he said.

"That's crazy!" said Malcolm. "Look, if you're coming all the way over from the Middle East, you're coming to make a statement. If you're gonna make a statement you sure as hell aren't going to make it in Minnesota. No one will hear you."

Malcolm put his finger on Chicago then traced it to New York. "No, I think it will be the East Coast." He walked over to his desk and sat down. "One thing's for sure. He ain't acting alone."

The car had been easily obtained. But it also had been chosen. It had been obtained because its doors were unlocked. It had been chosen because Amjad had tested only late model, popular cars with a familiar color. Once inside, before reaching down to hot wire the car, Amjad reached under the carpet pad and found nothing. He checked the glove compartment. Empty. He pulled down the visor. When the keys fell into his lap he thought, *amazing, these Americans. Why didn't they just leave the motor running and validate the parking ticket?*

He put the keys into the ignition and started the car. "Even a full tank of gas. Amazing." He drove to the attendant gate, paid the ticket and, refusing the receipt, drove away.

It was his third cup of coffee and it hadn't reached midmorning. Since becoming chief of police of Chicago, he had measured his intake of the juice from the java bean not in cups but in pots. His assistant entered the room.

"They're all on line one," he said.

The chief walked over to his desk and pushed the speaker button and then the button for line one. "I've got all of the precincts on conference call," he said into the speaker. "Something's come up and I want you all to hear it. We've got to act fast."

He took a sip of coffee. "Now I want you to sound off so I know you're all here."

The speaker chirped with the acknowledgments of the precinct captains. When they had completed the check, the chief continued. "We've had the CIA and the FBI track a terrorist to our lovely city and they've asked for our help." Another tip of the coffee mug. "As we speak, I'm having his composite faxed to each precinct. This guy is either acting alone or he has some help. If he has some help, someone here already, he may not need transportation. I want you to circulate his composite to everyone. I want an APB out on this guy. He's from the Middle East and probably will have like-minded and like-looking comrades. If you see any Middle East looking guys and they're going fifty-five and a half in a fifty-five, pull 'em over and check 'em out. Taillight doesn't work, pull 'em over. Forget to signal a turn, check 'em out. If they're parked an inch too close to the curb, check 'em out. If this guy is alone, he'll need transportation. Precinct 3, you've got the airport. Precinct 5, you've got the train station. Precinct 4, you've got the bus depot.

"Also, this guy was last seen at Memorial Hospital. I want any reports of a stolen car in that area forwarded to me immediately. Any stolen car could be a lead, but anything around Memorial I want yesterday!"

Another sip. "If you find him, proceed with caution. This man's wanted for murder. He was last seen two hours ago, so let's get moving. I want this town closed up tight!"

Windshield wipers slapped as Amjad rolled into the Safeway parking lot. It had been raining since he had left the hospital. But now the midmorning skies had darkened and the rain had increased to torrents. A few people had made a mad dash for shelter in the store but no one had ventured out into the parking lot, seeking to wait out the downpour. Toward the end of the third row the headlights of Amjad's Taurus fell upon another Taurus of similar color. Amjad pulled in beside it and turned his headlights off. He got out of the car and looked around. The dark rain had descended upon the parking lot and depopulated it. He reached into his jacket pocket, pulled out the stethoscope, and walked to the back of his car.

Disconnecting the metal frame from the rubber tubing, he bent down and used the newfound tool to unscrew the screws holding the license plate. Once the plate was loose, he moved over to the neighboring Taurus and exchanged rear plates. He moved to the front of the vehicles and repeated the procedure.

Back in the car, he opened the glove compartment and took out a map. After studying it a moment he laid it on the passenger's seat. He drove down Irving Road to 294. He then took 294 to I-94. The rain had let up and the skies were clearing. There was a rainbow to the west. He headed north on I-94 knowing that, aside from gas, there would be no stops until Minneapolis.

Lawrence Malcolm sat in his chair and swiveled away from his desk, eyeing the map of the United States. He looked at Chicago, then at New York. He noticed the myriad of cities along the East Coast and compared it to the open spaces of the Midwest. He had just put in a call to Eastern Division Manager, Lynn Broadwater, and was waiting for the return call. Malcolm was more envious of Broadwater than jealous. When the position had opened up he had put in for it but was passed over for Broadwater. Broadwater was young and capable. Although it was a lateral move and they held the same rank within the company, Malcolm knew he had been outflanked. Broadwater was on the fast track in management and the

Eastern Division was the right vehicle. Broadwater was being groomed for the top spot and it was only a matter of time. But Malcolm's envy did not get in the way of his work. He was a company man and he would work within the system and get the job done.

The speaker buzzed.

"Broadwater on one," came his secretary's voice.

Malcolm pushed line one and then the speaker button. "This is Lawrence Malcolm."

"Hi, Larry." It was Broadwater's voice. "What ya got?"

Malcolm disliked being called Larry and he presumed Broadwater knew it. But he decided to pass on this one.

"Lynn," he said. "We've got a situation here I'm sure you're aware of." He picked up a pencil and started drumming the eraser on the desk. "CIA gave us a line on a terrorist heading for Minnesota. He diverts the plane and lands in Chicago. Apparently this guy's got some nuclear designs somewhere but we don't know anything else. CIA thinks he's a loner but I can't buy that. Doesn't make much sense. One man can't do much by himself. Especially with his rather theatrical entrance. This guy didn't sneak in. He blew in! He's got to have some connections already here. Anyway, if he is a single, the locals have a better chance than we have.

We have to assume that he's an important cog in a machine that's already in place." More tapping on the desk. "Anyway we've got our boys out here but it wouldn't surprise me if he was headed your way. I mean, you have a much larger contingent of Middle Easterners there than we have here."

"So, you think that Chicago was just an entry?" the speaker crackled.

"That's the way I see it," answered Malcolm. "If the guy lands on the East Coast, he's got to clear customs. This way he makes a forced landing in an emergency situation and slips away in the confusion. Pretty ingenious, really. It's all in my report. I'll fax it to you today. Anyway, if it's nuclear, we're guarding the power plants. Doesn't sound like a bomb to me. But I still think you make a louder noise on the East Coast than you do here. Besides, the more militant ones are out your way."

"I hear you," cracked the speaker. "There's a few militant Iranian groups we've had our eye on and since the Gulf War some Iraqis here have been rattling their swords. We've got some people on them already. When can I expect the fax?"

"You'll get it within the hour."

"Look's like we've got our work cut out for us."

The chief of police walked over to the sink and poured out his coffee. He refilled his cup and walked back to his desk. "Man," he said. "I knew we had a lot of car thefts in this city…" He held up a handful of slips. "But look at this!" He took a sip of coffee. "And it's barely noon."

His assistant took the slips from him and was cataloguing them.

"But each one of these has to be checked out," he said. "Car thefts have top priority now. I mean, top priority!"

Sergeant O'Mally burst into the room holding a slip of paper. "Here's a hot one! Just reported. Ninety-one Taurus, tan, Illinois license NRU486. Taken from parking lot near Memorial Hospital."

"Holy mother of pearl," exclaimed the chief, taking the slip from O'Mally. "This is our man. Get an APB out on this *now*!"

The day had started out like her life had been lately: dark and gloomy. She had sat out most of the downpour beneath an underpass. But having achieved shelter late, her matted hair and soggy shoes bore witness to her tardiness. She had tried Chicago, but Chicago had treated her no better than her boyfriend. What she hated most was leaving her cat. But Mitzi would take care of herself. And besides, her boyfriend had treated Mitzi better than he had treated her. Yes, Mitzi would be okay. And it's not very easy hitchhiking with a cat.

As the rain stopped and the skies cleared, Ginny felt good about her decision. It was time to go home. She walked down the entrance ramp and on to the shoulder of the road. The sun was peeking through now. "Here goes," she said as she stuck out her thumb.

It was the seventh car that pulled over to the shoulder ahead of her. She picked up her duffel bag and sloshed her way over to the car. The passenger car's window came down.

"Where you going?" came the voice from inside.

Ginny pulled the wet hair from her forehead. "Minneapolis."

The door lock clicked.

"Get in," came the voice.

Ginny opened the door and got in.

Amjad took the car out of park and slipped it in to drive. He glanced at his mirrors and then at her.

"Better buckle your seat belt," he said as he pulled out and headed north.

Officer Logan had just finished with the accident report and was writing up a ticket for following too close. Officer Murphy was with the participants in the accident, consoling them that since there were no injuries and since both cars were drivable that everything would be all right. The drivers had exchanged information and now should report this to their insurance companies for further instructions. Officer Murphy did not like to give out tickets to people in situations like this. No one was hurt. Minor damage. Why make someone's day worse? Officer Logan had no compunctions. His attitude that "the law is the law" had put him on the precinct leader board in tickets given out. At least his sergeant would know that he was on the job.

Officer Logan finished with the ticket and looked out at the traffic. It never ceased to amaze him, this gawker slow down. There was nothing really here to see but everyone had to slow down for a look. And traffic would back up and come to a halt. He enjoyed the sense of participation. He enjoyed the feeling of power. He could, by turning on his flashers and just sitting there, alter the arterial flow of traffic. He could direct the heartbeat of the city. He always took a few more minutes with the accident report. And there was always the obligatory ticket.

Logan got out of the car and returned the driver's licenses, one of which was gift wrapped in a present from the clerk of court. Officers Logan and Murphy watched the two cars merge into traffic and pull away. They got back into the squad car and Logan turned the flashers off. As traffic flow began to improve, Logan pulled forward and merged into traffic.

"Another one?" asked Murphy.

"Yup," said Logan. "Following too close." He looked into his side mirror and switched to the left lane.

"You know," he said, "if more people watched what they were doing we wouldn't have all these accidents."

"Whatever," answered Murphy showing his distaste.

Murphy searched an endless train of cars for a distraction. Suddenly his gaze fixed on a car two lengths ahead in the right lane.

"What kind of car was that APB on?" he asked.

"I don't remember," said Logan. "Check the sheet."

Murphy pulled out his clipboard and read from the attached paper. "Ninety-one Taurus, tan, Illinois license NRU486, approach with extreme caution."

Murphy looked up at the car again. "Pull up," he said. "That tan Taurus up there on the right."

Logan started to accelerate.

"Not quite so fast," said Murphy, "Just enough so I can get the license plate."

Logan eased off a bit as they were still gaining. The car behind the Taurus backed off a bit, giving them a line of sight to the license plate. It showed an Illinois license plate NRU486.

"Holy shit!" exclaimed Murphy. "That's our man!"

Logan reached for the button to turn on the flashers.

"Wait a minute," said Murphy. "This is not the place. Not here on this freeway. Too many people here. Let's back off and follow him a while. We can call for backup and wait 'til he gets off the freeway."

Logan eased off the gas and pulled into the right lane three car lengths behind the Taurus. Murphy picked up his radio and clicked it on. "Central," he said anxiously. "This is 86. We have APB suspect in sight."

"Roger 86," came the speaker. "Describe suspect vehicle."

"Late model Taurus. Tan. Illinois License NRU486."

"Roger, 86. Stand by."

Murphy sat back in the seat. He felt his heart beat faster and his palms were getting moist.

"Eighty-six, what's your twenty?"

"I-94 northbound just past Irving Park Road."

"Roger that. Stand by."

Murphy let his right hand go to the gun butt protruding from his holster and then to the shotgun held upright just inside the passenger door.

"Eighty-six. Follow suspect vehicle only. Do not, repeat, do not approach suspect vehicle until backup arrives. Backup on its way. Keep this line open and advise your twenty as you go."

"Roger," said Murphy. "What are we dealing with?"

"Suspect wanted for murder. Possible terrorist. Considered extremely dangerous. Proceed with caution."

"You can roger that!"

Within two minutes another squad car had come up behind them quickly followed by another.

"Who the hell's in that car?" muttered Logan. "O. J. Simpson?"

The Taurus' right taillight flashed. Murphy clicked the radio.

"He's turning off on to Foster," he said. "Awaiting instructions."

Another pause. Then the speaker crackled. "As soon as suspect is off freeway, use your best chance and take him."

"Roger," said Murphy. His palms were clammy as he stroked the shotgun barrel.

The Taurus exited off the freeway, stopped at the entrance to Foster Avenue, and proceeded right. As the phalanx of squad cars approached Foster, Logan hit the siren and turned on his flasher. The Taurus pulled over to the curb and stopped. As Logan pulled up behind the Taurus, a second squad swung around them and skidded to a stop at an angle in front of the Taurus. The two officers exited the vehicle on the driver's side, pulled their weapons, and squatted behind the hood of their car, their weapons drawn down of the Taurus. Murphy opened the passenger door, grabbed the shotgun, and placed it through the window of the door. Logan flicked on the loudspeaker.

"You in the Taurus." He paused, but no response.

"You in the Taurus," he repeated. "Put the car in park. Open the door slowly and step out with your arms raised."

The officers in the squad car behind them had come up beside Logan and Murphy's car with their weapons raised.

"Come out with your hands raised," Logan repeated.

The driver's door opened slowly.

"Come out slowly," said Logan. Logan opened his door, got out, and pulled his revolver.

Out of the Taurus emerged a little old man in a flowered Hawaiian shirt and Khaki pants. His hair was white and his thin arms were raised and trembling. The liquid stain on his crotch was enlarging.

"What the hell," said Logan as he approached the little man.

When he got up to the Taurus he looked inside. In the back seat were three bags of groceries. In the passenger seat was an older woman with white hair and a checked gingham dress.

"George," she yelled at the old man. "I told you not to park in the handicapped zone!"

"What do you mean you've got the wrong car?" snapped the chief. "Yes I've checked. We've got the right license number. Have you checked the vehicle registration?" He switched hands on the phone and brought it to his other ear. "Well, check the registration and see if it matches the license plate on the car."

The chief took a huge gulp of coffee as he waited for a response from the other end of the phone. After a moment the voice at the other end explained that the license plate number on the registration did not match the license plate on the car.

"The son of a bitch switched plates," snapped the chief.

"Give me the license plate number on the registration. He'll probably be driving a tan Taurus with those plates."

The voice at the other end read off the license number. He wrote it down on a piece of paper and handed it to a sergeant.

"Get this on the wire now!" he said. "This guy's got to be alone. If he had someone here they wouldn't need to steal a car. The person here would have one already. If this was just kids on a thrill ride or some professional taking it to a chop shop they wouldn't go to the bother of switching license plates. No. This is our man. And he's traveling alone."

Chapter Eighteen
"To Going Home"

Amjad looked over at the pretty girl in the passenger seat next to him. "Are you coming or going?"

"What?" she asked.

"Are you from Chicago going to Minneapolis? Or are you from Minneapolis and going home?"

"Oh," she said, "I'm from Minneapolis." She looked down at her soggy shoes. "I mean I lived in Chicago for a while but I'm going home to Minneapolis."

Amjad looked down at her shoes. "Why don't you take your shoes off? I'll turn the heater on and open a window. Looks like you got pretty wet out there."

"Fine, I'd like that." She took off her shoes and wiggled her toes. "I didn't quite make it to the shelter on time."

"Yeah, it came down pretty good for a while."

"You're telling me!"

The heater felt good on her feet as she rubbed them against each other.

"You going all the way to Minneapolis?" she asked.

"Yes, that's my final stop."

"Hope you don't mind," she said. "Sure is nice of you to give me a lift."

"No problem. In fact maybe you could help me. Do you have a driver's license?"

"Yup."

"Would you like to drive for a while? It's going to be a long drive and I could use some sleep."

"Sounds great."

"Tell me when you're warmed up and ready."

"Oh, I'm ready now."

Amjad pulled over to the side of the road, hopped into the back seat, and lay down. Ginny slid over to the driver's seat, checked the mirrors, put the car in gear, and pulled out into traffic.

"Please keep it at the speed limit," he said. "I think my insurance may have lapsed and I'd rather not get stopped by the cops."

"No problem," she said.

Amjad really didn't need the sleep. He could have gone on alone. But he figured that they wouldn't be looking for a girl.

"Mind if I use your duffel bag for a pillow?" he asked.

"Not at all," she said. "Go ahead."

Amjad adjusted the bag under his head. He looked up at her wet matted hair. Even in the rain she was a beautiful girl. She reminded him of another beautiful girl he once knew. He remembered back to when he sat in the rain next to her grave site. And he thought of an island in the middle of a river in Minnesota. He turned over and went to sleep.

Wisconsin State Trooper John Gordon was at the end of his shift and heading south on I-94. It was his birthday and he was anxious to get home. Mrs. Gordon had promised to cook his favorite dinner tonight. Porterhouse steak, medium rare, mushrooms and onions. Baked potato with sour cream and chives. Cut wax beans. And for dessert, hot apple pie. It had been an uneventful shift. Two speeding tickets, one flat tire, and one stalled vehicle. But now he had his mind on the fixin's at home. He noticed a tan Taurus coming from the south and watched it pass by. He could tell it was a girl driving the car and noticed the Illinois license plate. He glanced down to the passenger seat at a bulletin to be on the lookout for a '91 tan

Taurus with Illinois license plate NRU486 and then another bulletin changing the license plate to 493DET. He hadn't noticed the number on the license plate but started to make mental calculations. It had been about a minute since they passed going in opposite directions at sixty-five miles per hour. They were two miles apart now. The next turnaround was a mile up the road. Four miles apart. By the time he got back up to cruising speed, five miles and five minutes apart. At one hundred miles per hour, it would take an other ten minutes to catch up. Fifteen minutes. And another fifteen minutes to get back to here again. Thirty minutes late. He looked at the bulletin again. Single male driver.

Unless this guy had a sex change, this ain't our guy, he thought. "Fuck it!" he said, and continued south toward his juicy steak, hot apple pie, and cold Budweiser.

"We're gettin' kinda low on gas," said Ginny over the front seat.

No response.

"Excuse me," her voice raised. "Hello!"

Amjad slid back into consciousness. "Um, what's that?" he mumbled.

"I said we're gettin' low on gas."

"Oh," he grunted. "Okay, pull over at the next gas station."

"There's a Food N Fuel up the road a bit."

"Fine. Great. I could use a bite."

"Me too."

Ginny drove the car to the exit ramp, pulled into the gas station and up to the furthest pump. Amjad reached in his pocket and pulled out a wad of bills. Gerald Spaulding had not liked traveler's checks. Certainly he had had credit cards but he had thought an ample amount of American dollars would be impressive if he ever found someone special on his trip. Unfortunately, he did not find love until the airport.

Amjad pulled out a one-hundred-dollar bill and handed it to Ginny.

"I'll pump the gas," he said. "Why don't you go inside and pay for it?"

Ginny looked at the bill, then opened the door to get out.

"I really don't like restaurant food," said Amjad. "Do you?"

Ginny paused. "No, not really. I'm fine with just a sandwich."

"Why don't you pick up a loaf of bread, some sandwich meat, chips, whatever you like. We can stop up the road and have a picnic."

"What do you want to drink?" she asked. "Beer?"

"No, just a diet cola."

"Sounds great," she said, and walked over to the store. Amjad watched her disappear behind the door before he got out of the car. He walked to the rear of the car and pulled the nozzle from its holding station. He held the nozzle erect with his right hand while his left hand opened the gas tank door and slowly unscrewed the gas cap. When the gas cap finally released its protective hold on the tank, Amjad lowered the nozzle, slid it into the tank's neck, and squeezed the handle. The nozzle jerked in response to its ejection of fluid which was hungrily accepted by the tank.

"That's it?" said Soran. "That's it? They got nothing?"

Covington looked back from the window and laughed. "Look's like a Chinese fire drill. FBI thinks it's a complex plot connected to some terrorist ring in the East and the Chicago police think it's a single. They end up using half the police force to arrest some eighty-year-old who shits in his pants."

"But we handed him to them," said Soran. "I mean we handed him to them! And they got nothing?"

"Like I said, it's like a Chinese fire drill."

Soran sat down in the chair in front of Covington's desk. "I don't know," he said. "I'm worried about this one."

Covington stopped smiling. "I'm worried too."

Interstate rest stops in the Upper Midwest are chosen for their beauty as well as their facilitation. Few city parks can offer the vistas of these open plains oases. The one Ginny and Amjad found themselves at was cut out of a forested hilltop comprised of white pine, Norway pine, and balsam with a gentle infusion of the maples, oaks, and birches. Even with the deciduous leaves still promised, the dominance of the conifers provided a spectacular setting. The parking lot was atop the hill complete with modern rest-room facilities and a huge map of Wisconsin and an arrow that told them they were here. A footpath led away from the parking lot to a pathway through the trees and down the hill. It opened up to reveal a pristine unpopulated lake with crystal blue waters under the bright blue sky. A single picnic bench was the only evidence that humankind had set foot here.

Ginny skipped down the path and put the bag of groceries on the picnic table. "What'll it be?" she yelled as she put her hand inside the bag. "Peanut butter, jelly, or peanut butter and jelly sandwiches?"

Amjad came down the path and entered the clearing. "What kind of choices are those?" he yelled back at her.

"Well," she responded. "You told me to get the groceries." She pulled a loaf of bread, a jar of peanut butter and a jar of jelly out of the bag.

"This way you get three choices," she said. "Peanut butter, jelly, or the chef's special, peanut butter and jelly."

Amjad smiled and sat down at the table. "What do you like?" he asked.

"Chef's special, of course. I'm the chef."

"Sounds good to me." Amjad reached in the bag and pulled out a six pack of Diet Coke. "How long you been cookin'?" he asked.

She grabbed a can of Diet Coke and freed it from its plastic fetter.

"Oh, I've been cookin' chef's specials since I was five years old," she said, and smiled. She undid the twist tie of the loaf of bread and reached inside. "You like the crust?"

"Not particularly," he answered.

"Me neither. You know, at home I make the sandwich and cut off the crusts."

She looked around the table and then in the bag. "Speaking of cutting, I forgot, we don't have a knife. How can I make chef specials without a knife?"

Amjad opened his can of Diet Coke and held up the pop top from the can. He straightened out the metal strip and grabbed the peanut butter jar. "Perhaps the chef could use some help from the maitre d'," he said as he spread the peanut butter over the bread with the metal strip.

"Saved by the pop top," she said as Amjad finished the job.

Ginny went around to the other side of the table and sat down on the bench facing the lake with her back to the table top. Amjad handed her a sandwich and sat down next to her. Ginny looked out at the lake and the blue sky and the trees.

"God, it's good to be going home," she said. "Heaven is not some ethereal place where angels sit around on clouds playing harps." She took in a deep breath and sighed as she let it out. "No, heaven is the north woods without the bugs."

Amjad passed her a Diet Coke and offered her a toast. "To going home."

They clicked cans and each took a swig.

"Exactly where is home?' he asked.

"My parents live in Eden Prairie, but I really don't feel like going back there right now."

She took another drink. "I have a girlfriend who has an apartment in Minneapolis," she continued. "I called her just before I left Chicago. She's going away for a week and wants me to stay at her apartment. She's got a cat and doesn't want to leave it alone for a week. I'm just leaving a dead-end relationship and I wanted to go back to Minnesota. But I really didn't want to stay with Mom and Dad so the timing was perfect. Besides, I miss Mitzi, so baby-sitting a cat won't be all that bad."

"Mitzi?" he asked.

"Oh, that's my cat. I had to leave it with my ex. It's a long story."

"Maybe you can tell me about it sometime."

"Yeah. Sometime. Right now I just want to sit in this beautiful place and think pleasant thoughts." She took a bite of her sandwich and washed it down with a drink of diet cola.

"Ya know," she continued, "I don't even know your name."

"Spaulding. Gerald Spaulding."

"Hi, I'm Ginny," she said, offering her hand. "And where might you be going?"

"Well," he said, "I've got a job at the University of Minnesota. I'm getting there a little early so I don't have a place to stay yet. I figure I'll stay in a motel for a while until I find a place."

Ginny thought for a moment. She looked up at Amjad. He was handsome and strong. Yet he seemed gentle and kind. But it was his eyes that fascinated her. They were deep and mysterious; penetrating yet somehow understanding. She had been hurt in Chicago and she could intuit that he had recently suffered a loss. She wanted to know more about this man. She could use a little kindness and understanding herself.

"It's really nice of you to give me a ride," she finally said. "You could stay with me a couple days until you get situated."

He looked at her and smiled.

"That is, if you don't mind sleeping on the couch."

"I'd like that," he said, "I'd like that very much."

"Here's to going home." She raised her can of Diet Coke.

Amjad looked out in the distance beyond the lake and the trees and the sky. "Here's to going home."

Malcolm slammed the receiver down hard. It was bad enough that he had a terrorist running around with barely enough manpower to cover it. But now Broadwater had pulled a power play and had requested that some of his men be sent to the East Coast. All this when there was no evidence that this Amjad character was on the East Coast or even headed there. *For Christ's sake,* he thought, *he landed in Chicago and was last seen in Chicago. You'd think the emphasis would be on where he was last seen. Perhaps with some of Broadwater's men, I could nab this son of a bitch. But no, I've got to give up some of my men. Broadwater's on the fast track to the top, all right, and he doesn't care who he steps on getting there.*

The phone rang, interrupting his train of thought. He picked up the phone. "Malcolm," he said.

"Malcolm, this is Covington, CIA," came the voice on the other end of the phone.

"How's it going?"

"Horse shit to middling," said Malcolm.

"What's wrong?"

"Well, we got a terrorist running around down here and I just got half of my men pulled out from under me and sent to the East Coast."

"The East Coast? I thought I told you our intelligence had him headed for Minneapolis."

"It's not my call. It's this Broadwater fellow out east. He's playing macho man with national security."

"Do you have enough people to cover it?"

"I'm pulling all my people into the Chicago area. If it is Minneapolis, unless we get some help from the local talent, we'll be shit out of luck."

"Holy shit!"

"Well I'm leaving two men up in Minneapolis but that's hardly enough to do the job."

"Damn. I'd like to send you some men, but you know our charter won't let us."

"Yeah, I know. We'll manage."

"I know you will. Say, I've got you on the speaker phone here and the fellow that broke this thing is sitting next to me. Phil Soran, say hello to Lawrence Malcolm."

"Hello, Mr. Malcolm."

"Hello, Phil."

"Just so we can update our files," continued Covington, "would you let us know how you are progressing?"

"Well," said Malcolm, pulling open a file, "we checked with the airline to see who was sitting in seat 30C. Turns out to be a fellow named Gerald Spaulding. We got the credit card number that he paid his airline ticket with, checked with the credit card company, and had them pull his application. They gave us his full name, address, date of birth, occupation, and place of employment. Seems he was an actor and worked for the Guthrie Theater in Minneapolis. With his full name and date of birth, we were able to check with the DMV in St. Paul, Minnesota, to get his driver's license number. I had them fax me a copy of his driver's license. We enlarged the photo on the license and can send it to you, but I can tell you now, it doesn't match the composite you sent us. We showed the composite to the airline crew and they confirmed it was Amjad and not Spaulding who was in seat 30C. My guess is that Spaulding is the stiff in Rome. The composite's pretty good, but I'd like a better picture."

"Why don't you check with the University of Minnesota?" said Soran with a raised voice. "He spent some time there. A guest surgeon or something. They should have a picture of him."

There was a pause. "We're on it," said Malcolm as he picked up a pen and jotted something on a piece of paper.

"I know you're not supposed to get involved. Internally, that is," continued Malcolm. "But I'll help you out and give you some information, you know, for your files. But you have to do me a favor."

"Name it," said Covington.

"If you come up with anything," said Malcolm, "anything at all. I'd like to be the first to know."

"Sounds fair," said Covington.

There was a click on Covington's speaker phone followed by a dial tone.

"God damn it," said Soran. "They're headed in the wrong direction."

"Looks that way." said Covington. "At least from our point of view. But who knows, they might be right. At least this Broadwater guy is covering his ass."

Soran rocked in his chair. "Sir," he said, "I'd like to go there."

"Where?" said Covington.

"To Minneapolis, sir. Both you and I know he's going to Minneapolis."

"Why, hell no. You're not going there. You're not a field man. You're an analyst. Besides, our charter doesn't allow us to operate in the United States. You know that."

"Yes, I know that, sir. But I'm pretty well caught up here. L2 and L3 are gone. Bolder can handle anything that comes up."

Covington picked up his pipe and tapped it in his palm.

"I've got a couple weeks vacation," continued Soran. "You know I'm from there and I haven't been home in quite a while."

"If you go there," said Covington, "you're off the clock."

"Yes, sir."

"I mean, you're not on company time."

"Yes, sir."

Covington swiveled his chair ninety degrees to square with the window. "I hear there's pretty good fishing in Minnesota," he said.

"Ten thousand lakes," said Soran.

"Pretty hard to find one fish in all that water."

"Not if you know the fish. Not if you know the terrain. Not if you know the bait."

Covington put the pipe to his lips. "Well, good fishing."

Soran got up and turned to leave.

"Oh, yes," said Covington. "If you catch a lunker..." he swiveled back to face Soran and leaned forward. "Stuff him!"

"Well, this is the place," said Ginny as she peered through the windshield at the apartment complex.

"Just swing on into the parking lot and park anywhere."

Amjad pulled the tan Taurus into the parking lot. "Which building?" he asked.

"Oh, the first one right there." She pointed.

"Why don't I let you out at the door and I'll go park the car."

"A true gentleman," she said. "I like that."

Amjad pulled up to the curb and stopped. "Which apartment?" he asked.

"Um," she paused, "302, yeah apartment 302. She told me where she hid the key. You go park the car and I'll get the place looking spiffy."

"Fine."

Ginny got out and, with the bag of groceries, disappeared through the front door. Amjad pulled away from the curb and drove to the far end of the parking lot. The headlights went from car to car until they finally rested on an older car sitting alone in the far corner of the lot. With its wheels up on blocks, it was obvious that this car had suffered the vestiges of winter and was awaiting the coming of spring. Amjad pulled up next to it and turned off the headlights. He got out and looked around. Sure that no one was around, he took out the stethoscope and, with the detached metal frame, unscrewed the screws holding the license plates of the parked car. He replaced the Taurus' plates with the Minnesota plates of the parked car and put the Illinois plates in the trunk of the Taurus. He drove back to the row of cars nearest to Ginny's friend's apartment and parked the car.

Inside the apartment, Ginny had made two more chef's specials and had complemented them with some potato chips that she had found in the cupboard. She opened two Diet Cokes and placed them on the table. There was a knock on the door. Ginny crossed the room and opened the door. As he stepped in, Ginny jumped up, put her arms around his neck, and kissed him on the lips. Caught off guard,

Amjad did not have time to return the greeting before Ginny disengaged the welcome, stepped back, and turned to show the kitchen table.

"Just like Donna Reed," she said. "Welcoming her man home from a long day's work. And you don't know how many hours I've slaved over the hot kitchen stove fixin' my man his supper."

Amjad laughed and walked to the kitchen. "I like it," he said. "But perhaps tomorrow we can go to the store."

Ginny had taken a blanket and one of the pillows off the bed and placed them on the couch. "I hope you don't mind sleeping on the couch."

"That was our agreement," he said.

"Well, I'm tired. I'm going to bed."

She reached up and gave him a kiss on the cheek and headed off to the bedroom. Amjad spread the blanket out on the couch and put the pillow at one end. He shut off the lights and stripped down to his shorts. He lay down on the couch and pulled the blanket over him.

Ginny lay in bed in a fetal position with her back to the door. She heard the door open but did not turn around. She heard a pillow land next to her head. The mattress tilted as it accepted the full weight of his body. She felt his knees come up to fit perfectly into the V formed by the back of her legs. His arm came over her shoulder as his left hand found and cupped her right breast. She lay still for a while measuring her own breath in anticipation, her shoulders hunched. She felt his breath coming in warm, gentle waves to the nape of her neck. When she heard his first faint snore she relaxed her shoulders and smiled. She clutched his hand, held it tight against her bosom, and nodded off to sleep.

Chapter Nineteen
"Give It to Tonto"

S orry to get you up so early," Soran said into the telephone.

"No problem," came the response from Bolder.

"I'm at the airport, waiting for my flight to Minneapolis."

"What's that?"

"Look, FBI's pulling everything out East and what's left is guarding Chicago. There's a few left in Minnesota but I figure I might be able to help. At least I can do more there than I can here."

"What if our man did head east?"

"Don't think so. I've been with this guy so long now I feel like I know him. I just know he's going to Minnesota."

"Cool. What can I do?"

"Covington knows I'm leaving but he can't help me. I've taken my two week vacation but Covington says I'm off the clock. I need someone back here to keep me posted. I also need an intro to the locals. Someone to show me around so I can keep up with current events there. FBI's no good. They know I shouldn't be poking around outside my jurisdiction, but I figure we might get some help from the locals. Might get a hold of someone who thinks it's pretty neat teaming up with

CIA. They also might not be as familiar with our charter. Anyway, I can't make the call. The call has to come from the office. Just in case they check up."

"I'm with ya."

"What I need you to do is to call the chief of police of Minneapolis or St. Paul and see if they can have a man meet me at the airport."

"What's your flight?"

"Northwest flight 111."

"I'll be on it within the hour."

"Thanks, man. I appreciate it."

"No problem. Good luck," Bolder clicked his gum, "and good hunting."

Morning came to Ginny even before she opened her eyes. She had grown accustomed to jumping out of bed immediately upon waking because, first she had someplace to be and, second, she had no reason to stay. But she greeted this day with sublime sloth. She even resisted opening her eyes as to prolong her indolence. And she was smiling. She could feel that she was smiling. The smile stopped just short of a giggle. She had not smiled for some time. It seemed like a month. Not since Tom started to… But that was long ago now. She had separated herself from him by time and space. And she was smiling again. She lay and listened to the rhythmical pattern of a light snore emanating from her intimate benefactor. She opened her eyes and rolled over to face him. He responded with a slight twitch in his slumberous cadence and then proceeded on undisturbed. She admired his features. Even in his relaxed state he was strong but gentle, forceful and yet kind. She liked what she saw. Was he as lost as she had been? Was he still searching for what she had just found? She leaned over and kissed his cheek. After two meals of peanut butter and jelly sandwiches, this man could use a good breakfast.

In her mind's eye she could see him hungrily devouring a dozen eggs and a side of bacon. *The way to a man's heart is through his stomach,* she thought to herself. *How trite. How true.* She would make him a good breakfast.

Their first breakfast together. She remembered that, last night, the refrigerator yielded nothing. But she still had the change from the one-hundred-dollar bill he had given her. She pecked his cheek again and slipped out of bed. She dressed quietly and walked out into the kitchen. The car keys were lying on the counter. She picked them up and headed out the door.

Ganyo hated these nonsmoking rules. It was bad enough when they limited smoking to the cafeteria. At least then he could sneak out, have a quick puff, and no one would be the wiser. But now the entire building was smoke free. Since he had become chief of police of Minneapolis, he couldn't very well run down three flights of stairs, have a smoke, and then run back up three flights of stairs every half hour. So he had switched to nicotine patches. They were not working well.

"Ganyo," he said gruffly as he picked up the phone.

"Is this the Minneapolis chief of police?"

"This is Chief Ganyo."

"Um, good morning, chief. This is Henry Jordan of the CIA in McLean, Virginia. We have a..."

"Give me your main office phone number and your extension," Ganyo snapped.

"What?"

"Your phone number and extension. You've got three seconds."

"Why, um..."

"Two seconds."

"Ah, 703-555-4787. Extension 107."

"I'll call you right back," Ganyo said, and hung up the phone. He picked it back up and dialed 1-703-555-4787.

One ring. Two rings.

"CIA, McLean," came the voice.

"This is Minneapolis Police Chief Ganyo. Do you have a Henry Jordan working there."

There was a pause.

"No. I don't see that name here."

"Can you tell me who is at extension 107?"

Another pause.

"That would be Bolder, John Bolder."

"Would you please connect me to 107?"

"Yes sir."

One ring. Two rings.

"Hello," came the receiver. Ganyo recognized the voice.

"Who is this?" demanded Ganyo.

"Who is this?" countered Bolder.

"This is Chief of Police Ganyo and you had better be John Bolder."

"Um, ah. Yes, this is John Bolder," Bolder said timidly.

"Listen you little cocksucker," yelled Ganyo. "You try something like that again and I'll have your job. You understand?"

"Ah. Yes, sir. Um, sorry sir."

Ganyo slammed the phone down. He tore the nicotine patch off his arm and grabbed his pack of Camels from his top drawer.

"I'm going for a smoke," he said, and bolted out the door.

"Chief Hardy," St. Paul Police Chief Hardy spoke into the phone.

"I'm looking for the St. Paul chief of police," came the receiver.

"This is Chief Hardy."

"This is...John Bolder from CIA in McLean, Virginia. We have a...."

"Wait a minute," said Hardy grabbing a pencil. "What's your main office number and extension?"

"703-555-4787, extension 107."

"I'll call you right back."

Chief Hardy hung up the phone, then picked it up and dialed the number.

One ring. Two rings.

"CIA, McLean," came the voice.

"Do you have an employee named John Bolder working there?" asked Hardy.

A pause. "Yes, we do."

"What is his extension?"

"107."

"Would you connect me please?"

One ring.

"Hello," said Bolder.

"Who is this?" asked Hardy.

"This is John Bolder," said Bolder as he held his breath.

There was a slight pause.

"This is St. Paul Police Chief Hardy."

Bolder closed his eyes and clenched his teeth.

"What can I do for you?" said Hardy.

Bolder pulled his phone down and sighed with relief. Bringing the phone back up he said, "Thank you, sir, for returning my call. We have a situation there. I mean, I'm sure you've been briefed by the FBI on the terrorist suspect being in your neighborhood."

"Yeah," said Hardy. "We're up to speed on that. But word is now he's heading east."

"That's always possible, but we think he still may be headed your way."

Bolder raised his left hand and crossed his fingers.

"We're sending a man to your town and I wonder if you could have someone meet him. He'll be active in the investigation."

"I thought you guys had no jurisdiction inside the United States."

"Well, yes sir, you are partly right there. Our charter when we were formed in 1947 prohibits us from gathering intelligence on citizens of the United States." Bolder rested the phone on his shoulder, raised his right hand, and crossed his fingers. "But there's an addendum to the Gulf of Tonkin Resolution that, by presidential decree, we are allowed to gather information and actually interdict a suspected foreign terrorist operating anywhere in the world, including the United States. So, if this jerk-off were an American jerk-off, we couldn't do anything about it. But since he's a foreign jerk-off, we'd like to help out."

There was a long pause as Bolder quickly considered what he might do after government service.

"So," said Hardy. "What can I do for you?"

Bolder let out a quiet sigh, grabbed the phone from his shoulder, and sat up in his chair.

"Like I said," he continued, "we have a man coming in and we'd like you to meet him and keep him up to speed. We will, of course, reciprocate with any intelligence that we gather at this end."

Yeah, sure! Hardy thought. "What's his name and flight number?"

"Phil Soran. Due in on Northwest 111 at 9:30 today."

"We'll get a man on it."

"Thanks. And if there's anything you need, anything at all, you've got my number."

Damn right I've got your number, thought Hardy. "No problem," he said, and hung up the phone.

Damn Feds, he thought. *First the FBI comes in here, sets up camp, and takes a couple of my men. And then when they want to send some of their men out east they pull a couple more. Now the CIA wants me to send another one of my men to baby-sit one of their guys. Who the hell do they think they are anyway? I've got a police force to run. Well at least this guy was half civil. At least he asked. Damn FBI just comes in here and commandeers what they want.*

Hardy pushed down a button on the intercom.

"Wasko, get in here," he said into the intercom.

Twenty seconds later the door opened and Sergeant Wasko entered the room.

"I just got a call from the CIA," said Hardy. "They've got a man coming in to help with this terrorist thing. They want us to send a man to pick him up at the airport."

"CIA?" said Wasko. "I thought they only..."

"Yeah, I know. It's a long story and basically I just don't have time right now." Hardy sat back in his chair.

"I'm sick and tired of these Feds poking around and taking my men," said Hardy. "Tell you what. They want a man, we'll give them a man. Let's send Tonto out there. The state can tell me to hire him and they can tell me to promote him, but they sure as hell can't tell me what assignments to give him."

Hardy wrote on a piece of paper and handed it to Wasko. "Here's the guy's name and flight number," he said. "Give it to Tonto."

Ginny was going through her mental list to see if she had forgotten anything. She had not taken the time to sit down and prepare a written list. She had tried to get enough groceries for a week, but she made sure she had at least gotten enough groceries for a good breakfast. Her mind lingered back to her lying beside him, staring into his masculine, weathered face as he floated on the wings of gentle slumber. This was a meat and potatoes man. No quiche and yogurt for this one. From her mental list she checked off eggs, bacon, bread, butter, coffee, and juice.

Satisfied that she met the morning's essentials, she pulled the Taurus into the groceries pick up lane. A seventeen-year-old with a green smock over his shoulders and the marks of puberty across his face strolled over to the car. Ginny rolled down the passenger window and handed the acne-faced teenager a numbered reclamation card.

"Where do you want them?" asked the teenager.

Ginny opened the glove compartment and pressed a yellow trunk release button. "Put them in the trunk."

He actually had two names, Billy Simpson and Billy Two Bears. His mother had been in the vanguard of the flower children generation, and to prove her liberalism or simply to piss-off her parents she had taken up sleeping with minorities. The issue of one of these trysts was Billy. She had known the father briefly. She had known that he was a Native American who had lived on the Prairie Island Indian Reservation. She had known that he was in the army. She had also known that he had left for Vietnam in a bus and had come home in a box, so she extended her last name to the boy.

But to be true to his bi-cultural heritage, she also wanted him to have a Native American name. Since the child's father was from the Mdewakanton band of Dakota Indians, she consulted the spiritual leader as to what to name the child. The spiritual leader consulted the spirits from the north, from the south, from the east, and from the west. He consulted the spirits from the past and from the present and from the future. The spirits had told him that the child would grow up to be big and strong. It should be a bear to symbolize this strength.

But the spirits also knew that this child was from two cultures, that he would benefit from the strengths of both cultures and would be hindered by the weaknesses of each culture. It would be Two Bears. The spirits told him that the name of the child should be Two Bears.

And so it was Billy Two Bears Simpson.

He had been raised white, with all the advantages of a white man's education. His mother had informed him of his bi-culturalism and his classmates would never let him forget. The taunts of half-breed were never far apart.

But the taunts and divergence did not dissuade him, and served as a reminder that he must work harder than the others to achieve his goal; that of respect. His mother's love and caring had provided the nurturing fields for his development. Through hard work and discipline he had excelled academically and had achieved his Bachelor of Arts in Law Enforcement.

His application to the St. Paul Police Department had been fortuitous. It had long been known that the department was a brotherhood of white Christian males and the entrance exams and hiring practices were skewed against minorities and women. When a civil rights commission exposed this inclination, the mayor had mandated that enough minorities and women be hired and promoted to achieve political correctness. So the hiring of Billy Two Bears Simpson was advised and his accelerated promotion was recommended, much to the chagrin of the brotherhood.

It was "Tonto" behind his back, and sometimes to his face, but he did not let it bother him. He had endured a lifetime of epithets. He could not break into the brotherhood. But he could be a good cop. And that's all he asked for.

Now Billy Two Bears Simpson was at the airport awaiting the de-planing of Northwest flight 111, holding a sign adorned with the name, Phil Soran. He felt more of a chauffeur than a cop. But he was doing his job as best as he could.

I wonder how he likes his coffee? Ginny thought to herself as she pulled the Taurus into the apartment parking lot. *Black,* she thought. *He's got to like it black. That seems to fit him.* She swung the car into a parking space close to the door and shut off the engine. Opening the glove compartment, she pushed the trunk release button. She got out of the car and walked to the back. She pulled two grocery bags out of the trunk and put her hand up to close the trunk when she noticed something. Two Illinois license plates were lying in the bottom of the trunk. *That's strange,* she thought as one of the bags slipped from her grip and fell to the pavement. "Damn," she said. "I hope I didn't break any eggs." She reached down and discerned that all comestibles were intact. She picked up the bag, closed the trunk, and headed for the apartment to cook her man some breakfast.

As the plane taxied to the gate, Phil Soran reflected on the last time he had been at this airport. How long ago it seemed. And yet there was still a pang in his heart. Had he broken her heart or had she broken his? Would he have done anything differently? Could he have done anything differently? He knew when it ended but he never could figure out when it started.

"Please remain seated until the plane comes to a complete stop," reminded the flight attendant, and people half out of their seats grudgingly returned. Within a minute the plane had halted and a minute later passengers were filing out.

Soran walked up the ramp and into the terminal. At the front of the gate area was a man in a chauffeur's hat with a sign that said TIPTON. Next to him was a tall, good looking young man with long black hair. His sign said PHIL SORAN.

"I'm Phil Soran." He walked over to the man and extended his hand.

"Detective Billy Simpson," said Simpson as he accepted the greeting.

"Nice of you to pick me up," said Soran.

"It's my job," assured Simpson. "Where to?"

"Well, first thing I've got to do is call my sister," said Soran. "I left in such a hurry I didn't have time to get a place to stay. My sister lives here and she can probably put me up."

"Sounds good," said Simpson.

Soran walked over to a bank of pay phones and picked up a phone book, studied it for a moment, then dialed a number. After two rings a female answered.

"Andrea?" asked Soran.

"No," came the voice.

"Is this Andrea Soran's number?"

"Yes, it is, but she's not here."

Soran knew that voice. An icy fist grabbed him in the stomach and squeezed.

"Ginny?" he asked as he swallowed hard.

"Yes. This is Ginny. Who is this?"

The fist clenched tighter.

"Phil? Is this Phil?"

The fist eased just a bit.

"Yes. Yes, its me, Phil."

"What are you doing in town?" she asked.

Phil's armpits were wet and he could tell his face was flush but the fist loosened a little more. "I'm here on business," he said, then caught himself. "I mean I'm here on vacation. Yeah, that's it. Sort of a working vacation." It was good to talk. The more he taxed his jaws the looser came the fist. "I made sort of last minute plans to come here and I figured I could maybe stay with my sister."

The fist was gone.

"Where is Andrea?"

"She's out of town. But she told me I could stay here until she got back. Sorry, but the place is kind of full right now."

"Tom?" he asked.

"Oh, no. Tom and I just didn't work out."

"Oh, sorry to hear that," he said, not really meaning it. "What happened?"

"I'd rather not get into that just now. We were just two different persons."

Phil had heard that phrase before, from the same person, in about the same place. "So, you'll be there for about a week or so?" he asked.

"Yup. Afraid so."

"Maybe I'll give you a call when I get settled and we can discuss old times," he said.

"Yeah, that would be nice." She thought fondly to a time long past. "I'd like that."

"Okay. I'll call you when I'm settled."

"Fine," she said, and hung up the phone. She poured herself another cup of coffee, turned to Amjad sitting at the table, and smiled.

"Seconds?" she asked.

Chapter Twenty
"Welcome to the Community of Cities"

B
ummer," said Simpson.

"Best laid plans," countered Soran as he turned to walk down the concourse.

"Tell me, detective," he said, "what exactly is your assignment here?"

"First of all, I'll let you call me Billy if I can call you Phil."

"I like that, Billy," said Phil, and patted him on the back.

"I do too, Phil." Billy smiled.

"Well, you're some kind of CIA dude. I'm supposed to inform you on this terrorist thing and then chauffeur you around."

"Doesn't sound too much like detective work."

"As you can see, I'm part Native American. And although I'm well qualified, the St. Paul Police Department does not like to hire minorities. Well, I came along at a time when they were forced to. I got sort of 'Operation Head Start' kind of thing, ya know. I'm well qualified, mind you, and I'd really rather work for it, but that's a tough nut to crack. Anyway, ever since I made detective, they've been giving me one shitty job after another."

He looked at Soran. "No offense intended," he said.

Soran smiled back, "None taken."

They reached the escalator.

"So," said Soran, "this chauffeuring me around, that means I don't have to rent a car?"

"As long as you're here," said Simpson, "and until I hear otherwise, I'm your man."

Soran turned and said a brief "thank you" to Bolder under his breath.

When they reached the bottom of the escalator, Soran turned to Simpson. "So, what's the latest on our visitor from the east?" he said.

"Well, not much," said Simpson. "FBI's in charge but they really don't have the manpower so they've enlisted the local talent. They're basically trying to cover the two nuclear power plants near the Twin Cities. They've enlisted Wright County Sheriff's Department and some members of the Minneapolis police to cover the Monticello plant and they've got both Goodhue and Dakota County sheriffs and St. Paul police to help cover the Prairie Island plant. Jurisdiction don't count for shit when the FBI's in charge. They just appropriate the manpower and nobody says boo."

As they arrived at the luggage carousel the light started flashing and the conveyor started to move.

"Anyway," continued Simpson. "FBI really doesn't think it's gonna happen here. They've pulled a lot of their men and headed east. The ones they have left are just basically covering their asses."

Simpson rolled his toothpick and chuckled. "Speaking of asses," he said, "where do you come in?"

Soran chuckled back. He liked this young man. He was easy going and quick of wit. He made him feel at ease. Soran could have played the sleuth, super-secret CIA James Bond sort of thing, but decided to play it straight. He felt that he could trust Simpson. And besides, he knew he was a terrible liar.

"I'm actually the guy that found our man," he said. "I've tracked him from Libya to Rome to Amsterdam to Chicago. I've been on this guy's trail every step of the way."

He spied his suitcase as it came down the ramp and settled on the conveyor. "CIA still thinks he's coming here," he continued, "so when the FBI decided to shift everything east, I decided to come myself."

Soran pulled the suitcase off the conveyor and put it on the ground next to him. He turned to Simpson. "Look. I've been with this guy for a long time. I feel I know him. He's coming here. I can feel it!"

Simpson took his toothpick and stuck it in his lower row of teeth. "Sounds fine with me," he said. "FBI is real thin. Police and Sheriff's Departments don't seem to be up to it. If you've got the inside track, I'm stickin' with you."

Soran picked up the suitcase and James Bond and Tonto headed for the parking ramp.

The Sears store on Lake Street had yielded a mid-length jacket and a set of screwdrivers. A tour of downtown Minneapolis and St. Paul had found one armory closed and the other too heavily guarded. Amjad had stopped at a phone booth and picked up the phone book. Under "Government Services," he found a National Guard Armory in a suburb of Brooklyn Park. Upon arriving there he found the armory to be conjoined with the Brooklyn Park Community Center. Amjad had walked into the building and noticed that the first corridor to the right was the National Guard office, and at the end of the corridor was the security door to the armory. The corridor straight ahead had led to the community center. Amjad had walked straight ahead to the community center and turned in to the first door on the right, which was marked "Men."

Inside the bathroom, he had observed two urinals and two toilet stalls. He had noticed the tile floor, the tile walls, and the suspended ceiling. He had walked out of the bathroom, out of the building, and turned around to confirm his mental notes. He had driven back to Sears to buy a Wonder prying bar, and two blocks later a Snyder's drugstore had supplied him with a dust rag, clothesline rope, and a bottle of ether. He now sat in the car outside the drugstore. Assured he had what he needed, he turned the key and headed the Taurus back to the apartment.

"Where to first, boss?" asked Simpson as he pulled the Oldsmobile up to the parking lot cashier. Soran looked over to see the handsome, dark young man with the high cheekbones and black hair cascading down to his shoulders. Soran had noticed the long hair in the airport but hadn't looked closely at it 'til now. Soran had always wanted to grow his hair long. Even for just a little while. Just to see how it looked. But even through college he hadn't let it slip much over his ears. And then when he went to work for the CIA, well, forget it.

"I'd like to look at both facilities to start with," he said.

Simpson handed the lady in the toll booth his ticket. "$4.25" appeared in red numerals. He gave her a five-dollar bill. She returned the change and raised the gate.

"No problem with the hair?" asked Soran.

Simpson pulled the car past the gate and into traffic. "Oh, sure. They give me some shit back at the station. Call me Tonto and such. But since I'm part Indian they can't do much about it. Besides, it makes me feel sort of…um…ethnic."

"Well, I like it," said Soran.

"Why don't you grow yours out?"

"Wrong ethnic group," said Soran running his hand through his hair. "From pictures of my grandfather, I'm lucky I don't have to wear a Heinie."

"Wouldn't make much of a scalp," Simpson said, and laughed. "Say," he continued. "You say you didn't have a place to stay?"

"Not yet," said Soran.

Simpson twirled the toothpick between his teeth. "You can stay with me if you like. That is, if you don't mind sleeping on the couch. I've got an apartment in St. Paul, though every now and then I slip back to the reservation. There's some mighty friendly ladies back there. Tell you what. You want to see both power plants. I'll take you up to Monticello first and you can look around. Then we'll go to Prairie Island. The power plant is right next to the reservation. I'll show you around. Who knows? You might just get lucky.

Traffic in New York City is always bad and today was no exception. Those that dare enter the labyrinth by day must understand that they have come to a place where civility has no meaning. They run the gauntlet of egocentric maniacs; ill-tempered, inconsiderate cabbies; and disdainful pedestrians.

Oblivious to the honking, taunts and single finger salutes, Mohammed inched the yellow rental van up the street. He turned into the parking ramp and took his ticket. He proceeded forward down to the third level and pulled the yellow van into parking slot C43 of the parking ramp beneath the World Trade Center. Jaquine, sitting next to him, reached around his seat and pushed one of the buttons on a little black box sitting on the floor of the van. The box had wires running underneath the curtain that separated the cab from the rear of the van. A light on the box went on. He twisted a dial and the digits 10:00 came on in red numerals. He pushed a second button and the numerals began to count backwards. The two men got out of the van, closed the doors, and began walking to sunlight.

Amjad lay on the couch looking out the window at the blue sky. The sky always seemed so blue in this climate at this time of year. This had been a very mild winter and, except for sparse patches, the snow had found its final resting place. The damp ground kept the dust from rising and allowed the air undefiled purity. It was only March, but there was an undeniable sense of spring in the air. The rivers had not frozen over and the ice on the lakes was, for the most part, gone. Winter had ended in Minnesota and the sun was high enough in the sky to bring the promise of an early spring.

"Why are you so deep in thought?" Ginny's voice intruded in his thoughts.

Amjad turned to see her coming toward him with each hand occupied by a can of Diet Coke.

"Would you like one?" she asked as she held out her right hand.

"Oh, yeah, sure," said Amjad, sitting up.

"What are you thinking about?"

"Oh, I was just thinking of some things I must do."

"Like what?" persisted Ginny.

"Some things," he said as he cracked open the can of pop. "Some things about the job I'm here for. At the University of Minnesota. Either today or tomorrow I'll be out late, so don't worry if I'm not home by the time you go to bed."

"I'm a big girl," she said. "I don't need to be tucked into bed. At least not all the time," she giggled.

Amjad took a sip of pop. "I've got to go out and get some things," he said as he got up.

Ginny took a sip as the phone rang. She walked into the kitchen and picked up the phone. "Hello," she said.

"Ginny?" came the voice.

"Yes. This is Ginny."

"This is Phil."

"Oh, hi, Phil. Good to hear from you again."

"Say, Ginny. I'm only in town for a week. We're going to drive by your apartment soon and I thought you might like to have lunch."

Ginny looked at Amjad as he put on his coat.

"Well," she said. "Yeah, I think that would be nice. Hang on a minute." She cradled the phone on her shoulder.

"Gerry, can you drop me off?"

"Yeah, sure," said Amjad. "No problem."

Ginny raised the phone to her ear. "Sure," she said. "Where and when?"

"Well," said Soran. "I just left Monticello. I'm on 94 but I could be on the 494 strip in half an hour. What's a good place near there?"

"How about..." she paused. "How about Friday's?"

"Highway 100 and 494?"

"That's the one."

"Okay. I'll see you in half an hour."

Ginny hung up and turned to Amjad.

"Sure you wouldn't like to have some lunch?" she asked.

"I'm really not that hungry, but I'll drop you off." He zipped up his coat and grabbed the car keys from the counter. "I've got some errands to run," he said.

The green numerals above the "Otis" sign read P3 as the World Trade Center parking ramp elevator eased to a stop. The doors opened and Mary Browne stepped out. She walked over to the bench, put her bag down, and reached in her pocket for her ticket. She took it out and examined the C44 that she had written in pen on the back. Mary Browne was very well organized. Whenever she parked in a ramp she would always write the number of her parking slot on the back of her ticket. Knowing the level number was never enough. She put the ticket back in her pocket, picked up her bag, and headed for parking slot C44.

Only two months pregnant, she was already shopping for the soon to be new arrival. She knew that Steven Browne had wanted a boy. When asked her inclination, she would always answer, "ten fingers, ten toes," although she was already thinking pink. She would wait until the ultrasound which would dictate the color of the bedroom. Whatever color, it would be busy. A wallpaper border of soft and cuddlies. Baby bears would be good. And lots of stuffed animals. A warm crib full of stuffed animals and colorful mobiles to hit and grab and giggle at. And a padded rocking chair to while away the hours with her new meaning of life.

Mary Browne reached parking slot C44 and noticed her car parked next to a yellow rental van. She shifted the bag to her left arm as she unlocked the car door with her right hand. As she opened the door, the bag slipped and she grabbed it with her right hand as the door banged into the side of the yellow van.

"Oops." she said.

There was a click, a flash of light, and Mary Browne ceased to exist.

Chapter Twenty-One
Ships Passing in the Night

When Soran first saw Ginny come through the door, he didn't know whether he should extend his hand or wrap his arms around her to give her a hug. His palms were not sweaty and his stomach, though not quite ready for food, felt near normal. He had wondered how he would react at this moment and was pleasantly surprised at his aplomb. She had left him some years ago. He actually had thought it was his idea. Although they had lived together, she had gotten in the habit of going out to parties without him and not returning until the wee hours of the morning.

He had accepted her stories about having drunk too much and in the interest of safety, she had opted to sober up before venturing home. But when the returns stretched into the late morning hours, he had decided that mischief may have been afoot and that she had best stay with her sister for a day or so until her self-examined actions would lead her back to him. He had thought that it was his idea and a bold statement at that. A statement that was sure to remind her of what she had to lose unless her behavior was modified. He had not known that she had already made up her mind to leave and was only waiting for a convenient time. Now he had provided the excuse. When she left she did not come back.

Soran put his hand out. "Good to see you again," he said.

She took his hand with a warm and firm grip. "It's good to see you, too."

Soran turned to Simpson.

"This is my friend Billy Simpson," he said.

"Nice to meet you," said Simpson as he reached for her hand.

"Nice to meet you, too," she said, and looked around. "So, do we have a table?"

"Yeah, right here," said Soran as he led her to the second table from the door.

"Good," she said. "I'm famished."

Lawrence Malcolm peeled his orange as he sat at his desk. Malcolm always saved his fruit for last. A whole-wheat sandwich, a carrot, a cup of yogurt, and fruit for dessert. He had finished with the peel and was sectioning the fruit when he was interrupted by the intercom.

"Mr. Broadwater on line one," blared the speaker.

Malcolm put the sections down, wiped his hands with a napkin, and picked up the phone.

"This is Broadwater."

Malcolm noticed the urgency in the tone and the lack of the mocking salutation. "Larry, they've blown up the World Trade Center."

"What's that?" asked Malcolm incredulously.

"They've blown up the fucking World Trade Center."

Malcolm sat back in his seat. "Who…when?"

"Your man and his gang. I'm sure of it," said Broadwater. "It's got to be Muslim extremists and guess who just got in to town."

"Do you have any leads?"

"Not yet, but it won't be long. I knew I should have asked for more men. I've got to get more men."

"But you've taken some of my men already."

"But I need more. I told you he was coming to the East Coast, but no, you said Chicago or Minneapolis. Midwest my ass. He's here. And they may have just started. I need more of your men!"

"I don't know how much more I can give."

"I've already put in a request to the director. You'll be informed shortly."

"Damn it, Broadwater. You're going to leave me here naked. What if it's just a coincidence and he's still here in the Midwest? We won't have the manpower."

"Don't worry about that," said Broadwater. "He's here!"

The talk had been small. Ginny had not talked about Tom and Soran did not discuss the reason for his vacation. Simpson was amiable and witty. The knot that Soran had anticipated in his stomach was supplanted by the croissant club sandwich and he felt totally at ease by the time he had finished half of his second Iced tea.

"Well, it's great to be back in Minnesota," he said.

"Yeah," she agreed. "I guess I could say that too."

Ginny finished the last bite of her quiche.

"It's amazing we came back on almost the same day," she said. "And ran into each other right away."

Soran took a last sip from his ice tea. "Almost as if we were star-crossed," he said, and smiled.

She smiled back a warm smile. Soran leaned back in his chair and put his napkin on the table. "Looks like two glasses is my limit. This iced tea really runs through me."

"I seem to remember that," she said.

"Will you excuse me while I go see a man about a horse?" He got up and headed for the men's room.

Ginny turned to Simpson. "So," she said. "How did you meet Phil?"

Simpson moved his chair sideways. "Well," he said. "We were just..."

He glanced up at the multiple TV sets which had all switched from the various basketball games and were all flashing "Bulletin." His eyes became fixed on the TVs when he continued..."it's that we just..." The flashing "Bulletins" on the TVs were gone and the reporter was at the news desk. The volume of the TV was turned up.

"Wait a minute," he said, and pointed to the nearest TV.

"This is Brook Donald live from New York," said the reporter. "Today New York City joined the community of cities like Beirut, Berlin, and Belfast whose membership is only that they share the devastation of international terrorism. Today a bomb was exploded beneath the World Trade Center. The size of the bomb is not known but it is thought to be equal to several hundred pounds of TNT. Many are dead and many are injured..."

"Oh, my God," said Ginny as her jaw dropped.

Simpson rose from the table. "I've got to call in," he said. "Where's the phone?" Ginny pointed toward the bathrooms as Simpson turned and walked away. Ginny stared at the TV with her mouth agape and her arms limp at her sides.

"Hello, Ginny," came a voice from behind her. "Are you ready to go?"

Ginny looked up at Amjad. She pointed at the TV. "They've just bombed New York," she said.

"Who?" said Amjad.

"Terrorists, I suppose," said Ginny.

Amjad looked at the TV. "Too bad." he said. He looked down at Ginny. "Are you about ready to go?"

Ginny glanced at her empty plate. "Yeah, sure," she said slowly. "But I've got to wait for my friend to say good-bye." She put her napkin on the table. "I'd like you to meet him."

Amjad looked back at the TV. "I'm afraid I'm double parked, I'll go wait in the car. I'll meet him some other time, I'm sure." Amjad turned and walked out the door.

Ginny picked up her purse and put it on her lap as Soran came back to the table.

"Sorry," he said. "Had to wring out the old sock." He looked at Ginny and she was not smiling.

"They've blown up the World Trade center in New York," she said, nodding at the TV.

Soran sat down in his chair and leaned back. "Holy shit!" he said.

"Say, look," said Ginny. "I've really enjoyed seeing you again, really. But I've got to go. My ride's here."

"I've really enjoyed seeing you again, too," he said as they both stood up from the table. He offered his hand to her. She looked up at him, pushed his hand aside, and threw her arms over his shoulders.

"It's good seeing you again," she whispered, and kissed him on the cheek. She loosened her grip and picked up her purse. She turned and walked toward the door. When she reached the door, she turned, smiled at him, and waved. He watched her walk through the door, get into a tan Taurus, and drive away.

Chapter Twenty-two
Ordnance

Ginny had a smile on her face. She couldn't help it. She didn't know where it came from and she wouldn't send it away. It had been years since she had seen him. She actually had forgotten about him. It had been eons ago when he took center stage in her life. But so many things had changed. So many things had happened. And yet he looked as she would have pictured him to be. Not older but more mature. More sure of himself. She had loved him once. But she had run off with another. She had treated him badly. And she had been treated badly in return. Had she come full circle? Had her indiscretions been pardoned by her own pain? Was she to be held forever accountable for her former immaturity? She had loved and she had suffered and she had cried and she had learned. Once again she had touched him and held him and kissed him. And she had felt the passion surge. And the smile was upon her face once more. She was intrigued by the man sitting next to her, but she felt warmth for Soran.

"I have to go to the university today to see about the job," said Amjad.

Ginny was suddenly back in the car. "I'm sorry. I was daydreaming."

"I said I have to go to the University of Minnesota today," he said. "It's about the job." He turned the Taurus into the apartment lot. "I may be home late tonight. Please don't wait up for me."

He pulled up to the apartment door. Ginny did not lean over to kiss him but rather squeezed his hand gently.

"Fine," she said. "Good luck." She got out of the car, opened the apartment outer door, and bound up the stairs, still smiling.

John Bolder was digging through his desk for a pack of Spearmint. He had three sticks of Spearmint in his mouth already but he could only find Juicy Fruit. If he didn't find another pack of Spearmint he would have to mix and match. He had mixed Spearmint and Doublemint with limited success, but Juicy Fruit would be a hard sell. In the third drawer, his hands fell upon the familiar feel of a five pack behind a ream of paper. "Aha," he said as he withdrew the familiar green package.

As he sat back and pulled the string on the gum package, the phone rang. He flicked the end cap off with his right thumb while he picked up the phone with his left hand.

"Bolder," he said into the phone.

"Hey, Bolder. This is Soran. What's new?"

"The shit's hit the fan. That's what's new."

"Yeah, I saw it on the news. What's going on around there?"

Bolder undid a new stick and put it in his mouth. "FBI thinks it's all New York."

"How bad is it?"

"Bad. Real bad. Apparently this Broadwater fella in New York is on the way up and this Malcolm guy in Chicago is on the way down. So Broadwater is pullin' everyone from the Midwest to cover his ass in New York."

"Jesus. Everyone?"

"Everyone they can get their hand on. They figure they've at least got something in New York. All they've got is a ghost in the Midwest. This guy has vanished. It's just possible he went east rather than west. They're banking on it. They figure there has to be a network here and they need the manpower to crack it. Even if he is in your back yard, they don't think that one man can do much. So, for the most part they're leaving it up to the locals. Hell, you might as well go fishing."

"Damn it!"

"How are things there?"

"They're okay. This morning I went to a plant north of the Twin Cities and now I'm at one south of the Twin Cities. Security looks okay, but I don't know what's going to shake down now that New York's getting all the attention."

"Did you bring your pole?"

"Actually, I'm right next to the Mississippi. 'Spose you'd like me to bring you back a couple of walleyes."

"Don't suppose you got any catfish in that stream?"

"I'll see what I can do. Actually this is a rather interesting place. This nuclear plant is right on the Mississippi River. Right next to an indian reservation. I've teamed up with this police detective who is half Sioux. His dad was from this reservation. He's going to show me around."

"Watch out. You might become blood brothers."

"After this week that might just happen."

Sergeant Everson was busy filling out form MNG1/4. There had always been forms for sergeants in the National Guard to fill out, but the cutbacks in the regular army had increased reliance on the National Guard. With increased reliance comes increased forms. The National Guard had always prided itself on being prepared to stand in if called upon, and filling out endless forms was part of the job of a supply sergeant.

One of the offsets of the cutbacks was that new armories, wherever possible, be combined with other government buildings to share the cost of new construction. The combination armory and civic center that she was assigned to was a prime example. Rather than have an armory in a dilapidated building in the center of a city with high land values and correspondingly high property taxes, the armories were being sent out to third-tier suburbs with lower land values and greater ease of access.

Sergeant Everson finished form MNG1/4 and started another form. She did not notice a man enter the door and proceed down the hallway toward the civic center, then turn into the first bathroom on the right.

Amjad entered the bathroom and noticed a man standing in front of a urinal. He proceeded toward the toilet stall as the man stepped back and zipped up. Amjad entered the stall, closed the door, and sat down on the toilet seat. He heard the water splash into the sink and then turn off. A paper towel was ripped off as the dispenser recoiled. Steps walked to the door. The door opened and closed and there was silence.

Amjad opened the stall door to make sure the room was empty. He stepped on the toilet seat and raised himself to the top of the stall walls. The suspended ceiling was only five feet above the top of the stall walls. He put his left knee and then his right foot to the top of the stall. Then his left foot came up as he straightened up and reached the ceiling. He lifted the two-foot-by-four-foot panel section of the suspended ceiling above its grate and slid it over to the side, creating a two-by-four-foot hole. Amjad put his head into the hole, pulled a flashlight from his pocket, and shined it into the darkness above the ceiling.

There was no crossbeam support member next to this panel section. But the light fell on a crossbeam support girder one section over. Amjad pulled the original section back into place and, balancing on the top of the stall wall, inched his way down the stall wall to the next panel. He lifted that panel and slid it aside. He reached up, grabbed the support girder, and pulled himself up. With his feet around the girder, he held on with his left hand as he bent down, and slid the ceiling panel section with his right hand until it slipped back into place. Amjad righted himself on the girder, and sat up. He shined the flashlight around until it landed on the air conditioning duct. He took off his jacket, laid it on the panel, and waited.

Lawrence Malcolm sat at his desk looking up at a picture of Amjad he had push pinned to a cork board near his desk. He looked at the dark, handsome features and into the brooding, determined eyes. In a way, he admired this man. This man was driven. He was obsessed and he was doing something. Malcolm realized that in ten years he would be sitting behind the same desk, peeling an orange similar to the one he was peeling now. But the man in the picture was actually doing something. Causing events. Living his life on the edge, ready to kill or be killed. For a cause. A cause Malcolm did not know and was sure he would not agree with. But at least he had a cause.

Malcolm finished peeling the orange, divided the wedges, and put them on a napkin on his desk. He sat back, glanced again at the picture, and turned to his roll-a-deck. He fingered through the cards until he stopped in the Cs. He picked up his phone and dialed.

Two rings and a click.

"This is Covington," said the voice at the other end.

"Hi, Wes," said Malcolm. "This is Lawrence Malcolm."

"Oh, hi, Mr. Malcolm," Covington answered. He knew Malcolm well enough to call him Lawrence and he also knew him well enough to know that Lawrence appreciated being called Mr. Malcolm.

Malcolm paused just long enough to let a slight smile cross his face as he accepted the gratuity.

"Call me Lawrence," Malcolm finally said. "Say, I wanted to thank you for the work you've done on the Amjad Mustafa case."

"All in a day's work," said Covington.

Malcolm picked up an orange wedge and split it. "Word is you've got a man down here," he said.

"Just one of my men taking a little vacation," said Covington, "Hell, he's from there anyway. Guess he just got homesick."

"It's okay, really. We could use a little help. You know, of course, I can't help him officially and he can't really help us, officially."

"Hell, I told him to bring his fishing pole."

"Right. But if he does stumble on to something..."

"You'll be the first to know."

"Do you think this guy is connected to the bombing?"

"Our guess is, no. We think it's just a coincidence. We've been following this guy for some time. And if he was connected to a network we'd have dug that up. No, this guy's traveling alone."

"What's his motive?" Malcolm asked.

"Revenge, we figure," said Covington. "We've discovered that his family was killed in the Gulf War. He was recruited and trained by terrorists in Libya. We moved in on them and just by sheer luck, he slipped by. Damnedest thing. You've been briefed on the rest."

"So, you still think he's going to Minnesota?"

"That's our best guess. We know he's been there before. He must have seen something there that piqued his interest."

"Power plants?"

"Who knows. Maybe he's going to genetically engineer some kind of super mosquito and unleash it on the world. I'm not saying that the mosquitoes are big in Minnesota, but I did see one there with three wood ticks on it."

"No, really. Best guess?"

"Check the power plants. Especially the one northwest of the Twin Cities. The one at Monticello. The prevailing winds in that part of the country are from the northwest and he may feel he can get to the cooling system and cause another Chernobyl. With the winds blowing in the right direction, it could be devastating."

"We've already checked that out and there is no way that could happen here. We've got too many safeguards."

"I know that, but he may not. Anyway it's my best guess. I understand you guys have pretty well packed up your tents and headed east."

"Yeah, Broadwater is sure Amjad is part of the World Trade Center bombings. Maybe even the head of the operation."

"That figures."

"He's just trying to protect his own ass. Anyway, he's going to release Amjad's picture to the press as head of the gang. It'll be on CNN tonight and in the newspapers by tomorrow morning."

Sergeant Hultga coughed as he reached for his handkerchief and coughed again.

"Still got that cold?" Sergeant Everson asked without looking up.

"Can't seem to shake it," replied Hultga as he coughed again into his handkerchief.

"Must have the same thing Corporal Barry has," said Everson. "He just called in sick. Well, at least you'll have a nice quiet night to yourself."

Everson got up from the desk and gave Hultga a wide birth as she passed him on her way to the door. "Good night, sergeant," she said.

"Good night, yourself," Hultga responded, and coughed again.

He went around the guard desk and sat down. He watched Sergeant Everson pass through and lock the outside door to the armory-civic center complex.

Sergeant Hultga looked around and observed everything in working order. He blew his nose into the handkerchief and put it into his shirt pocket. He looked around again and, assured that he was alone, took a bottle of cough syrup from another pocket. He squeezed, twisted, and slid off the childproof cap, took two large gulps, and started the graveyard shift at the National Guard Armory.

Amjad picked up his flashlight and shined it on his watch. 2:30 A.M. Amjad turned the flashlight off and put it back in his coat. He picked up the coat and put it on. He took out a screwdriver, pried up the ceiling panel, and slid it aside. The room below was dark. He turned on the flashlight and checked the location of the stall wall. Leaving the flashlight on the panel he lowered himself down to the stall wall. He reached up and picked up the flashlight and put it in his pocket. Reaching down, he found the top of the stall with his hands and lowered himself to the floor. He walked across the room and slowly opened the door. The hallway to the civic center was dark, but there was a light at the end of the hallway that led to the armory.

Amjad walked slowly down the hallway until he came to the corner and peered around it. At the guard desk was a man leaning back in his chair with his head resting on his chin. A portable TV was on the desk but its volume did not rise above the snoring coming from the man in the chair. Amjad reached in his coat pocket and withdrew a bottle of ether and a hand towel. He opened the bottle and poured the ether on the hand towel. He turned the corner and walked toward the guard desk. The sergeant's snoring increased as Amjad neared. When he reached the desk, Amjad went around behind the sergeant and placed the ether-soaked towel beneath the sergeant's nose. Amjad poured more ether onto the towel and held it closer. He held it there for thirty seconds and the sergeant's arms released to his sides.

Amjad put the hand towel on the desk and searched the sergeant's pockets. In his shirt pocket he found a plastic card with a magnetic strip tape on the back. On the front was the marking "first door." He looked over to the door leading to the armory and noticed the locking device was operated by a magnetic plastic card. He walked over to the door and slipped the card through the slot in the lock. A green light flashed and the latch clicked. Amjad opened the door and stepped into a short hallway which ended with another door. Amjad walked to the other door and turned the door knob. A light flashed on a panel next to the door. "ENTER CODE PLEASE" was flashing above ten numerals. Amjad pushed 1, 2, 3. A light flashed again and the letters "INCORRECT CODE" appeared. Amjad pushed 2, 4, 6 and the letters "SECOND INCORRECT CODE. PLEASE WAIT TWO HOURS BEFORE ATTEMPTING ENTRY." Amjad walked back out the door and over to the sleeping sergeant. He put the magnetic strip card back in the sergeant's pocket.

Amjad checked the sergeant's breathing and, assured he was out, walked down the hall, turned the corner and walked to the bathroom. He opened the bathroom door and turned on the lights. He walked over to the stall, stepped on the toilet seat, and raised himself to the top of the stall wall. Raising up he pushed the ceiling panel up and slid it aside. Reaching up to the girder, he raised himself up. Sitting on the girder he took the flashlight out of his pocket and searched the air conditioning duct until he found a seam. Crawling along the support girders, he came to the girder next to the duct. He took a tin snips out of his jacket pocket and wedged one blade into the seam and twisted. As the seam in the duct flexed, he squeezed the tin snips. The snips put only a small cut in the duct but this allowed him to push the snips in further and squeeze again. This cut was larger. Large enough to twist the snips to a right angle with the duct, and quickly he had cut a flap in the duct three feet wide and two feet high. He preyed the flap up and crawled into the duct. In the cramped duct there was barely enough room to move but he pushed the flashlight along in front of him and inched forward. The metal smelled of tin and his flashlight showed small clouds of dust released with every movement. As he breathed in another cloud of dust, his nose twitched and his breath came in short spurts. He brought up his right hand to stifle the sneeze, placing his forefinger beneath his nose and pushing up hard. The sneeze was moderately suppressed but the action caused his head to reflex upward and bang against the top of the duct. His left hand went surveying the top of his head, feeling a small bump. He corrugated his brow, sniffed hard, and, with a mild expletive, moved forward.

Soon the duct took a right angle. It was now heading directly to the armory. He followed the duct until he came to a vent. Pointing the flashlight down the vent he saw that the duct had passed through the wall and he was now above the armory. There were boxes stacked beneath him. He brought out the tin snips again and quietly cut through the wire mesh over the vent. Quietly, he bent the wire mesh back. The hole was big enough for him to crawl through. He slipped through the vent feet first until he hung by his hands. He let go and dropped to the floor.

A red light was flashing on the panel behind Sergeant Hultga, signaling that the motion detector alarm in the armory had been triggered. It was accompanied by an alternating buzzing sound. In his ethereally induced sleep, Sergeant Hultga was no more aware of it than was Amjad.

It did not take Amjad long to find what he was looking for. He put the flashlight down next to a crate labeled LAW ROCKET. With the wonder bar from his jacket he pried open the small crate and exposed two LAW rockets. He put the top back on the crate. The C4 explosive was just as easily found as were the detonators.

With his prizes in hand, he walked back to where he had landed under the vent. He piled crates one upon another under the vent until the top one was five feet below the vent. Climbing up the box of crates with his crate of LAW rockets and C4 explosives, he reached the top. He put the rockets and C4 through the vent and into the duct. He pulled himself into the duct and turned his flashlight to the duct behind him. There was a seam in the duct about three feet away. He made one cut in the seam and bent the tin back. Then he made another right above it and bent that back as well. He pulled the rope from his waist and put one end through one hole in the duct and treaded it back through the other. After tying off that end of the rope, he pulled hard. The rope held. He crawled back to the vent and let himself down on the box of crates. Pulling on the rope hard, he found that it still held. He crawled down the box of crates and put the crates back to their original position.

He pulled once more on the rope. It still held. He pulled himself up the rope, hand over hand until he reached the vent. Pulling himself into the vent he pulled the rope up and tossed it aside. He bent the wire mesh back down over the vent and pushed his booty in front of him until he was back over the bathroom. It was a simple matter for him to retrace his steps back to the bathroom, out the hole in the vent, through the open ceiling panel, and into the bathroom in the Civic Center. After he had replaced the ceiling panel he opened the bathroom door and turned out the lights. He walked with his crates in his arms to the front door. He put the crates down and walked back to Sergeant Hultga.

As he approached the sergeant's desk, he could hear the alarm buzzing and saw the flashing light on the panel behind the desk. He walked behind the desk and pushed the reset button on the panel. The light went out and the buzzing stopped. He reached over to the sergeant's waist and removed a set of keys. He walked back to the front door and found the correct key on his third try. After he had unlocked the door, he walked back and replaced the key ring on the sergeant's waist. He opened the drawers of the desk and found a nine-millimeter Colt automatic pistol and put it in his jacket pocket. Picking up his hand towel from under the sergeant's chin, he walked to the front door, picked up his packages, and disappeared into the night.

Chapter Twenty-Three
Soldiers of Time

Ginny woke with the same smile with which she had gone to bed. Meeting an old love had stirred feelings in her she had not had in quite a while. Barring abuse, one usually remembers the good from an old relationship. The soldiers of time wage war on inconsequential trivialities. That which had once loomed so large is given succor by the soft memories of foregone enchantment.

She had had her differences with Soran before but she still felt the warmth of long ago stir within her when she was with him. She felt she had two men in her life now, no mater how tangential. After Michael and Chicago, she did not need encumbrances. But she did need assurances.

She moved in her bed and felt Amjad's body curled up next to her. She tossed off the covers and sat up. Amjad grunted and slowly opened one eye.

"You were out late last night," said Ginny.

"Yeah," he said sleepily.

Ginny stood up and stretched. "Well I'm ready to meet the day. Can I get you breakfast?"

"Yeah, sure," said Amjad as he rolled over on his side again.

Ginny slipped into her jeans and a sweatshirt and walked out to the kitchen.

She quickly made two bowls of instant oatmeal and two glasses of orange juice and set them on the table. Amjad walked into the kitchen, patted Ginny on the behind, and headed into the bathroom.

Ginny sat down and took a drink of juice.

"The paper," she said to herself.

She got up and walked to the front door, opened it and retrieved the morning edition of the Minneapolis *Star Tribune*. She walked back to the table, sat down, and raised her juice glass as she opened the paper. As she gazed at the front page, her grip loosened and the glass fell to the table spilling juice about the paper. A large picture of Amjad Mustafa was centered on the front page in an article on the bombing of the World Trade Center in New York. Her disbelieving eyes read that he was believed to be involved, if not the leader of the bombing. This article explained that he had diverted a plane and landed in Chicago, the same day she had met him. The paper went further to say that he was believed to be driving a tan Taurus with Illinois license plates.

Ginny started to tremble as she heard the toilet flush. She remembered back to the two Illinois license plates in the trunk of the Taurus when she pulled out the grocery bags. The bathroom faucet turned on and water splashed in the sink. Ginny's whole body was shaking now as she tried to stand up but found she couldn't move. The bathroom faucet turned off. Ginny finally found the strength to rise but just stood there, her gaze fixed on the bathroom door.

The bathroom door opened and Amjad appeared. Amjad looked at Ginny who had turned pale as a ghost. He noticed her hands were trembling. Amjad walked over to the table and looked into Ginny's face and then down to the paper. Ginny's heart was racing and she swallowed hard. Amjad's eyes turned to blackened steel and his jaw tightened. He put his hand out to her neck, but she brushed it aside and bolted for the door.

Amjad caught her in two steps and grabbed her by the throat, the thumb and forefinger of his right hand closing like two pincers above her larynx, cutting off her air supply. Ginny coughed and gagged but Amjad kept his grip. Ginny's hands shot out and flailed about his head and shoulders. Amjad picked her up and dragged her, kicking and flailing, into the bedroom.

He pushed her down on the bed, keeping his grip on her windpipe. She grasped at his shoulders with both hands while she choked. Her eyes watered and pleaded as he picked up a pillow with his left hand, covered her face, and pressed down. Her nails dug into his shoulders as he pressed harder on the pillow. He saw her breasts heave as she arched her back. He thought back to the first time he had seen her, drenched in the rain but still spunky and full of life. To the rest stop when she skipped down the path to the picnic table and turned with a smile. To the time he had held her in his arms as he drifted off to sleep. He remembered long ago in a faraway land that he had once cared for someone.

Ginny felt the grip on her windpipe loosen as the pillow was lifted from her face. She gasped and coughed for air. She put her hands to her throat as she felt the air gush into her lungs. She looked up through blinking eyes to see Amjad's fist descending to meet with her forehead. There was a shower of golden stars against a sea of red, then fade to black.

Chapter Twenty-Four
Sweat Lodge

C hief Ganyo once again had the nicotine patch on his left arm. He would rub it occasionally. He missed the oral gratification and singular mannerisms of smoking. But he knew smoking was killing him and he was determined to quit. The patch adhering to his arm would placate the addiction and the rubbing would substitute for the tactility of the cigarette. The mannerisms he would leave to the carrot sticks in his upper right drawer. The phone intercom interrupted his thoughts.

"St. Paul Chief Hardy on line one," squeaked the box.

Ganyo picked up the phone and brought it to his ear. "Ganyo."

"Ganyo, Chief Hardy here. Have you seen today's paper?"

"Lookin' at it right now," said Ganyo.

"We've got our men loaned out to help the FBI and now they think our man is in New York," said Hardy.

"I don't give a shit what the FBI says now. If they're pulling their troops to the East Coast and they come out in the paper saying that our man is in New York, I'm not going to have my men spread thin chasing a ghost."

"It's not just FBI," said Hardy. "I had the CIA send a man here and they enlisted one of my men to baby-sit him. Some addendum to the Gulf of Tonkin Resolution or something."

Ganyo leaned back in his chair and let out a howl.

"What...what's going on?" asked Hardy.

Ganyo put his feet up on the desk. "Hardy, my man, you've been had."

"What do you mean?" asked Hardy.

"The same son of a bitch called me with the same rag and I tossed him out on his ear. There is no addendum to the Gulf of Tonkin Resolution. I don't know who your man is baby-sittin', but it ain't kosher."

"Son of a bitch," said Hardy in disgust. "This shit has gone on long enough. I'm pulling all my men back. I'm not chasing any ghost."

"I've already given the order," said Ganyo. "This little party's over."

Billy emerged from the community center and walked over to the car. Soran reached over across the driver's seat and opened the door in anticipation. Billy slid in and closed the door.

"Got some good news," he said.

Soran breathed deeply. "I could use some good news," he said.

"I've talked to a couple of the elders," said Billy. "Told them you were here to help them. To help preserve the land and the river from the bad guys. Anyway, they would like to meet you."

Billy put the keys in the ignition and started the engines. "They are going over to the sweat lodge," he continued. "They would not mind if you come along."

"Sweat lodge?" asked Soran.

"Yeah, sweat lodge," answered Billy. "Sort of like a red man's sauna. Only this has much greater religious significance. They usually don't let outsiders partake. It's a real honor, I assure you."

Soran buckled his seat belt. "Well then, I'm honored."

They entered the lean-to through a canvas door. It was pitch dark inside, and Billy took Soran by the arm and led him to a seat. In the minutes that it took for

Soran's' eyes to adjust to the dark no words were spoken but he could hear the breathing of others. A hole had been dug in the center of the sweat lodge and hot rocks placed in the hole forced stream upwards. The heat seemed to permeate his skin and the air was heavy with the smell of sweating bodies. Billy leaned over to him and spoke softly.

"We are with two of the elders, Red Eagle and Crooked Wing. Elders in our culture are revered. They pass on much knowledge and possess much wisdom. Make sure you are respectful when in their presence."

Soran nodded in the dark, not sure if anyone observed his acquiescence.

A low voice from across the lean-to spoke. "Billy Two-Bears has told us about you, how you have come to try to help us protect the land. You are welcome here."

"Thank you," Soran stammered. "Sir," he added.

"I am Red Eagle," came the proud voice.

"Very pleased to meet you," Soran fumbled. "Honored. Really."

"We are Mdewankanton Dakota tribe," sounded the voice. "Dakota means friend. You are welcome here. But tell me, why did you come?"

Soran looked into the dark and began to make out figures. "I have reason to believe that a person may be coming here to blow up the nuclear power plant next door."

"A white man?" asked Red Eagle.

Soran was taken aback. "Why, yes," he said. "I guess you would call him a white man."

"Figures," answered Red Eagle in disgust. Red Eagle said two sentences in his native language and someone next to him laughed.

"So," he continued, "you noticed we have our community next to a nuclear power plant?"

"Yes," said Soran. "Couldn't help but notice that."

"I suppose you wonder why would we stay here."

"Well no," Soran stumbled, "I mean yes. Yes, that would be a logical question."

"We stay here," Red Eagle's voice grew somber, "because this is our land. This is our land. This is all we have left. We are of the Dakota tribe of the Sioux Nation. There was a time when our numbers filled the land. Our nation covered many of your states. Yet there were no prisons here. There were no jails. There was no need. We are an honorable people.

"Look at the white man. He builds more prisons and more jails. And the more he builds the worse his crime becomes. Just think of the Sioux. An entire nation and not one jail. No need. Because we had honor. We had respect.

"But to truly understand why we stay here you must understand our culture. We believe that the Great Spirit Wakantanka created the world and everything in it. His spirit runs through all living things. There is peace and harmony through all living things. This world was like heaven on earth to us. We had everything that we needed and we were the caretakers of what we had. We only took what we needed and did not waste anything. The buffalo gave us meat and clothing and the land gave us herbs for our medicine. The streams and rivers ran clean and the fishing was plentiful. We had everything we wanted. And we kept the natural laws of Wakantanka.

"Then came the white man. At first we welcomed the white man. But then they took our land. And they changed the land. They plowed up the plains and they cut down the forests. If a mountain was in their way they would tear it down. If a river confronted them they would change the course of the river.

"Then they took more of our land. We fought to keep our way of life, but we could not prevail. They put us on a reservation, took away our buffalo, and told us that they would provide for us. But they did not provide for us. The warehouses of the BIA were brimming with food, but our people were starving. When we went and told them to give us some food because our women and children were starving, they told us to eat grass. We rebelled and killed some people and they killed more of us and took more of our land.

"Now we are here. This is the land we have left. It is our land. Here we keep the spirit of Wakantanka alive. But then the white man builds a nuclear power plant right next to us. The plant is three blocks away from our community center. And the power lines with their electromagnetic waves are a block away from our houses where our children play. They buy up the land around us. Now the fish in the river have mutated. The medicine we get from the land is weaker. The children cannot swim in the river.

"We cannot eat the fish from the river and the climate has changed because of the steam released from the power plant.

"They have offered us money to buy the land. So why do we stay?" His voice rising. "Because this is our land!" His voice trailed off, then started again. "I am an old man. I will go to see my ancestors soon. What am I to tell them? That I sold their land, their children's land, their children's children's land, for the white man's money? No! This is our land. Without our land we are nothing. We will stay!"

Soran's eyes had become accustomed to the darkness now. He could see the images across the rock pit. The perspiration was running down his face, dripping from his chin. He put his head down and sweat fell from the tip of his nose and landed on his thigh. He looked at the sweat beading up on his skin, his pale, white skin, the white skin of his ancestors, and felt ashamed.

Chapter Twenty-Five
The Cask

Mornings are special in Minnesota when spring comes early. The snows that caked the land, like the frosting of the season, have melted and long since entered the ground to feed the ravenous appetite of new green life. The rivers and streams have loosed their icy fetters and the straining of their banks gives evidence of the coming season. The air is crisp and clean yet is quickly warmed by the rising sun. Paths of frost hide in the shadows, teasing the sun with their presence. Birds were singing their praise of the light as a tan Taurus drove eastward toward the sun.

Billy came around the side of the couch, put his hand out, and shook a sleepy shoulder.

"Wha…who..." Soran grunted.

"Time to get up," said Billy.

Soran opened his eyes and looked up at Billy. "What…what time is it?" he asked sleepily.

"Time to get up," answered Billy. He walked over to the chair, picked up Soran's pants, and threw them at him.

"I just got off the phone." Billy picked up some socks and tossed them on the couch next to Soran. "Seems Chief Hardy has talked to your people back in Virginia," he said. "He says I should bring you in right away. Says he can't wait to talk to you."

"Oh, shit," Soran said beneath his breath as he sat up and put on his socks.

Amjad could see the Native American community center on his right as he drove toward the nuclear power plant. He could see the power plant straight ahead of him as he came to a stop sign in front of the guard's gate. Everything was as he remembered it. He thought back to when he had been here before. He was at the University of Minnesota Hospitals learning the latest transplant techniques. His American hosts were so proud of their country that they wanted to show him how it worked, how it ran. They took him to the state capitol to show him democracy in action. He remembered being surprised at the open discussion and protest.

That particular day a group of people were protesting the storing of nuclear waste on the Prairie Island Power Plant facility. They talked about how catastrophic it would be if the waste found its way into the Mississippi River, the longest river on the continent. He remembered their saying what a precarious place to put nuclear waste—not just near the river but actually on an island, an island near the headwaters of the Mississippi River. They talked about half-lives and nuclear devastation that would last for centuries. The other side talked about all the jobs that would be saved if they could store the waste on the island. He remembered thinking no one would be so foolish.

His hosts had told him of America becoming less dependent on foreign oil. They spoke of advances in solar energy, wind energy, geothermal energy, and nuclear energy. And they had taken him on a tour of a power plant on an island on the Mississippi River.

The engineering was impressive, state-of-the-art. He asked about where they kept the spent rods of nuclear fuel. They had assured him that they were seeking approval of dry storage in permanent casks. But until they had the approval from the Department of Energy, the nuclear waste was stored under about a half million gallons of water in a cask next to the power plant.

Amjad turned the car to the right and followed a road next to the power plant. The road curved around to the left and headed toward the river. As he approached the end of the road he pulled over and stopped. He got out of the car and opened the trunk. He pulled out a box, a shovel, and two army green cylindrical metal tubes and crossed the road. The small wire fence created no problem for him as he headed up a small hill. When he reached the top he could see the large storage cask between himself and the river. The cask was surrounded by an empty moat leading to a dike by the river. He put the tubes down and with his shovel and box of C4 explosives and detonators, headed for the dike and the cask.

"Goddamn protesters," said Billy as he took the flyer off his windshield, crumpled it up, and threw it on the ground.

"Now, Billy, let's not litter," said Soran as he picked up the paper and put it on the seat of the car. "What is this anyway?"

"Oh, it's just the protesters. They come around and put these flyers on our windshields protesting the nuclear power plant being here and the storage of nuclear waste."

Billy started the engine and put the car in gear.

"They mean well," he continued. "And I support their cause. But do they really have to put these things on our windshield all the time. I mean the litter…"

Soran picked up the paper and unfolded it. As he read it he realized that this was not your run of the mill, end-of-the-world propaganda. The paper simply explained that when nuclear fuel is used up it has to be stored. This is not a simple task, as the by-products can have tremendously long lives. One of the by-products of nuclear fission is plutonium. This element has a half life of 24,400 years. A half life is the amount of time it takes for fifty percent of the original activity to decay; after ten half lives, one-one thousandth of the original radioactivity—an amount still dangerous—would remain. So with its half life of 24,400 years, plutonium 239 would remain dangerous for a quarter of a million years, or twelve thousand human generations. And as it decays it becomes uranium-235, its radioactive "daughter," which has a half life of its own of 710,000 years.

The storage of these wastes creates a real problem. The power plants are seeking authority to store these wastes in dry storage casks but the radioactivity of these wastes would eventually outlast the stainless steel containers that house them. But even that would be a vast improvement over the current means of storage. Now the nuclear waste is temporarily stored in forty-foot-high casks filled with about five hundred thousand gallons of water. While they have been waiting for the Department of Energy's approval, these casks now contain twenty years of waste. While the D.O.E. drags its feet, the situation becomes more critical. The typical large nuclear reactor creates about thirty metric tons of nuclear waste each year. This power plant has been producing waste for twenty years. So there is somewhere in the vicinity of six hundred metric tons of nuclear waste sitting on an island in the Mississippi River and if that waste were to…

Billy honked the horn of the car and Soran looked up to see Red Eagle and Crooked Wing standing beside the road. As the light haze fought a doomed battle with the early morning sun, he could see that they were dressed in their finest ceremonial costumes. They each raised a hand as Billy drove by. Soran watched as their eyes followed the car.

The dew from the morning mist that had gathered on the top of the car windows streaked down the glass, tear-like, as Soran watched them disappear into the haze.

"What was that?" he asked Billy.

Billy's eyes turned back to the road. "I don't know," he answered. "I've never seen them like that before."

Billy pulled his car past the Native American community center and onto the side road that would take them to Highway 61 leading to the Twin Cities.

"First time you've slept on an Indian reservation, I bet," he said. "How did you like it?"

Soran rubbed the back of his neck with his right hand. "Actually," he said, "I was hoping to stay a little longer."

Billy turned on to the main road. "'Fraid that's not possible," he said. "If you'd like to learn more about our culture, I could bring you back later."

"Fine," said Soran stretching his back. "I'd like that." He rubbed his arms with his hands.

"Say," he continued. "I really appreciate you getting me into the sweat lodge. I enjoyed meeting Red Eagle and Crooked Wing. It was quite an experience."

He rubbed the last of sleep from his eyes and continued. "I'm really sorry about what happened to your people."

Billy laughed. "I think the problem was that we never declared war on America. We had treaties with the white man but he kept changing the rules. Then they would kill some more of us and take some more of our land, get another treaty, and change the rules again. We never got a chance to formally declare war on America like the Germans and the Japanese. Hell, if we'd have had a chance to declare war before we lost to America we would have had a head start on the Germans and Japanese and maybe you'd be buying Native American cars and TV sets."

Soran forced a smile.

"Come on, Phil," said Billy. "Even Native Americans can have a sense of humor."

Soran looked at Billy quizzically.

"We'll be okay, Phil," Billy said. "But I do wish they would just leave us alone. We get our strength from the land. Our spirituality lives in the land. Now the land is getting weak because of the power plant. I wonder if they would have built the power plant there if we were a community of white people."

Billy stopped at a stop sign, waited for two cars to pass, then pulled out and accelerated.

"It's bad enough," he continued, "but now we have to live with the nuclear waste, too."

Soran stopped rubbing his eyes. "What do you mean?" he asked.

"Nuclear waste," said Billy. "The power plant produces nuclear waste. It's got to be stored somewhere so they store it on the island."

Soran's hands dropped to his waist and his stomach started to churn. "The island?" he asked as his eyes opened further.

"Sure," said Billy. "Prairie Island. Where do you think we've been staying the last twelve hours?"

"I guess it was dark when we came last night and I really didn't notice," said Soran.

"I thought it was just a name. I didn't realize it was actually an island. But the nuclear waste, how is it stored?"

"Well," said Billy. "They're trying to get permission for permanent dry storage casks but that hasn't come through yet. So in the meantime it's stored in water-filled casks until they find out what to do with it."

"Are these casks being guarded?" Soran blurted.

Billy looked at Soran. "Not really," he said. "We figure any terrorist would be after the nuclear reactor in the plant itself. And we figure no one would want to steal the waste because they would have to pull it out from under a half a million gallons of water. By now the water it's stored in would be radioactive itself."

Soran's stomach became knotted and he could feel goose bumps on the nape of his neck. "Oh my God," he said staring straight ahead.

"What is it?" asked Billy as he gave Soran a glance.

"Oh my God, Billy. Turn the car around."

"Why. What the hell is it?"

Soran grabbed Billy by the shoulder. "I know what he's after," he said. "Now turn this fucking car around!"

Amjad walked back up the hill until he reached the two army green cylinders. He turned and sat down. He could see where he had buried the explosives in the dike. Looking at the cask he could make out the arc of C4 clinging to its side. Amjad took one of the tubes and removed the rear cover. He extended the tube as the sight popped up. Setting the tube down next to him, he looked around and felt the warmth of the rising sun on his face. He could see the river running swiftly alongside the complex. The trees that lined its shore had just started to show their buds. He wondered if he would live to see the buds turn to leaves. He thought back to a time in Baghdad when a guided bomb had landed on a building creating a hole for a second guided bomb to go through and destroy all that he had lived for. He might indeed live to see the coming of the leaves. But his wife and child would not. He picked up a small electronic box and flipped a switch. A green light came on and he moved his thumb to a red button in the middle of the box. He closed his eyes and thought of long ago.

Billy brought the car to a stop sign in front of the power plant gate. He took a right and followed the road that would take them to the river. As they approached the end of the road, Billy slowed down. In front of them, pulled over alongside of the road, was a tan Taurus. Billy brought the car up behind the Taurus and stopped.

They got out of the car and approached the Taurus, Soran from the passenger side and Billy from the driver's side, with his gun drawn. Billy reached the driver's door and opened it. Soran looked through the passenger window and saw Ginny lying in the back seat, her hands and feet tied and duct tape covering her mouth. Ginny's eyes were wide with terror. Soran flung open the door. He leaned inside and ripped the duct tape from Ginny's mouth. Ginny gasped for air.

"He's...he's..." Ginny blurted out.

Soran put his hand on her cheek. "Yes, we know who he is."

Suddenly one explosion then another rocked the area. Soran looked up and saw the dike for the safety moat had been breached by one explosion and there was smoke and debris coming from one side of the storage cask. Soran looked up on the side of the hill between them and the storage cask and saw Amjad raise a small tube to his shoulder. The end of the tube exploded in flames and he watched the rocket's trail as it sought the cask. The rocket's trail ended right next to the hole opened by the C4 and exploded. The hole in the cask was much larger now but no water seemed to be escaping. Amjad reached down and picked up the other tube.

Billy was halfway up the hill by now. He stopped, raised his gun, and fired. A bullet struck Amjad in the right shoulder and spun him around. He dropped the tube, pulled a nine-millimeter Colt from his waist, and shot three times. One bullet hit Billy in the right arm and another pierced his abdomen. Billy fell to the ground, the gun tumbling from his hand. Amjad turned around and picked up the tube again as Soran rushed up the hill toward Billy. Amjad pulled the safety pin from the rear of the LAW rocket and the rear cap fell off. He pulled the extension tube back as the sights popped up.

Soran was at Billy's side and picked up the dropped service revolver. Amjad brought the LAW rocket to his shoulder and peered through the sight to locate the hole in the cask. Just as he found the hole and put it in the cross hairs, a bullet smashed through his left lung followed quickly by another that tore through his neck. Amjad slumped to his knees in pain, but straining, brought the tube slowly back up. The cross hairs were again on the cask but now Amjad could also see the red shoe; a girl's red shoe. He saw through the shoe to put the cross hairs on the hole in the superstructure of the cask and put his finger on the trigger. As he depressed the trigger another bullet hit him in the right side, causing him to flinch as the rocket left the tube. He followed the trail of sparks and smoke and flame as the rocket sped toward the cask. But the spasm had altered the trajectory by a few degrees and the rocket passed over the cask and exploded on the bank of the river. Amjad fell forward to the ground, thrusting his hands toward the cask, blood gushing from his mouth.

"No!" he yelled through the blood. "No!" His hands grasped as if trying to reach out and touch the cask but his fists could only clutch soil and grass.

"Daddy," a voice from behind and above him. He slowly, painfully turned over, blood streaming from his mouth, neck, and side. He lay back on the mound looking up. The daylight had vanished and the colors and hues of the day were fading as if they were being drained back over the horizon. He felt cold. A gray cloud was descending toward him, filling up what was left of the sky. As the cloud reached him, a girl appeared out of the cloud and floated right above him. A pretty girl dressed in a pink dress and a bonnet. And red shoes.

"Daddy," the little girl said. "Daddy, we're waiting for you."

Amjad painfully raised his arms to the girl. Blood was flowing freely from his mouth and nose. "Fatima," he spurted through the blood, "Fatima," as he reached up, took hold of the girl, and pulled her to his breast.

Soran reached the top of the rise of the hill and saw Amjad on his back, eyes fixed skyward in a glassy stare. His arms crossed over his chest and through the blood, a seemingly peaceful smile on his face. Soran raised the revolver and shot two more times. The corpse flinched as each bullet entered its body. Soran stood over Amjad's body gasping for breath. Dropping to one knee, he bent forward, his left arm reaching to the ground to help support himself as he searched for air. The ground felt cool and damp to his touch and he smelled the freshness of spring coming from the ground. As his panting slowed and his breath returned, he turned his head skyward and noticed the beautiful blue of a spring morning sky, spotted only by a few white, puffy clouds and a grouping of birds swooping and swaying in playful harmony with the gentle breeze. The tops of the trees swayed like many-fingered hands rising from the earth offering the promise of green gifts to come. The grass had shaken off its blanket of brown and zestfully showed the color of new life flickering off the heavy dew in the sunlight. In the distance he could faintly hear the echo of beating drums, the heartbeat of a living land.

He took a deep breath and felt the freshness that could only come from early morning air. As he closed his eyes, he held the breath in for just a moment longer, then let it out slowly. He turned to Amjad; the arms crossed on his chest as if clutching some hidden treasure, the eyes fixed at some distant focus, the mouth finding in death a peaceful smile.

Soran reached over and put his hand on Amjad's eyes, closing them with a caress. "What have we done to you to bring you this far?" he asked in a voice slightly above a whisper. He closed his eyes, slowly shaking his head. "What could we have done?"

He turned from Amjad and looked toward the cask, smoke and flames billowing from the fractured outer casing, the inner casing apparently still intact. And beyond the cask, the breached safety dike and the river. He could hear the rushing of water. He could see the mighty river straining at its banks as if it could, by a simple act of will, have anything that it wanted. To reach out, enfold it in its watery fetters and carry it along as it started its 2300 mile journey to the sea, knowing full well that, once started, nothing, nothing under heaven or on the earth could stop it.

"My God," Soran said as the gun slipped from his hand. He turned to Amjad lying on the cold, wet ground, then back to the cask, and then to the river.

"My God," he repeated as his breath tightened to short spurts. His jaw dropped and his cheeks felt cold and clammy, its blood having been drained. Chills went racing up his back, his scalp tingled. He closed his eyes.

"Oh, my God."

Epilogue
The Future

Daytime does not give up easily. From beyond the horizon it desperately sends fingers forth that grasp the wispy clouds in fists of scarlet indignation. Boldly at first, displaying the crimson, gold, and pink in remembrance of its past dominion. Then as the strength is spent, the grip loosens, the colors wane and give way to the grays and purples that herald the coming of the night.

With the darkness comes the beating of the drums. The rhythmical patterns which echo throughout the valley as if measuring the heartbeat of the land itself.

Along the Upper Mississippi Valley campfires blaze as the dancers cast their shadows into forever. The ceremony is a song. A song of long ago when their numbers filled the land and their medicine was strong. They were the caretakers of the land and the sky and the trees and the grass. And the river. Now their numbers are few and their medicine is weak. They are the last to honor the Great Spirit, Wakantanka. They are the last to keep the balance. And they wonder if the creatures that survive extinction and evolution will remember them.

And they dance. They still dance.

Note to the Reader

Prairie Island is an island in the Mississippi River approximately forty miles southeast of the Twin Cities of Minneapolis and St. Paul. It is home to two entities: the Prairie Island Indian Reservation and the Prairie Island nuclear power plant. The typical large nuclear power plant creates approximately thirty metric tons of nuclear waste per year. This plant has been operating for more than twenty years. The waste is stored under water within the plant in large storage pools. The storage pools within the plant have reached capacity. Without a national storage site, the plants have had to look for alternative ways to store the waste. So the waste is being brought outside the plant for storage in temporary casks.

In 1982 the United States Congress passed the Nuclear Waste Policy Act. This act was to create a permanent disposal site for the nuclear waste being created by nuclear power plants. The task fell to the Department of Energy. The original date was set for 1985. It was later set back to 1989, then to 1998, 2003, and now is set for 2010. It appears that the current projected date of 2010 is hopelessly optimistic. Meanwhile, the buildup of waste continues.

This book is a story about nuclear terrorism. As I did not want this to be a "how to" manual for terrorists, I have deliberately altered the substantiality and dimensions of the casks. But that does not diminish the danger of having nuclear waste stored on an island in the Mississippi River. Near the headwaters of the longest river on the continent.

To order additional copies of this book,
please send full amount plus $4.00 for
postage and handling for the first book and
50¢ for each additional book.

Send orders to:

Galde Press, Inc.
PO Box 460
Lakeville, Minnesota 55044-0460

Credit card orders call 1–800–777–3454
Phone (612) 891-5991 • Fax (612) 891-6091
Visit our website at http://www.galdepress.com

Write for our free catalog.

NORMANDALE COMMUNITY COLLEGE
LIBRARY
9700 FRANCE AVENUE SOUTH
BLOOMINGTON, MN 55431-4399